CH TO HIS OWN

THE ASIAN SAGAS BOOK 2

PETER RIMMER

ABOUT PETER RIMMER

Peter Rimmer was born in London, England, and grew up in the south of the city where he went to school. After the Second World War, aged eighteen, he joined the Royal Air Force, reaching the rank of Pilot Officer before he was nineteen. At the end of his National Service, he sailed for Africa to grow tobacco in what was then Rhodesia, now Zimbabwe.

The years went by and Peter found himself in Johannesburg where he established an insurance brokering company. Over 2% of the companies listed on the Johannesburg Stock Exchange were clients of Rimmer Associates. He opened branches in the United States of America, Australia and Hong Kong and travelled extensively between them.

Having lived a reclusive life on his beloved smallholding in Knysna, South Africa, for over 25 years, Peter passed away in July 2018. He has left an enormous legacy of unpublished work for his family to release over the coming years, and not only they but also his readers from around the world will sorely miss him. Peter Rimmer was 81 years old.

ALSO BY PETER RIMMER

∾

Cry of the Fish Eagle

Vultures in the Wind

Just the Memory of Love

Second Beach (A Novella)

All Our Yesterdays

∾

THE ASIAN SAGAS

Bend with the Wind (Book 1)

Each to His Own (Book 2)

∾

THE BRIGANDSHAW CHRONICLES

(*The Rise and Fall of the Anglo Saxon Empire*)

Echoes from the Past (Book 1)

Elephant Walk (Book 2)

Mad Dogs and Englishmen (Book 3)

To the Manor Born (Book 4)

On the Brink of Tears (Book 5)

Treason If You Lose (Book 6)

Horns of Dilemma (Book 7)

Lady Come Home (Book 8)

~

THE PIONEERS

Morgandale (Book 1)

First published in Great Britain in July 2020 by

KAMBA PUBLISHING, United Kingdom

10 9 8 7 6 5 4 3 2 1

PROLOGUE

The Second World War had been over for nine years and the British Empire was dissolving rapidly. Power had gone East and West with communism and the dollar on their way to success and the British left with an almighty overdraft, a tax system that penalised anyone who made any money and the flight of the best brains out of the country. But not every family with capital despaired: the Beaumonts, whose ancestry reached back to 1066 on the same piece of land, had weathered the storms. Henry, the oldest son, had been killed on the Normandy beachhead, so when Sir Thomas had died, the bachelor, Reggie, had taken on the baronetcy. The first of the new breed of British businessmen, Reggie had insured the family against death duties to make sure Merry Hall stayed in the family for the next generation: Beau, Lorna, Raoul and Karen, Geoffrey's children; Adam and Tammany Jr, Tug's children by his Malay wife; and Roz, the family rebel.

PART I

MAY TO DECEMBER 1953

1

Zachariah Booth, his real name and the one he used on stage, was sitting in the open window frame on the second floor bedsitter, bored out of his mind. Down the road, Blake Emsworth was walking back from the Earl of Buckingham, his paisley harem pants exposing his sandaled feet. He was bored, having nothing to do with the rest of his life. He watched as a taxi turned off the Bayswater Road and stopped outside number twenty-seven.

The moment Tammany Beaumont climbed out of the taxi and stood up to her full height, each man's boredom evaporated. She wore red capri pants and a white silk shirt that showed off the fullness of her breasts. Her hair was long and black and to the watching Zach and Blake her legs seemed to reach all the way up to her armpits. She looked up at Zach in his window, smiled, and carried her suitcase up the ten steps to the front door of the digs.

Zach got off his windowsill and smiled benignly to himself. "Zachariah Booth, your luck has just changed."

WHILE TAMMANY WAS STARTING out on her career as an actress, her first cousin Beau was lifting his cricket bat to the crowd as he walked back to the pavilion at Lords; he had scored twenty-six runs in the Eton-Harrow match. He raised his bat twice more to the applause, which increased as he reached the boundary.

"Well done, Beaumont," said the captain, patting him on the back. "Jolly good show. You and Ainsworth have given us a first-class start. Can't have Eton beating us two years in a row."

By the time Beau was seated on a fence to take off his pads, he was surrounded by people paying him compliments.

FOUR MILES away as the crow flies, in a well-appointed second-floor flat, Lorna, Beau's sister, was being entertained by her aunt Isabel, a lady not talked about at Merry Hall other than in the servants' quarters.

"You can have another cup of tea but I am having a drink. How was the presentation?"

"The Queen smiled and shook my hand."

"Mother presented you?"

"I was terrified."

"You realise what 'coming out' means?"

"Meeting people. Making friends."

"Nonsense. With your looks and my help you can succeed despite your lack of money."

"Oh, but I'm..."

"Listen. You're a debutante for one season. You have to decide what to do with your life. Give me that."

She studied the list to Lorna's coming out ball, which was planned for August, chuckling to herself over four of the names, marking others with a cross and some with question marks.

"Do you like men?" she asked.

"Yes," answered Lorna in surprise.

"Did I ever tell you about our uncle Reggie's American partner? Married your aunt Pippa and took her off to America. He always said, 'I made myself some enquiries', which is what I will do about the ones with question marks. The others I've crossed out you can ignore. They'll be looking for the 'uglies' with money. Let me have a look at you. Your dress is sexless. You've got to show them something in a way the Queen would think decent."

Isabel collected two sheets of drawing paper from the top drawer of her bureau and with two sharpened pencils beckoned Lorna to follow her to the dining-room table where she began to draw in quick, firm lines. After five minutes she stood back.

"Pure white. Ankle length. This new material has the texture of silk and doesn't crease. Hangs over your body without clinging. This drawing is the front of the dress. Halter neck within inverted V from your throat, baring your shoulders and freeing your arms. All the other girls will be wearing ball gowns. This is the back. Bare from the waist up. One silk petticoat underneath."

"My strap will show."

"You won't be wearing a bra."

ADAM BEAUMONT, Lorna's first cousin and brother to Tammany, blue-eyed in contrast to his otherwise oriental features, was standing to attention in front of the station commander at Royal Air Force Hednesford where he was undergoing his basic training. At nineteen he was self-assured.

"At ease, airman."

Adam stamped his feet apart and partially relaxed, waiting for the sentence to fall.

"What's all this about refusing a commission?"

Adam said nothing, tracing his mind back to an earlier interview with the squadron commander.

"I didn't think I'd be good enough, sir," he said, recovering his wits.

"For us to decide, young man. Why don't you think you're good enough?"

"I had a bad time at school, sir. Ridicule. That kind of thing. My appearance, I mean. The officers' mess..."

"Officers are men, not schoolboys."

"Yes, sir."

"Every man should be proud of his parentage."

"That I am, sir."

"Good. Then show it. You will attend the officer selection board at the Air Ministry on Friday."

ON THE MORNING of the ball, the sun rose blood red behind the woods, reflected in the window panes from Merry Hall. Tammany woke at nine o'clock with the sun on her face and got up to go down to the river for water. Walking barefoot through the woods, she sang to herself, swinging the billy can and wondering at the beauty of everything she saw. Bending over the riverbank where the water was flowing and free of floating leaves and twigs she washed the coffee dregs out of the billy can and filled it with water for their tea. They had come down from London by train and camped out for the night.

HALF AN HOUR LATER, on the gravel driveway in front of the main entrance of Merry Hall, Beau and Charles Ainsworth watched the trio push their bicycles towards Merry Hall.

"Who are those men Tammany's brought with her?" Beau asked his grandmother Beaumont. "Breeding will out." He looked towards the vista of the woods and rolling farmland with the spire of Ashtead church in the distance where he and the rest of the family had been christened for centuries. He had completely missed his grandmother's look of dislike as she turned away.

"Come on," he said to Charles, "let's get some fresh air. We'll ride up to the Downs and take a gallop round the course. Nothing serious... Did you see them?" he added contemptuously as his feet crunched the gravel, his free hand smoothing the well-combed hair with the perfect parting.

"Is your uncle coming down?"

"You never know."

"Father wants a word with him."

"You shouldn't ask me."

"If you could make the introduction, old chap."

"Haven't they met? Uncle Reggie isn't very social."

"Why doesn't he get married?" asked Charles.

"Heaven forbid," said Beau, making a sweep of the estate. "I like this place... What on earth is he doing here?"

He stopped as a Norton motorcycle came through the gates at the end of the long driveway up to the Hall, the rider in RAF blue, the strap of a crash helmet flapping under his chin.

"Thought we'd got rid of him for a while. Motorcycles are so common."

And he feigned not to have seen the wave from Adam.

"Motorcycles and strange men. Just shows you," he said, missing the sight of his younger cousin, Roz, disappearing into the woods with one of the house guests.

Roz LED the man deep into the woods and when she found her secret place she was surprised to see wisps of smoke rising from an old wood fire.

"Someone's been here," said the man, looking around in trepidation.

"They're not here now," said Roz turning to him. "Come on," she said a few minutes later, "we can make out here." She lay down on the moss where Tammany had slept and opened her arms for him, her pleated skirt falling back to show the soft plumpness of youthful thighs.

TAMMANY MET Lorna in the corridor on her way to show Zach and Blake their bedrooms.

"These are friends of mine. My cousin, Lorna. It's her ding. Zach and Blake."

"They can't go like that," said Lorna, pulling back as Zach doffed his imaginary hat and bowed from the waist, his long hair falling forward.

"Your servant ma'am," said Zach, and Blake tried not to laugh.

"What's that?" said Lorna, pointing at Blake's trousers.

"Harem pants."

"You can't..." she began.

"Did a box arrive for me from Montague Burtons?" said Tammany.

"Yes."

"Evening wear for the men. Uncle Reggie... "

"Well that's something," said Lorna, going past and giving her cousin a look of annoyance.

"My very own pleasure, cousin dear," replied Tammany theatrically to her cousin's departing back and shrugged. "Now you've met one of my family," she said and led them off to their rooms.

"HELLO, DARLING," said Lady Beaumont, putting up her cheek to be kissed. "What's all this?"

"Hi, Gran. Forty-eight-hour pass. They're sending me to OCTU. Isle of Man."

"Slowly. Not so fast."

"Sorry, Gran." Adam grinned down at his grandmother.

"That's wonderful."

"There's a good chance of me failing the course."

"You won't... Tammany's here. Pavy said..."

"Where?" and he was off up the stairs to the door.

"In her room, I'd expect. She caught the train..."

"Thanks, Gran," he said, and he shot into the house, leaving his motorcycle on its stand and his grandmother smiling.

"Who was that?" said Lady Hensbrook coming around the house from the direction of the conservatory. Lady Hensbrook was the other grandmother.

"Adam. He is going to OCTU."

"Tug will be glad."

"Boy told me he wanted to stay in the ranks."

"People change their minds."

"I'm glad. It just might put Beau in his place. Geoffrey says National Service Commissions in the RAF are few and far between."

"Reggie was right. Better to have the dancing in the library so they can spill over onto the terrace."

AT TWELVE-THIRTY, Beau was told of his cousin's success and hit his leg viciously with his riding crop.

"Maybe he'll fail the course," consoled Charles.

"Not Adam. Once he's made up his mind."

"You'll have to get the Sword of Honour when you go in. Shouldn't be difficult."

"If Adam doesn't get it first in the Air Force. Why can't he go back to Asia and leave me in peace? We'd better go and study the invitation list. If one has to get married in this life one might as well make it worthwhile."

"Have you seen your cousin?" asked Charles, who was not looking forward to coming face-to-face with Isabel's daughter.

"Roz? Now there's a sexy bit. That'll make a good bang one of these days. She takes after her mother. Aunt Isabel must have been a looker in her day."

"Still is," said Charles, causing Beau to look at him.

"You fancy my aunt? Don't make me laugh. She's old enough to be your mother. Who goes for old women when there are plenty of young ones offering it around on a plate?"

"You've had it properly?" asked Charles curiously.

"Plenty of times," said Beau, who was a virgin.

"I've never had a young one. They always push me away. Say *I'm* too young."

"Not me," said Beau, missing the point. "Here comes Roz." He waved, causing Charles to follow suit. "Who's she with?"

"He was down at breakfast."

"Old enough to be her father," said Beau jealously.

"Hello Beau," said Roz. "How's my handsome cousin this morning? This is Benedict. Hello Charles. Haven't seen you for ages," and she laid clear emphasis on the 'seen'. "Benedict, this is Beau and Charles. I've been showing Ben the estate," she said with an air of propriety.

"Marvellous," said Charles, looking the man in the eye to see if anything had happened.

"Wonderful," said Benedict, who had regained his composure the moment he had pulled up his trousers, there being something said for a public school education.

"We'd better go in to lunch," said Beau, which was a relief to everyone as they moved off the lawn onto the gravel driveway towards the steps.

ZACHARIAH BOOTH APPEARED for luncheon wearing a high-necked sea-green shirt and drain-pipe trousers that exposed his socks. On his feet were a pair of chunky brogues. Blake Emsworth was wearing his harem trousers, with his hair tied back in a ponytail. Tammany was delighted with both of them and choked on her soup when Beau made a late entrance and was confronted by Zach.

"How is the acting going, Tammany?" enquired Lady Hensbrook from the top of the table, which caused everyone to look up and take note of the conversation.

"Very well, thank you, Granny Hensbrook. I had my first lesson in mime on Thursday." She struck a pose that nobody understood except Zach and Blake but at which everyone smiled politely and went back to drinking their soup, making certain not even a trace of a slurp could be heard.

Roz was purposely sitting at the other end of the table to Benedict and was chatting up another unsuspecting victim while receiving sidelong glances from both Charles and Beau, who were seated three places up on the other side of the table.

Tammany had also tied her hair in a ponytail and was wearing an old white shirt and rolled-up jeans, which her grandmother Beaumont put down to her now being in the theatre. She hoped the girl would look a little better at the ball and couldn't begin to imagine what her friends would show up looking like, then thought about it and decided it did not matter, that it might unstuff some of the stuffed shirts, though she doubted it.

"What school did you go to?" asked Beau, as Zach was presented with a plate of roast chicken.

"Are you asking me if I went to a public school?" asked Zach. "Because if you are, I didn't. I was educated in South Africa." He let them all go back to their food before adding, "We were evacuated. A lot of the kids from the East End were evacuated," and leaving it at that.

Blake Emsworth, totally engrossed with Tammany, had taken no notice of the other guests at the table.

"Don't I know you?" said Charles Ainsworth, causing him to tear his gaze from her at last and look straight at his father's partner's son.

"Possibly, Charlie," he said, causing Charles to wince, a fact noted by Roz for future reference. (No one his age screwed her mother and got away with it.)

Charles kept his attention on Blake.

"You look a bit ridiculous in that gear. What do you do for a living?"

"Play the guitar at the Earl of Buckingham."

"Still strumming away."

"I enjoy it. How are your mother and father?"

"Well, thank you."

"If you see any of my family you might mention you've seen me. Are you going into the firm?"

"Yes."

"Bully for you."

"What does that mean?"

"That you will make a very good stockbroker."

"You can't go on playing guitar in the local pub."

"Maybe not," he said, and his eyes rested gently on Tammany.

"Are you going into the firm?" asked Charles.

"Like this?" said Blake in mock amazement. "I don't think so. But I have some ideas. One just came to me."

"What's that?" asked Tammany.

"Later."

"Any chance of it making money?" asked Zach hopefully.

"Not for a long time. But it involves you."

"You've got me a job?" said Zach.

"You don't work?" asked Beau with the trace of a sneer.

"Very occasionally," said Zach.

"May I enquire what you do occasionally?"

"No," said Zach rudely, going back to his chicken and Brussels sprouts.

"You're very quiet, Adam," said Beau, trying to keep the conversation going.

"I try not to talk when I eat," said Adam, who had changed into civvies before lunch.

"I believe congratulations are necessary."

"Not until I finish OCTU. You'll have the same problem."

"I suppose so," said Beau in a way that indicated he would not.

By mistake, Lorna caught Zach's eye and he gave her a big wink.

"Marvellous lunch, Lady Beaumont," somebody said, and the conversation became more generalised.

"We'll take horses after lunch," said Tammany to Blake. "You and Zach can ride?"

"I can," said Blake, looking at Zach.

"Bareback," said Zach. "Essential if you want to break into the movies."

"You in the movies, Mr...?" said the girl on his right, who had studiously avoided him up until now.

"Booth. As in the gin. Miss...? No. Not yet."

"Oh." The girl turned away.

. . .

It was a five mile ride from Merry Hall, through Epsom Downs, which formed a small part of the racecourse. From there it was a mile and a half to the Wheatsheaf. They arrived at two-thirty, an hour before it closed, hitching the horses near to the front door.

"We'd better behave tonight," said Tammany after Zach had downed his first pint.

"How would you like me to behave?" asked Zach.

"The perfect English gentleman."

"I will act the part to perfection... Now, what's up your sleeve, Blake?" asked Zach.

"A musical. We three are going to write a musical that will return London to the heydays of Coward and Novello. We'll out-musical the Americans."

"What's it going to be about?" asked Tammany.

"I have no idea. That's your department. Yours and Zach's. I'll write the music. I wouldn't have asked you if I didn't..."

"Be serious."

"I have never been more serious."

"Good. We'd better get the nags back. The lady has to get herself ready."

"So do you," said Tammany.

While the three horses were trotting back Indian file along the bridle path, Lorna was throwing a tantrum in front of her mother, who was telling her that if Norman Hartnell was good enough for Queen Elizabeth, he was good enough for her daughter, and she was not going to be allowed to make an exhibition of herself in that thing her sister had run up for her, and that was final.

"But Tammany's got one," Lorna said.

"Have you seen it?"

"Well, no," she said sweetly.

"There isn't enough material."

"That's what I thought, darling Mummy. It's sensational. Aunty Isabel may have a reputation of being a very naughty girl but she is also a very good dress designer. Any young girl with a good figure will wear her clothes and I am not having that cousin of mine upstaging me at my own 'coming out' dance... How do I find a husband in something that would suit Granny Hensbrook?"

"Don't be rude."

"You know what I mean."

"Your father..."

"Is not here."

"Your uncle..."

"Will love it."

"He paid..."

"He'll be around at that dress shop trying to buy it."

"Let's have a look. I never did understand your generation. Ever since the war..."

"Everything has changed," finished Lorna, who had got down to a hipster petticoat and was pulling on the dress.

"What about your bra?"

"You don't need a bra," she said, adjusting the dress in front of the mirror before turning back to her mother and parading around the room, leaning sideways, picking up a book from her bedside table, spinning as if in a dance to prove she would not be embarrassed.

"I see what you mean," said Georgina when Lorna stopped. "Maybe my sister has found a vocation."

"It won't be right without your approval."

"Your grandmothers will have heart attacks," she said, and they laughed together, Georgina's a little strained, while Lorna went back to the mirror and piled her blonde hair up on top of her head, giving length to the dress.

"Tammany can never compete with that," said Georgina quietly.

"Oh she'll be good... Does Adam have evening dress?"

"Uncle Reggie sent him to his tailor."

"He'd be good looking, in an oriental way, if only he knew how to dress."

"You're as bad as your brother."

"They deserve it."

"Personally, I think you're both jealous," said her mother and poured herself a gin from her private stock.

KAREN, eleven years old, and the youngest of the cousins, sister to Lorna, Beau and Raoul (he had sensibly gone straight off on a summer holiday with a friend) was used to being spoilt by Granny Hensbrook, Granny Beaumont, Georgina, Pavy the Butler, Doris Breed the cook and an assortment of housemaids, scullery girls, head gardeners, under gardeners, garden boys and the chauffeur. For the past two days no one had paid her any attention. After careful inspection, she had chosen the tallest fir tree that skirted the gravel driveway close to the Gothic front door.

Georgina, having given in to her oldest daughter, had turned to take a breather from the ball and come face-to-face with her youngest child, who had climbed the conical fir tree to the very top of its tapering strength and was now clinging on for dear life with both hands, for all the world like a fairy on a Christmas tree, swinging precariously with the whippy bend of the treetop and radiating fear and panic from every cell in her young body

Georgina's first reaction was to scream, but she managed instead to turn for the door, gritting her teeth and telling Lorna, who was still inspecting herself in the mirror, not to look out of the window.

Meanwhile downstairs, Granny Hensbrook, who was the more highly strung of the grandmothers, had seen her grandchild's predicament and lost her nerve, something she never allowed herself in non-family circles. She shouted for Beau to do something, which caused him to stand and gaze up at his sister swaying in the breeze. Charles had the presence of mind to think of a blanket and reacted first, running off to look for one.

At this point Zach, Blake and Tammany rode up the driveway and Zach got halfway up tree before the branches were too thin to take his weight and he came down the slight slope of the fir tree like a train on a ski slope. Fortunately he landed on his bottom on the grass, ramming his coccyx where it should never have been rammed and causing him to let out a cry of agony which made the young girl at the top sway even more precariously. Three of those in the gathered crowd began calling for an ambulance.

Inside, Pavy, who had never been known to panic, was telephoning the Ashtead Fire Brigade, who left immediately, the crew delighted by the prospect. Everyone in the village knew about the ball and many earned extra money by contributing in some way. The big red engine with the longest of extension ladders (which was exactly what was needed) came out ringing its fire bell vociferously. The crew, mostly young, were interested in getting a look at the flock of young girls, half undressed in their ball gowns. Everyone on board the engine was fervently hoping that nothing else would come up that night.

Meanwhile, the under gardener had leant the longest ladder that could be found at Merry Hall halfway up the tree, and Beau, Charles, Blake and a semi-recovered Zach, who at six foot seven inches was too tall for the job, were dancing around the tree gripping the corners of a moth-eaten blanket that Zach thought unlikely to do the job. Each time Karen swayed with the breeze, the blanket team moved to position themselves where they thought she would fall, and as four sets of eyes were looking up and working independently the result was erratic.

Lady Beaumont, having inspected the kitchens, now arrived at the front door and surveyed the panic. "Everybody calm down," she said in a stentorious voice. "The fire brigade is on the way. Karen, just you hang on, darling, and granny will have you down in a jiffy," which turned out to be a little longer but calmed the girl, which had been the intention.

Upstairs, Lorna was wishing she had never been presented to the Queen in the first place and was convinced the first guests would arrive with the fire engine, which turned out to be correct. Two young guests in an MG sports car, not yet used to the social circuit, were early and as the roads were too narrow to get off to let the fire engine pass, had been chased all the way to Merry Hall and up the driveway, the bell clanging threateningly above their heads.

Within minutes, the fire brigade had rescued Karen, who had succeeded in her ambition of gaining the full attention of everyone at the hall, along with the fire engine crew and the two early guests.

"Come along then. Everyone get ready. Hello, I'm Lady Beaumont, Lorna's grandmother," Lady Beaumont said to the guests. "Pavy will serve you a glass of sherry. Very sensible to arrive early. By nine o'clock they will have to park behind the stables. My youngest granddaughter has just seen fit to cause a scene and will go to bed without her supper," she added, and the child in question was still too frightened to complain.

"How's your arse, old man?" Blake asked Zach.

"Bloody sore."

"We were proud of you," said Tammany.

"You came down quicker than you went up."

Just then Adam came back from a solitary walk along the river, coming to a sudden, puzzled halt at the sight of the fire engine in the driveway.

"We better think about getting ourselves ready," said Tammany, and they all trooped into the house. As they did so, the band, which had come in by the tradesmen's entrance, struck up from the newly erected dais in the library and the music echoed down the length of the old corridors, poking vibrations into corners that were not normally so disturbed.

"Hello," said Blake. "The piano is out of tune."

"People won't notice," said Zach.

"They're meant to be good," said Tammany. "You want to play, Blake?"

He shook his head. "Tonight I'm escorting the prettiest girl in the country."

2

*A*part from the height there was no resemblance. Zachariah Booth stood in line waiting to be announced by Pavy, who stood at the open double-doors leading into the high-ceilinged drawing room and thence through similar doors onto the polished wood-block floor of the library that had been chalked for dancing with the centre bookshelves dismantled and removed, leaving a space big enough for eighty couples to dance in comfort.

Off to the left of the drawing room was the dining room, which led into the conservatory, greened to the glass-paned ceiling with tropical plants. In the dining room, on every conceivable surface, including the long mahogany centre table that could seat thirty guests, were silver dishes, crockery pots, silver trays and copper trays, tureens of all sizes crammed with exotic food. Whole fresh Scotch salmon with frills and tucked in beds of new potatoes sprinkled with parsley; bright red lobsters, fat claws still plunging forward on the plates; oysters, open and ready to eat, which had been delivered that afternoon in barrels of ice; pyramids of pineapples; cold roast goose; partridge by the dozen, pickled from last year's shoot; and the centrepiece, a wild boar that Chuck Everly, Reggie's American business partner, had sourced from Wisconsin, transported in a truck to a landing strip, flown to New York in a light aircraft and taken on board a four-engine Constellation to Heathrow where the Merry Hall chauffeur had been waiting with the Bentley. There it was, tusks included and a large apple stuck in a surprisingly small mouth, richly crackled to a red-brown and done to a mouth-watering turn, its natural juices under the crackling ready for the majestic blade that would be wielded by Pavy at ten o'clock.

And over everything, the fragrance of gardenias flown in by Reggie's business correspondent from Hong Kong and driven down with the wild boar. Light caught in a thousand facets of the crystal chandeliers, the one in the drawing-room six feet wide, dancing and jingling in the summer breeze brought in with hothouse scents through the open doors of the conservatory which led out to the sloping lawns and rose beds on the east side of Merry Hall and thence through the tall elms, crow-roosted, to the fields, the woods and the river.

Zach smiled to himself. Everyone was giving Pavy a small visiting card which the butler looked at through his glasses and read out in a good voice that everyone could hear. On Pavy's left were the grandmothers shaking hands with the guests but otherwise no sign of the family.

"Are the shoes pinching?" asked Blake.

Zach ignored him, a baleful, sardonic expression on his face that he had spent some time perfecting in front of the mirror. He was immaculate in a well-fitting dinner jacket, his cuffs protruding one-eighth of an inch, crested cufflinks in evidence, his hair stuck down with Brylcreem to disguise the length and his patent shoes a brilliant shine. Zachariah Booth was playing the part to perfection. He handed Pavy his card, (the one he had printed on Friday morning without telling Tammany), flicking it out without looking, waiting for his name and entrance.

"The Honourable Zachariah Booth," announced Pavy, and Zach came forward to shake by the hand first Lady Beaumont and then Lady Hensbrook, neither of them having the slightest idea that he was the unsuccessful tree climber and corner man on the blanket they'd witnessed in action only a short time ago.

"Mr Blake Emsworth," he heard Pavy announce behind him, and together they moved among the upper crust of English society, ostensibly to see and be seen.

ADAM BEAUMONT, uncomfortable in his tailored dinner jacket and standing back from the guests in the farthest bay window from his grandmother, recognised Zachariah Booth for the man on the end of the blanket and looked around for Tammany. The rooms were filling up, which increased his discomfort. He disliked being paraded in front of strangers who would come forward to the man but changed in mid-stride when they looked into a face that was different to their own.

He had concluded by the age of ten that people were more comfortable in a pack, and when he had looked around for one of his own he had become bewildered at the rejections, some forceful, some coy, but mostly plain, downright rude. There had only been his sister and they had grown up together at Merry Hall, creating the children's world as they wanted it to be and making up in their imaginations the other companions of their childhood. They had had hundreds of friends living in the woods. Now, he had recognised there was nowhere to hide, that a man needed friends, but he, Adam, did not have any.

There had been the Scotsman, Flicker Burns, who had taught him how to flick a safety razor blade across a room and embed it in the wooden door a quarter of an inch; but that had been because of the way his face bones were structured and the way a public school accent had been grafted on, apparently falsely, which had caused them to fight on the small square of grass outside the hut and no one had won as they slugged on and on until neither hit anymore and Flicker had become a brief friend and the only person on camp who had been pleased he was one of the eleven for the air ministry selection board. Were the lower classes less conscious of his impediment, more human? Tammany seemed to get away from the problem as she was so pretty and had a way of making capital out of her colour. But now he was going to the Isle of Man and Flicker would find someone else to fight with and teach to flick a razor blade.

He shifted onto the other foot and watched the stream of his adversaries being announced to their world by Pavy until finally Beau took the line, tall, confident, liked by everyone, basking in the success of his school days. Adam was glad he had come in through the French windows and had found his corner to stand in and watch, there in body but never part of them, and he wondered if he ever would be. Should he go out East and find the other side of his parentage? There were uncles and cousins, even a grandfather that his father had talked about, but when his twelve-year-old face had lit up at the expectation of friendly relations, his father had told him he was an Englishman and a Beaumont and though his mother had been the most beautiful woman his father had ever seen and was missed every day of his father's life, she was of the East and he, the son, was of the West. He, Adam, was an Englishman.

His father had gone on living in Penzance, an almost total recluse, mourning Adam's mother's death and painting her portrait and creating on canvas the house they had all lived in on the lagoon, the long bungalow on the lawns leading through the tropical foliage to the soft sand and the warm blue sea and there he was in his father's paintings: Adam at one and a half crawling on the sand; Adam at three; Adam at five, but never older. The Japs had come and stopped all that and Adam's world had crashed around him. There was too much wanting in his father and nothing that he or Tammany could do to break it down, and they had tried. He wondered if both his parents had died then: that Horoshini (yes, he knew his name) had tortured both of them to death. Maybe they had all lost part of their lives...

He was going to OCTU... That had been decided. He would work and fight his way for his commission so they would have to look him in his slanted eyes and recognise him for the man he was.

This brought a smile of confidence to his face and he turned to go off and get himself a beer, and in turning all but bumped into a girl who came up to the lower part of his chest, all frills and petticoats. She looked up at him in the expectation of common ground but began to turn away in the ensuing silence.

"Hello," he said, having just made up his mind to overcome his side of the embarrassment.

"Ah," she said, smiling back now at the confident, very Asian smile Adam was giving her. "You must be a friend of Sir Reginald's partner, Mr Kim-Wok Ho. My father told..."

"I'm his nephew."

"Mr Kim-Wok Ho's?"

"Sir Reginald's."

"Oh, yes," and the shutters came down again as if she had opened the wrong door by mistake and found someone else on the lavatory.

"And his heir," said Adam, who was going to be a British Officer and was sick of all the nonsense.

"But that's not possible," she said.

"Why?" he asked coldly.

"Beau told me he would inherit everything as it passed down to the next male heir and as Sir Reginald is a bachelor..."

"My father is older than Beau's."

"Legitimate heir, I think was..."

"Did Beau say...?"

"All he said was that your mother and father were never married." She turned her back on him to look for unsullied company and he was left alone. He was totally stunned. There had been sniggers, whispers behind his back all his life, but no one had come out and called him a bastard to his face. So Beau really wanted Merry Hall... Now that he knew exactly where he stood it gave him confidence and he strode across the centre of the room to get himself a beer, and a beer it would be and none of those champagne cups that floated blueberries and strawberries at you as if you were having a fruit salad instead of a drink; and for the first time in his life he did not bother to see what kind of impression he was making. If Beau wanted a fight he would take pleasure in giving him one.

Roz Beaumont, having convinced her grandmothers that she was old enough to be seen at the ball, even if she was too young to be formally announced by Pavy, had also come in through the French windows. What she had not said to her elders was that she had borrowed her mother's make up and got her mother's Carnaby Street partner to run her up a party dress that would 'give her a chance with the boys'. She had seen Adam have words with the little snob she'd taken an immediate dislike to and had started off to talk to him herself but he'd walked off across the room for his beer. The best she was able to do was stare daggers at his adversary, causing six pairs of male eyes to take her in with obvious approval, which then gave her the courage to make her solo, side-door appearance. She made a beeline for the little bitch who had by then turned her limited charms on a tall, lanky thing that drooped over at the top to give everyone the best view of his limited chin. The chinless wonder, seeing her coming towards the group he was lucky enough to be part of, stopped paying any attention to the bitch. His jaw slackened and his droop increased, which caused the bitch to turn round and see what he was staring at.

"I am Rosalyn Beaumont," she said to the bitch. "I saw you talking to my cousin."

"I thought Lorna's sister was...?"

"I'm the other cousin."

"I didn't hear you announced."

"I wasn't. I'm sixteen."

"Good Lord," drooled slack-jaw, looking down the front of Roz's dress at her breasts in no way encumbered by a bra, causing his good luck to overcome his overbred manners as he stared until Roz pulled back one of her shoulders to cut off his view. By then she had the men's attention and had shut out the bitch.

"What were you talking about to my cousin?" she asked, bringing the girl back into the circle. "He's my favourite cousin," she said sweetly and truthfully.

"We were just talking."

"Arguing seemed more to the point."

"Would you like a drink, Miss Beaumont?" managed slack-jaw, hoping it would make her move and show him the best pair of breasts he had ever seen. Roz looked up at him and smiled, saying nothing, telling him with her expression that she knew exactly what he wanted and he was not going to get it. She was a firm believer in giving men something only once and he had seen quite enough to keep his dirty little mind in turmoil for the evening. She waited until he was almost at the point of repeating himself.

"A small glass of the fruit cup, thank you," she said, and turned her charms on the next man, still not having found her target for the evening in the ever increasing crowd. Within five minutes the men were fighting over her and the women were no longer trying to be polite. With everything nicely stirred up she smiled at them all and said she hoped they would all enjoy the evening. It was only the Geoffrey Beaumont side of the family that wished to be part of society but for the life of her, looking around at them all en masse for the first time, Roz could not think of one good reason why. And then she saw Charles Ainsworth and gave him a brief but pointed look before turning her full attention to the next group of men.

THE BUTTERFLIES in her stomach were bumping into each other as Lorna stood back from the line of sight where Pavy had paused from announcing names. Most of the guests had arrived. Lorna had watched the arrivals from her second-floor bedroom window as the cars drew up at the entrance to Merry Hall and the escorts left the car engines running while they came round to open the doors for the debutantes to step out in their swirls of dress and petticoats and, hopefully, a trim waist and creamy shoulders free of acne. She had turned back many times to the mirror and looked at the simple lines and the contrast of her own dress, which left her free and gave pleasure to her movements. The cut was perfect and drew in faint lines the curves of her body.

"This is it," she said, taking a deep breath as she began to walk forward in the manner in which her aunt Isabel had coached her. Her hair was up and twisted into a bun, drawing the hair taut from her forehead and hiding none of her beauty. As she moved, a book could have balanced on her head.

ZACHARIAH BOOTH WAS TRYING, unsuccessfully, to slacken his jaw when Lorna was announced, causing Lady Beaumont and Lady Hensbrook to look to the left and receive the first eyeful of their granddaughter.

"She's positively naked," said Lady Hensbrook in horror.

"Positively," said Lady Beaumont as the slow motion drama began to unfold in front of their eyes and the flash of the society photographers' cameras went off one after the other in high delight while Lorna continued through to meet her guests.

"Miss Lorna Beaumont," announced Pavy in an even if slightly cracked voice that hid his fear of the social disaster about to unfold.

The front ranks of the guests fell silent first, the others turning to look up as Lorna, in her white braless dress, floated across the parquet floor, smiling at the faces that looked back at her in awe, being female, and hunger, being male, shading down to disgust, being the 'uglies', to sheer lust from half a dozen of the men.

A wave of silence brushed away from Lorna until it reached the back, where Zach was standing slack-jawed at last as he looked over the tops of the heads at the near perfection of this woman at the height of her beauty. Being sensitive to an audience, he took in the situation quicker than the others and, nudging Blake, began to clap, which caused a ripple effect that spread as people, who a moment before were embarrassed, were now able to clap, giving those with a genuine eye time to appreciate what they were seeing and join in with the applause.

The band, who had been standing up for a better view, were signalled to play, and Zachariah Booth, in the full swing of his part and almost believing himself the son of a baron, came forward through the guests to claim the prize that was rightfully his. Lorna, having earlier seen from whence salvation came, fell easily and gracefully into his arms and began to dance, floating on her success, until she finally looked up into the smiling, bearded, well-groomed face that she did not recognise. Much relieved, Zach let himself study the flawless beauty of the young woman dancing so perfectly in his arms.

"What's your name?" she asked.

"Zachariah Booth. The honourable. My father is Lord Barnstable," he replied, which put her completely off the track.

"Is he very wealthy?"

"Very," said Zach, and he had a vision of his father in waistcoat and shirtsleeves selling tins of unlabelled carrots as pears off his barrow in the Portobello Road.

He was tempted to suggest she came and met his friend, Blake Emsworth, but thought the two together might click in her memory and so gave her up to her brother, who was furious with his sister for jeopardising his reputation.

As Beau was about to make a tart remark, his eyes fixed on Tammany, who was then being announced by Pavy and coming forward in a dress similar to Lorna's but in a rich red that contrasted the darkness of her skin and picked out a sheen of blue from her black hair that was pinned to one side, displaying one glorious ear from which a single, long oblong earring was suspended, the same rich red colour, surrounded by what looked like diamonds. The dress clung closely to a full body and in particular to the firm, heavy breasts that pushed at the silky material and gave their shape a free view of the room: once again the guests, started off by Zach and Blake, were clapping, and this time the photographers were after Tammany.

Upstaged and at the back of the room, Roz cursed her age but vowed her mother would design her a dress like that one.

"Who made that dress?" demanded Lady Hensbrook, having pursued her granddaughter until she could speak to her alone.

"Aunt Isabel," said Lorna.

"Isabel! I don't believe it. All she does is socialise."

"And design clothes."

"Tammany?"

"Same. Have a look at little Roz over there. The teenage look. Aunt Isabel."

"Do you think she makes any money out of it?" said Lady Beaumont, who had joined the conversation and was always more practical.

"I think she will now," said Lorna, nodding at the newspapermen who were crowding Tammany.

"Well, my goodness," said Lady Beaumont, looking from one to the other of her three grandchildren. Tammany had turned to look for Blake. They smiled at each other but as she turned she had accidentally pushed her left breast hard into the red silk.

"That's the sexiest thing I've ever seen," said Charles Ainsworth, following the line of Beau's stare.

"Your mask will come off," said Tammany to Zach, noticing the way he was looking at Lorna.

"She didn't recognise me, so I added a few bits to the story. She likes rich, titled gentlemen."

"None of which you are."

"She's smashing."

"My cousin is made of ice and ambition."

"People are never what they appear to be except that brother of hers. I have a permanent itch to flatten him and we haven't been introduced. The way he looked at you was bloody insulting."

"No swearing,"

"Wouldn't it be nice to take some of that gorgeous food out onto the terrace and sit at the comfortable table for four."

"She won't have supper with us."

"Yes she will."

"She's the big lady tonight. She'll find someone with a title and lots of land."

"I have a title and..."

"Zach!"

"Your idea I should be a gentleman."

"It's gone too far if..."

"Here she comes. Don't forget your part."

"There are tables on the terrace," said Tammany. "All set up on the two sides of the hall."

"Splendid," said Zach. "Hello, Lorna. I was telling Tammany I was coming over to ask you to have supper with us on the terrace."

"You've met each other?"

"How could I not meet the two most adorable women in the room. You haven't met Blake, I suppose? He's attached himself to Tammany for the evening."

FOR SUPPER, Adam had been taken in tow by Roz, much to the chagrin of all the men who had been given the privilege of a peek at her bust. Roz was particularly amused with the avoidance treatment being dished out to her by Charles but was happy to wait her time, knowing well she had his full attention. If there was one thing she disliked it was cocky nineteen-year-olds making free with her mother.

"Why did that bitch upset you so much? What did she say?" she asked Adam.

"It wasn't what she said but what Beau had told her. I'll wring his neck."

"You had better lay off the beer and come and have some supper. Who is that tall streak of wind taking Lorna to supper?"

"The Honourable Zachariah Booth. I think our cousin is going to learn something tonight."

"She is very beautiful."

"Where did all these waiters come from?"

"The village."

"Never seen half of them before. Ah... That'll do fine, thank you," he said as he took a glass of wine. "Your good health."

"You should not mix beer and wine."

"How would you know, young lady?"

"When you live with my mother you grow up fast. Do you like my dress? Mother..."

"It's very nice, Roz. It will be your turn to be presented next."

"No thanks. I see enough of these creeps in the general course of things without cultivating them."

"You have a point."

"Glad about your commission?"

"Haven't got it yet."

"You will."

"You've always been nice, Roz."

"So have you. Just ignore Beau."

"Some things you can't."

"Such as?"

"Telling that bitch I'm a bastard."

"He wouldn't. Granny...."

"He did."

"They say there's always a rotten one in every family."

"He wants Merry Hall," said Adam.

"Let him have it. Do you want Merry Hall?"

"No."

"What you want to do?"

"Join the trading section of Beaumonts. Train in the Far East. Be a strong link between East and West. Maybe both sides will trust a half-half. The perfect go-between."

"Sounds more fun than pigs and cows."

"It's the principle."

"Principles should never be stood upon."

"You've learnt a lot for a fifteen-year-old."

"I'm sixteen! My mother...."

"Of course. I better come and see her. I've only met her twice."

"Better not," said Roz, imagining the worst. "Come and get some food and leave that wine glass alone."

"Cheers, cousin," he said, drinking it down and following her into the dining room, where people in hordes were bending over the buffet. "We'll take a bottle through to the terrace and split it together."

"Adam," she giggled. "Are you going to get me tight? I'll tell Granny Beaumont."

"Wouldn't do that if I were you. She'd want to split the bottle three ways."

"The band's terrible."

"Probably not. It's what they have to play."

BY ELEVEN-THIRTY THE buffet had been removed and the noise level had risen so that it was difficult to carry on an intelligent conversation. Reluctantly, Lorna left Zach at the terrace table to circulate.

"Can't we go and relax somewhere," said Zach. "I'm beginning to feel like a boring drip."

"Granddad's study," said Tammany and led them away auspiciously to visit the powder rooms. "Port or old brandy? Very special. The room is stuffy but quiet... I've never seen Lorna like that."

"Actually," said Zach, as he followed them down the corridor and into the old study with its heavy leather chairs and racks of dust-covered bottles and the grandfather's butterfly collection, "she's a rather nice girl. I'll pour."

"What a lecherous bunch," said Tammany.

"Part of the price of beauty," said Zach, handing her a glass of port and pouring one for himself and another for Blake.

"I've got an idea... About the musical," said Tammany. "Why don't we set a musical in the original Merry Hall? My ancestor came over with William the Conqueror and there's quite a bit known about him. Married a local Saxon who gave him seven sons. All very romantic as she was the original squire's daughter so through the female line we've probably been here forever. The costumes were beautiful in those days. We can use the forest. Hunting songs. Love trysts. Banquets – they ate a lot. Call it *1066*. Ballads. You like writing ballads, Blake. A roving minstrel. A fat abbot. Even a band of friendly robbers who sneak out of the woods every now and again to have a good meal and a laugh with old Sir Henri. Maybe one of the sons can fall in love with the robber-king's daughter. Robber-kings always had beautiful daughters."

"A bit of magic," said Blake, who had forgotten his port and was pacing up and down the room. "A Merlin of the eleventh century. There must have been one if we research. The costumes will be exact and the ballads true to the period. All the laughter of Merry England."

"Set it after Sir Henri had been here a while," said Zach, whose professional mind had woken up. "Everything settled down. Give the impression of a happy family who expect to find their children's children in the same spot hundreds of years later. Give them a magical blessing that all will be well forever. No strings attached. We want a thoroughly nice Merlin who hands out everlasting happiness without strings attached."

"Lots of lutes and flutes," said Blake. "We'll start tomorrow. You'd better not drink that port or you'll have a hangover and you can't write top-class musical plays on hangovers. Clear head. That's the thing."

"This one is to celebrate."

"All right."

"*1066*," said Zach.

"*1066*," said Tammany.

"You're a PRICK TEASER," said Charles Ainsworth.

"Oh, Charlie, you look so funny in your shirt tails," said Roz from the other side of her bed.

"And don't call me Charlie."

"All right, Charlie. But those socks and garters are just terrific. Do you wear them when you play cricket?"

"Of course not. Why did you ask me up here?"

"To show you my photo album. You seemed very interested down...."

"I thought...."

"What, Charlie?"

"Well, you know."

"What, Charlie?"

"Don't call me Charlie."

"Why not?"

"You're thoroughly irritating."

"Then why did you come up?"

"You know."

"You think because I know you've been with my mother that I was asking you up for...?"

"Well, what else was...?"

"To show you photos, sweetie."

"I'll bet you're a virgin."

"Maybe, maybe not."

"Then why?"

"Because I don't like nineteen-year-old twerps making out with my mother and I wanted to teach you a lesson. But you can have a look at my panties, Charlie."

"All right... Go on then.... Go on."

"Do you want to see?"

"Yes."

"Why?"

"It's sexy."

"There. Did you have a good look?"

"Yes. Now, come on."

"Oh, no, Charlie. We agreed just a look."

"You're a virgin."

"I was with Mr Benedict Bellamy this morning at eleven o'clock if you must know. You saw us coming out of the woods."

"I don't believe..."

"Ask him. It will blow what's left of his hair off."

"Why Ben?"

"Because he's a pompous idiot and I wanted to make a fool of him."

"You let him go the whole way?"

"Well, not quite, but nearly."

"Why tease, Roz?"

"'Cause I like it. Seeing somebody really randy turns me on."

"I'm randy, Roz."

"I'm sure you are but you also kick over my mother's furniture in the middle of the night and that turns me off."

"Ben's old," said Charles, stressing the old.

"So is my mother."

"She asked for it."

"And you obliged."

"I prefer..."

"Younger girls?"

"Of course."

"You'd screw anything that moved."

"That's crude."

"Maybe."

"How old were you?"

"When?"

"When you first had it."

"That would be telling," said Roz, sitting on her side of the bed.

"Can't we Roz?" he said, wheedling.

"No."

"I've never been so randy."

"Good. That was the idea."

ADAM HAD SEEN Roz leave with Charles and had asked some of the wallflowers to dance without any success and then gone into the bar to drink beer as he was fed up with the wine. The snippets of conversation he overheard were so boring he did not bother to join in, not that he would have been accepted. In Adam's mind, everyone knew him as the Beaumont bastard and ladies who had been presented at court did not associate with men whose parents had failed to get married. He hated everyone except his sister and maybe Roz. No, he hated her too after she had gone off with that toffee-nosed friend of Beau's. What the hell, he'd have a couple of beers and go back to camp tomorrow and take a bottle of champagne. Pavy'd give him a bottle and he and Flicker would drink it. They'd sit right on that same patch of grass. What the hell did all these people mean to him when he and old Flicker were going to drink champagne together?

"Give me one of those quart bottles, barman. No glass, thank you. Just take out the stopper. That's my man. Good evening, ladies." He took the bottle of beer out onto the terrace and down onto the lawn and down the path between the herbaceous border and the noise grew further away and the lights were left behind him as the oaks drew closer with the night.

"GOOD TURNOUT," said Beau, surveying the guests. "Most are here that matter. Checked the list with Pavy... Roz not as old as you thought?"

"Shut up," said Charles.

"Temper. Good to get a duck every now and again. Increases the old concentration. Plenty more down there." They were standing behind the empty bandstand.

"Most of the oldies have left," said Charles. "Your uncle didn't come. Father will..."

"Sorry, old chap. There will be a next time. Pavy said Uncle Reggie phoned. Something about flying to America. Business bores me. That one over there is a bit tight. Not bad looking. Know her?"

"Which one?"

"You see Tammany?"

"Difficult not to."

"The group next to her. Against the pillar. Talking far too much. Head on one side. Sure sign."

"Felicity Cholmondeley. Hot, that one. Porchester senior says he made her but you know Porchester. What can you lose?" Beau watched the girl and his cousin Tammany at the same time.

"His brother is a twit," said Beau.

"Who?"

"Porchester minor. Odd family."

"Interbred... Think we'll get into the Guard's first eleven straight away?"

"Last week's game will help. Had an approach from Surrey Colts..."

"That's a good start. Your father played for Surrey?"

"Couple of times... Better get off. Band's coming back. Hello, chaps. Getting enough drinks? I'll have some beer sent up. You can play what you like now. The older generation has gone to bed... You should jive with Roz, Charles. She is very good and in that dress it'll be quite a sight. Did you see Adam? Took a bottle of beer and went off into the woods. There must have been a lot of timber in Sarawak. Have you heard of Lord Barnstable?"

"No."

"Neither have I. The invitation didn't go out to the Honourable Zachariah Booth either. Wonder who he is? Reminds me of someone. There was a plain Zachariah Booth on the list and mother never gets a title wrong. Pavy says he read it off the man's card so it can't be... Excuse me, I better chase my younger sister back to her bedroom. She is behind that drape in her pyjamas. Ah, Granny Hensbrook's spotted her. Lucky not to break a neck this afternoon. Feel like some tennis tomorrow?"

"Marvellous."

"Ten o'clock. Some of the houseguests will play later. Forget about her, Charles."

"Little bitch."

"Mustn't say such things about my cousin." Beau was smiling, pleased with himself. 'Tammany is not wearing a bra,' he thought.

'Who's the creep that's been following her around?' And it was only then that he recognised Blake and Zach. 'The bohemians... To hell with Tammany.'

"Excuse me," he said to Charles, "I'm going to have a word with my sister."

"Don't forget Felicity Cholmondeley."

"First things first." But he continued to wave and smile at people he recognised, pleased with the sudden blushes of two of the prettier girls.

"AH, THE YOUNGER BROTHER," said Zach, recognising the confrontation as Beau made his way through the group, slightly pushing Lorna. "Careful," said Zach, without the banter in his tone.

"You know it's against the law to use a title that doesn't belong to you?"

"Certainly. I played Macbeth once and the Honourable Bertie in *The Importance*... Tonight it is the part of the slack-jawed aristocrat."

"You should get out," said Beau.

"Why? I was invited."

"You can't..."

"Why not? Lorna herself said I couldn't come in my usual style."

"You're the bohemian," said Lorna. "You're not...?"

"Let us talk outside," said Zach, turning to Lorna.

"You'll do nothing..." said Beau, which caused Zach to bend down to the level of his head.

"You're out of your depth, sonny boy, but please give me the opportunity."

"What's the matter, Zach?" said Tammany, joining the circle with Blake in tow.

"Nothing. Lorna and I need some air."

"You know who he is?" said Beau.

"Of course. He's been beautifully behaved. You should mind your manners."

"Not with Lorna."

"I think your sister picked one of the few men in the room."

"He's an..."

"Imposter...? No. An actor. And a good one. We share the same digs. Calm down, Beau. You look quite puffed up. Go and find a nice young thing to dance with. They're all dying to dance with the great cricketer. And congratulations on your seventy-six runs..." Beau turned his back on her. "Oh, dear. I've upset my cousin."

"We'd better rescue Zach," said Blake.

"Leave them. It wasn't all acting." She watched Zach move away through the guests and said to Blake, "Come and dance. They're playing jive. You can jive?"

"A man who writes musicals who can't jive?"

"Can you do the over and under?"

"Of course."

"I hope this dress..."

"You're wearing pants?"

"Don't be silly."

"In the clubs I've been..."

"Will you take me?"

"There's 100 Oxford Street. Chris Barber's. Humphrey Lyttelton's. I'll sing lunch in the Earl for extra money. You better get out of those high heels."

"Okay, Buster, let's give it stick."

"Why the hell can't you be Lord Barnstable's son," said Lorna.

"Because there is no Lord Barnstable."

"You've made a fool..."

"I was going to tell you and then Beau..."

"That horrible, horrible moment and you saved me and so tall and then rich and going to be a Lord. It's what I want, damn you. Why can't you be rich?"

"Why can't you be sensible?"

"I'm being sensible."

"I'm still Zachariah Booth."

"Don't you see?"

"An out of work actor isn't any good to you."

"Why couldn't...?" And she hit him on the chest.

"Lorna, there are plenty of men. Go back in there and laugh it off as Tammany's practical joke, which is all it was. Tell the bohemian story. Do you want me to go and change?"

"Don't do that, for God's sake."

"Don't swear. I've heard your grandmother..."

"It was damned unfair."

"I'm sorry, Lorna. The joke backfired."

"Yes, it damn well did." She pulled away from him and walked down the steps of the terrace onto the lawn, Zach watching her. He watched her for some time.

"Come and have a drink," said Blake, who found him still staring across the lawn. "It's free."

"Nothing is free. Nothing is ever free, Blake. But I'll have one nonetheless." And he laughed, falsely.

"That's my boy. Women are..."

"You're a fine one to talk."

"She's different." Zach left it at that and went inside and had the barman pour him a Scotch.

BEAU WAS wrong about one thing. Adam had not gone into the woods to commune with the timber but to drink a large bottle of beer and then go back and fetch another one, neither of which helped the twisting in his gut which by the end of the second bottle was as taut as a piano wire. He was seething mad with his cousin and the alcohol had removed his better judgement so that when he went back into the house at two-thirty in the morning for his fourth bottle, the party was coming to a close but Beau was on the dancefloor with the young girl who had reported to Adam that he was a bastard. Adam waited until the dance was over and his cousin was walking out onto the terrace where a bottle of German hock was sitting in an ice bucket along with Charles, Felicity

Cholmondeley and four glasses. Adam followed, bottle of beer in hand, and sat down at the table uninvited. The girl who had been dancing with Beau, and who Roz had correctly labelled as a bitch, tried to get up from the table.

"Cheers," said Adam, waving his beer bottle at them. "Wonderful party. All the right people. Well, a couple maybe who shouldn't have been allowed but generally a good sampling of the peerage and their offspring. Wouldn't you say so, Beau? Most gratifying."

"What do you want?" said Beau rudely, pouring wine into the glasses.

"I've been waiting all evening to see you two together. No, please don't get up. Your evidence is vitally needed. Sit down and drink your wine."

"Adam! Do you mind?" said Beau. "Charles and I..."

"The inseparable twins. Now, my dear," he said, turning to the bitch, "would you mind repeating your story?"

"You've been drinking."

"Undeniably. Please, my dear. What was it you so kindly told me earlier this evening?"

"If you must," she said, turning on him nastily. "You are illegitimate."

"And who was so kind as to impart this information?"

The girl did not answer.

"I did," said Beau.

"Now the dog is at bay."

"Don't call me a dog," said Beau. "Your mother and father were never married despite what Uncle Tug says. He would. He was forced to bring you back from Australia after the war. You had nowhere to go. My uncle is a man of honour. Who can blame him for taking a mistress in Sarawak? There weren't any white women. Bringing you back and bringing you and Tammany up was commendable but it doesn't make you any less of a bastard in the true and figurative sense of the word."

"Lord Gray confirmed they were married."

"He was First Officer but not a witness and you know as well as I that the records of marriage and birth were lost when the Japs overran Sarawak."

"They were married."

"You've got to prove it, cousin, which you can't, so until then you are a bastard in my eyes and the eyes of the College of Heralds and I am heir to Merry Hall and the Baronetcy. Only legitimate heirs of Sir Henri de Beaumont can inherit. Don't blame me. Blame the laws. Or, failing that, blame your parents for not getting married. In the meantime, please leave my table as I don't feel like drinking with the family by-blows just now."

"They were married," said Adam.

"Prove it."

"I will. To spite you. To prove that my mother was not a white man's concubine."

"You said it, dear boy. Now would you mind pissing off. Excuse the expression, ladies, but it's the only language they understand."

"Grandmother..."

"Don't go crying to your grandmother. You're meant to be a man. Go and have another beer and get thoroughly drunk. You bore me."

And there was nothing else left for him to do.

"What a twit," said Charles.

"That he's not," said Beau. "Just a bastard. Cheers. Now no one will be in doubt. I love those old titles. So specific. As rich as he is, there is nothing Uncle Reggie can do about it."

"How old is your Uncle Reggie?" asked Charles.

"Forty-six."

"He can..."

"Never. Married his business years ago. Doesn't even have time to visit the Hall and he owns the place for the moment. Confirmed bachelor. Felicity, come and dance with me. The night is but a pup."

"I'd love to, Beau."

"Have you been round the Hall?" he said, leading her away from the table.

"No."

"I'll show you. The grounds first."

"And then."

"Where would you like to visit?"

"Come and dance. It's a slow one. You'll work it out by the end of the dance. I think you two were going to fight. Men fighting makes me excited... Not like that. Closer. That's better." He pushed against her and she pushed her crotch hard against his erection and danced him slowly round the darkened floor, her right hand constantly stroking the back of his neck.

"Your bedroom or mine?" she said. "House guests privilege."

"Mine," said Beau huskily. "It's nearer."

3

*T*en days later, Rosalyn Beaumont turned sixteen and asked her mother if she could leave school. She had taken her school certificate in the summer term and expected to pass, and after that, in her mind, what was the point of school?

"And what are you going to do, young lady?" asked Isabel.

"Oh, I've worked that all out."

"Please let me into the secret."

"Mum, stop treating me like a child. I know a lot more about life than you think."

"You do?"

"I'm not that innocent, you know."

"What do you mean?"

"My business, Mum."

"What on earth are you talking about?"

"I met a boy at Clacton, when we visited. He ran the dodgem cars."

"And?"

"He taught me a few things."

"Are you serious?"

"Yes, but I was careful. Let's face facts, mother dear."

"Don't mother dear me."

"Why did it always have to be the males' need and the subject we girls shouldn't talk about?"

"I see."

"I'm nothing like you, Mother. Not yet."

"Rosalyn! And if you leave school?"

"Oh, Mum," said Roz, giving her a hug. "I love you. You're so practical."

"Sometimes one has to be. But Roz, don't grow up too fast. Life has stages. Don't burn them away too quickly or you'll end up sour. Don't you want to stay a schoolgirl a little longer?"

"No."

"Don't you want to go to Switzerland? Uncle Reggie said he'd..."

"No."

"Oxford? Girton? Your school marks are very good."

"No, thank you."

"Secretarial college?"

"No."

"What then?"

"I'm going to turn your dress shop into the biggest swinging teenage clothes boutique in London. We're going to get all the kids wearing the gear I had on at the ball. Look at the *Tatler*. You saw Tammany and Lorna but have another look and you'll see your daughter. Mum, we caused a sensation. We can sell those designs to the chain stores."

"Who told you all this?"

"My friend, Pen..."

"Nonsense. She's fifteen."

"Well, a man I know..."

"Go on."

"He's in business. Promotions. Own company at twenty-three."

"Your boyfriend?"

"Kind of."

"I see."

"Well, I showed him the press clippings and he couldn't believe it and wanted to know how many more designs the designer had up his sleeve and when I told him it was my mother he laughed and said no old woman could design for the kids and I said you weren't old."

"Wait till I get my hands..."

"You keep your hands off him, Mother dear. That's the first rule if we're going to be in business."

"I don't believe it," said Isabel, laughing. "You in business with me!"

"And Ted and Lorna."

"What the hell has Lorna got to do with it?"

"She's the model. The way she carried it off was a sensation. I couldn't..."

"She's nearly nineteen."

"At twenty I wouldn't be able to walk into a crowd of strangers and have them clapping. It was touch and go but she did it. I don't think Tammany could have got away with the first entrance and she's in the drama business. Ted's going to do promotions campaigns. Create a label. A name. Throw parties that will overflow into the street. Have a lot of good looking girls walking around in our gear and chatting up the chain store buyers."

"What do you know about chatting up? That's..."

"Vulgar? No, Mum. It's fun. I love chatting up guys and to do it you need the right gear. Ted's slogan is going to be 'kick the bra'. He'll have an advertising campaign showing the girls dangling their bras over their shoulders. And only good looking models... That earring of Tammany's. We'll make them. Accessories, Ted says, can make a big difference. Give the kids six outfits for the price of one."

"Where did you meet Ted?"

"I don't remember, Mum."

"Ted who?"

"Cornwell."

"Where did he go to school?"

"Well, he left."

"Expelled?"

"Good Lord, no. He went to the board school and learnt to read afterwards, I mean..."

"A strong accent?"

"Strong but cute. Mum, he's got brains but he doesn't have any capital and this is the opportunity he's been waiting for and he's right. Makes sense. You don't even know how good your designs are. To you it's a hobby to pass the time."

"I'm going to have a cigarette."

"Have one of mine."

"You smoke! I suppose you have a light?"

"Yes."

"Where are you going to get the money for promotions and advertising?"

"And a factory. Ted's adamant."

"He is, is he? And the capital?"

"Uncle Reggie will jump at it."

"Uncle Reggie has better things to do than piddle around with a dress shop."

"This is big, Mum. Ted says we can sell to the Americans. Compete with the French. The Fifties and Sixties are going to be the British look. Others will follow. Carnaby Street will be full of designer boutiques. Everybody's sick of the war and the rationing and never having a good time. Ted says the kids want to play around a bit before they take life seriously. Do you blame them? Look at Dad. He wasn't old. Did he have much fun?"

"Your father liked horses... Maybe you're right. It's a new era. Henry's biggest goal in life was to win the Derby... Maybe I was born twenty years too early. This new wacky society you dream about would have suited me fine."

"Design what you would like to have worn. What you missed."

"That's an attractive idea."

"You can wear your clothes, Mum. You've still got a figure."

"How kind of you to mention it."

"I'll tell them we're sisters. You'd look great in Lorna's dress.

Maybe a belt. Different shoes. Jewellery. You could have stopped that ball. How old are you, Mum?"

"You know perfectly well. Forty-two ."

"From now on you're thirty-two. Think young. How's that?"

"What's the time?"

"Five o'clock."

"I need a drink."

"Can I bring Ted up?"

"Where is he, for God's sake?"

"In the car downstairs."

"You've worked out costs and profit projections, whatever they are, I suppose," she said sarcastically. "Reggie says they're important."

"That's the bit we haven't done. We need you to tell us how long it takes to make a dress on an assembly line and how to buy material in bulk. Where to buy thread, buttons, you know."

"How long have you been going out with Ted?"

"Two weeks. Why?"

"Wow! Do you just talk business?"

"Don't be ridiculous, Mother. When you see what he... Come on."

"Why not... You think they'd sell?"

"Like hot cakes." Roz moved to the window and threw it open.

"What does he drink?"

"Gin and tonic with a slice of lemon. Ted's on his way up in the world." She leant out of the window and looked down onto the street and let out a whistle. "We're in, Ted. The old lady..." She turned back, said, "Sorry, Mum," then looked down again. "Come up," she called, then turned back to her mother.

"We can all go round and see Uncle Reggie afterwards."

"He's still in America."

"He's always away."

"Yes," said Isabel softly, as her daughter went to open the front door. "He always was."

She waited expectantly until the door opened.

"This is Ted."

"Hello, Mrs Beaumont. I think you're the greatest dress designer in the world."

"Why, thank you," said Isabel, giving him a wry smile. "Gin and tonic, I believe."

"That would be smashin'," he said, looking at the dining room table. "Pure bleedin' genius. Sorry, ma'am. Language always out when I'm excited. Smashing, that's what they are. Hear that Rozy, got the 'g' on the end that time. Rozy's teaching me to talk right..."

"You seem to be teaching each other quite a lot. Where did you meet?"

"I picked her up, Mrs Beaumont... These are really smashing," he said, turning back to the drawing. "Hear that, Rozy? Got the 'g' again. Sounds funny, smashing with a 'g'."

"Where?"

"Richmond ice rink, Mother. Penny and..."

"Ice rinks or street corners. What's the difference? I believe you can write, Mr Cornwell?"

"Call me Ted."

"If we wish to share anything with Sir Reginald we will require a written report."

"I like things on paper myself. Clears the thoughts." He unlocked a slim, black briefcase and took out five sheets of typed paper. "The headings are 'market', that's who we want to sell to. Then 'cost'. We can't sell to a kid something he can't afford. The rest's all 'ere. We'll have our problems but if it don't work on paper it won't work neither."

"We'll have to work on that last sentence," laughed Roz, handing Ted a gin and tonic.

"You ain't... I mean you haven't got yours, love."

"Mother?"

"Help yourself, Roz," said Isabel, taking in the 'love' and the way he looked at her. "Give me that report."

"This copy is for you, Mrs Beaumont."

"Very efficient."

"I don't like muck ups, Mrs Beaumont," he said, stumbling over the 'm'.

Isabel suppressed a smile and sat down at the head of the dining room table to read.

"When's Uncle Reggie..." began Roz.

"Don't interrupt."

"Sorry, Mother." She went to the side table to pour herself a brown sherry, taking one of Ted's offered cigarettes without thinking.

"I put the lighter on the bureau," said Isabel, without looking up from her reading.

"Thanks, Mum," said Roz, and she tiptoed across the Persian carpet and flicked the heavy silver lighter three times before it caught and then dropped the cigarette out of her mouth onto the floor. Ted picked it up, lit it, and handed it back. They smoked and drank in silence until Isabel put the report down on the table.

"I'll work out the costs with my partner. Uncle Reggie is back tomorrow. Ring him at his flat, Roz. He takes more notice of you than me. He always thinks I'm after something."

"But you are," said Ted, surprised. "Fifty thousand pounds."

"Not money. Reggie doesn't worry about money. He'll have that report checked out by four people and the figures by his accountant. If the mathematics say yes, you'll get your fifty thousand pounds with some rather neat strings attached, one of which will be fifty-one per cent of the shares for Reggie. In return you'll get your money and the full clout of Beaumont Limited. You two will be employees with share options and Mandy and I will split the forty-nine. The problem is design. You have a lot of faith in me, Mr Cornwell."

"Ted."

"I hope Reggie has the same amount. We haven't always agreed with each other. What are you doing, Roz?"

"Phoning Uncle Reggie. He once told me he often came back unexpectedly from a trip to surprise his staff."

"Here's your drink, Mrs Beaumont," said Ted.

"Chin-chin," said Isabel wearily. "Now what the hell have I got myself in for?"

"A lot of fun. We're all going to have a lot of fun."

"Maybe."

"Hello," said Roz. "It's Rosalyn. Are you going to be at home in ten minutes, Uncle Reggie...? Good... How's school? I've left... No, Uncle Reggie I was not expelled and please don't laugh like that... I'll catch a taxi... I'll tell you what it's about... You're a darling... Bye bye." She put down the phone and immediately picked it up again and dialled for a taxi. "When you say a time to Uncle Reggie you have to mean it. Get downstairs, Ted, and grab a growler if it comes first. Mother, put on some lipstick and those dark stockings."

"I don't believe this is happening," said Isabel as Roz collected the press clippings.

"You don't have a date, do you mother?"

"Not tonight."

"Maybe Uncle Reggie will take us all out to supper."

"That would be nice," said Isabel. She had gone into the bedroom, where she was rolling on her stockings.

"If not, Ted will take us. There's only one thing Uncle Reggie will have to change. Ted wants shares."

"How about a fee payable to his company?"

"That might work."

"A percentage on sales. Overrider or something."

"Mum, I always thought you were dumb."

"Thank you, darling."

WHILE TED (much to his surprise), Isabel and Roz were sitting down to dinner at the East India Club with Sir Reginald Beaumont, who had argued their concept in his Whitehall flat for an hour before agreeing to put it up to his new-business management team, Lorna was being shown to a seat by the maitre d'hotel of the Berkeley. The man had wrung his hands appropriately and smiled with delight when recognising his patron. What Lorna did not see was the smile dropping off his face the moment he entered the kitchen to give the order for lobster bisque and a half bottle of hock; the Honourable Edward Hemming tipped well.

"Good-looker outside," he said to the chef. "Where does that idiot find them?"

"Money."

"Put a bit of extra pepper in the bisque."

"Careful."

Meanwhile, Edward was surveying the room to see if he should recognise anyone. He saw a man he knew at Lloyds but chose to ignore him; the man had gone to a minor public school.

"I was in one of your uncle's boxes this afternoon," he said to Lorna, referring to his job at Lloyds. "Wrote me a line. Does he ever visit the room?"

"Where? Who?" said Lorna, who had switched off.

"Sir Reginald Beaumont."

"Probably. I don't know. Excuse me a moment..."

Edward got up to move back her chair solicitously in the way a gentleman had been taught. His expression was correctly bored.

After waiting five minutes, Lorna came back. She had been long enough to put him in his place but not long enough to be thoroughly rude.

"You know how it is," said Lorna sweetly, causing Edward to curse under his breath, having now to make up his mind whether to take her out again or let it go. She took a sip of the wine before picking up her soup spoon. "Bon appetit," she said politely, giving her escort a smile but avoiding eye contact. That trick of her Aunt Isabel's was dangerous.

THE DAY after Lorna had successfully avoided going back to Edward Hemming's flat, Adam Beaumont looked around hut eleven at the fifteen exhausted officer cadets seated on their perfectly made beds.

"I did not ask to be made senior cadet so don't give me looks. I've had them all my life. Half English and half Asian so let's get that one out the way. Three cadets have withdrawn from the course and less than a hundred are expected to pass. Anyone want to pull out? We are now in August. The weather is good. This hut is made of tin which by winter will be too cold to touch. Last year the sea froze one hundred yards out. The squadron commander told me this afternoon that the first week is easy and after that he builds up the pressure until you crack or you pass out on the 19 December. It's a big man who stands up now and says he can't make it." Adam waited, looking from one cadet to another. One coughed, some stared ahead, some tried to smile.

"I'll never get through," said Percy Wade.

"Why not?"

"You've got to be physically strong. I'm so stiff I won't get out of bed tomorrow."

"You'll toughen up."

"They'll throw me off eventually. I like the idea of the commission but not like this."

"Percy, we can go through to Burke now. This is the last chance to go off voluntarily... No one else...?"

"I can go on my own. Hope you all pass. Been good being with you. Best part of the course. I'm sorry..."

"Have a good crossing on the ferry."

"Good luck."

"Same to you." The hut door opened and closed and they listened to the sound of his boots hitting the pathway.

"Right," said Adam. "That's it. That's the last guy who fails from hut eleven. We have to help each other. Officer qualities. OQs. You'll hear plenty about them. Today we did the obstacle course. Four teams of four. George, you led one and didn't even try to get over the electrified wall."

"I couldn't see how."

"Harry had a go and botched it. Left the dummy on top of the wall but nearly made it. At the water tanks all of us fell in and I asked Burke how it was done and he smiled. 'Some things are impossible'. If one of us gets into shit, don't stand back like that lot from Green Squadron did this morning. Get in and help. Pull out. Next time it'll be your turn to be dragged out. Oh, and everyone volunteers to play sport. Everyone goes to church whether you believe in it or not. Smile and look cheerful. And no one thinks of failing. We've got a PhD in mathematics and George who plays rugby for Gloucestershire. Talent there is plenty. Pool it and we're all through. Any questions...? Let's get supper. At least they feed us properly."

ON THE DAY at the end of September when Beau joined the army for his two years of national service and exchanged his aristocratic haircut for a shorter one, his sister, Lorna, was walking through the ripe corn fields to the west of the thirty-acre field accompanied by three Merry Hall Pointer dogs. A slight breeze made golden waves out of the cornfields and the touch of winter rustled the beech trees to her right, sending the occasional beech nut to the carpeted floor. A short, intermittent summer was over. Only Lorna of her generation was left at the Hall, Karen having been packed off to boarding school. She called the dogs and skirted back to the house for the confrontation. Reaching the herb garden, she let herself through the wooden gate and walked into the house, already darkened by the shorter evenings.

"You missed supper," said her mother as Lorna walked into the drawing room.

"Need a fire soon," said Lady Beaumont, who was threading different coloured wools through a pattern to make a cushion cover. Granny Hensbrook had nodded off in the opposite chair and Lorna was conscious of the strong scent of tobacco plants that had been planted outside the window to perfume the room in the evenings.

"Sorry, Mother."

"There's a glass of milk and a biscuit on the side table."

"Thank you, Mother."

"Why didn't you go to the Hemming dance?"

"Because Edward is a prig."

"Very eligible."

"Very priggish."

"Don't be rude."

"Sorry, Mother."

"You'd better sit down if you've something to say, Lorna," said Granny Beaumont, pushing her glasses back onto the bridge of her nose.

"Gran, were you presented?"

"No, I was not. Lot of nonsense. Met Thomas when he came back from India on leave."

In the ensuing silence, the grandfather clock in the hallway ticked loudly and a fluting sound came from Granny Hensbrook, who had taken a second gin and tonic before supper.

"I'm not going to any more dances," said Lorna, which caused Granny Beaumont to stop in mid-stitch and her mother to look up.

"Why ever not? Have you found someone?"

"No one, Mother."

"Then you must carry on going to them."

"They're all the same."

"Of course they are. Young gentlemen have a resemblance."

"No chins, no talk except about themselves and only one thing on their minds."

"Nonsense," said her mother.

"You don't have to go out with them."

"It's a stage. Find one eligible enough, marry him and everything will fall into place."

"Hello, Charles," she imitated. "Nice to see you. Usual table. Jolly good. I've met enough head waiters in three months, thank you."

"Wait until you settle down."

"You met Father playing tennis."

"I was lucky. The war lost us a lot of eligible bachelors."

"I'd prefer to be unmarried."

"What are you going to do?"

"Take a course in modelling."

"Modelling," said her mother, "is the first step towards prostitution. Disporting your body in public."

"Aunt Isabel..."

"Don't mention my sister in this house."

"Mother, for goodness sake don't be so old-fashioned," she said, which caused her grandmother to cough. "Roz's boyfriend is opening a shop..."

"Roz! Boyfriend! She's still at school."

"She left on her sixteenth birthday."

"Did she?" said Granny Beaumont, nodding and dropping her glasses onto the needlework. "Damn."

"Mother!"

"I said damn, Georgina."

"What?" said Lady Hensbrook.

"Go back to sleep, Mary," said Lady Beaumont.

"I don't mind my sister going to the dogs," said Georgina, "but I won't have her..."

"She's not going to the dogs," said Lorna nicely. "Far from it. Ever since Uncle Reggie put fifty thousand pounds into the business."

"What business?" said Lady Beaumont, folding her glasses.

"Designer clothes. Carnaby Street. They're going to make a fortune."

"Who is 'they', Lorna?" said her mother.

"Aunt Isabel, Mandy, Roz, Ted and of course Uncle Reggie. He'll make more than..."

"He usually does, dear," said Lady Beaumont.

"They want me to be the house model."

"Over my dead..."

"Quiet dear," said Lady Beaumont. "Let the child say what it is that she wishes to say."

"Your father would..."

"Malaya is a long way away," said Lady Beaumont, referring to her son Geoffrey, a brigadier in the British Army. "What is a house model, Lorna?"

"I wear the house designs. Fashion shows. Functions. Impress the chain store buyers."

"How?" said Georgina.

"By showing off the new designs to the best advantage. Roz is already..."

"What did I say?" said Georgina.

"Does it pay well, Lorna?"

"Not really, Gran, but that doesn't matter. It's the excitement. The people. Selling the new stuff. Seeing the kids wearing it later."

"Where did you learn to talk like that?" said Georgina, who was sitting bolt upright in her chair.

"Well, Ted..."

"Who is Ted?"

"I told you. Roz's boyfriend. He's twenty-four and knows a lot."

"He's what!"

"Twenty-four, Mother."

"Disgusting."

"Roz doesn't think so."

"Don't be rude." This caused Granny Beaumont to put on her glasses and find a spot in the needlework where she had left off.

"Anyway, he's only just turned twenty-four."

"How a niece of mine..."

"This is the second half of the twentieth century."

"And what exactly does that mean?"

"Things change, Mum."

"Don't call me Mum."

"Sorry, Mother. The war changed a lot. Ted says England won't have an empire soon."

"Won't have an empire!"

"Attlee gave away India."

"Attlee was a socialist."

"Things have changed. Girls are going to work. They don't sit at home and have tea parties. There's a big world out there and I won't be locked up in some country estate to breed children. If it wasn't for Uncle Reggie's business acumen the Hall would have gone out of the family by now. He was the first to go into business. He saw the change coming. It took them an hour to persuade Uncle Reggie that Isabel's designs..."

"So now it's 'Isabel'. You call your aunt by her first name?"

"Roz calls her Isabel."

"I don't believe it."

"When Isabel's dressed up she doesn't look a day over thirty. We're going to turn over a million pounds this season."

"How much?" said Lady Beaumont.

"A million pounds, Gran."

"Lot of money."

"Reggie says..."

"Not 'Reggie' as well," said Lady Beaumont, biting her lip.

"Yes and he doesn't look forty-six. How someone hasn't nailed him down I'll never..."

"What a vulgar expression," said Georgina.

"It would solve all this nonsense with Adam and Beau," said Lady Beaumont.

"It is not nonsense, Mother. If Tug was never married then Beau is the heir to Merry Hall."

"Tug is not a liar. Gray confirmed the marriage and so did that ghastly wife of his and she would have loved to have proved otherwise... 'Consorting with natives,' I think she would have put it."

"That's exactly what..."

"Consorting finishes when marriage starts. Reginald went out to Sarawak to find out and met the DC before Tug fell out with him and the man started trafficking in drugs. I have told Adam that unless Reginald produces an heir he must go to the East and obtain affidavits from that man Marshbank and the doctor. They were the witnesses. Lord Gray has retired and elected to stay in Kuching as he can't afford to live in England, which makes a nonsense out of forty-five years in the Colonial Service. He will certainly help Adam."

"Why are you doing this, Mother?" said Georgina.

"Because if Beau's father was here he would do the same and give his son a damn good hiding."

"You prefer Adam to Beau?" said Georgina.

"Certainly. Far nicer boy. We will not have a legal wrangle should anything happen to Reginald. Anyway, the Hall could never survive without Reginald's personal fortune."

"Everyone seems to be against me," said Georgina.

"Not at all. But I think it's an excellent idea for Lorna."

"Thank you, Grandmother," said Lorna.

"What's all this," said Lady Hensbrook.

"You can wake up, Mary. Your granddaughter's to become a model."

"Which one?"

"I don't seem to have a say in the matter," said Georgina.

"And you can still please your mother by going to some of the dances," said Lady Beaumont to Lorna.

4

*A*t ten past five the following evening, Zachariah Booth was sitting in the only chair in Tammany's bedsitter with his booted legs out of the window resting on the sill when the doorbell rang from downstairs.

"I'll go. You two carry on," he said to Tammany and Blake. Engrossed, neither of them had heard the bell or Zach and took no notice as he left the room.

"All right, all right, I'm coming," he called, climbing down the stairs thinking of the next scene. They had split the work. Tammany wrote the words to the songs in conjunction with Blake, and he wrote the screenplay. He was enjoying the fantasy of a musical and it gave him something to think about. Once again he was out of work. He opened the front door of twenty-seven and gaped. "The debutante!"

"Can I come in?" said Lorna.

"Have dinner with us. Vegetable stew. Your cousin cooked it."

"One of my favourites. You were right. Lot of stuffed shirts. I think I prefer the bohemian look," said Lorna, grinning.

"Who is it?" called Blake. "We've got a problem, Zach. Need help."

"Lorna. She's come to join the party." He turned back and smiled broadly at Lorna.

"Don't get ideas, Zachariah Booth. What's Tammany up to?"

"Writing a song."

"A song?"

"Yes, with Blake."

"Does he still wear his outlandish trousers?"

"Tammany made him a new pair."

"Hello Baxter," said Lorna as the dog jumped up at her.

"You two know each other?"

"Yes, he was born at the Hall."

"Hi," said Tammany, looking down the stairwell. "Come on up. Stew's ready. Got any money, Lorna?"

"Ten pounds."

"Marvellous. We can all go to the Earl of Buckingham."

OCTOBER WAS DRAWING TO AN END, and the weather was closing in nicely on the Isle of Man. The officer cadets in hut eleven were at the end of their tether but holding on by willpower, and Beau was in the last week of his square bashing. Isabel had recently completed her summer range and the staff and friends at thirty-six Carnaby Street had gathered together to see the results. The six house models were ready. Music played around the large room from a side entrance through which the models would enter to the stage. The lighting was perfect, Ted having brought in a lighting engineer to create a warm, intimate effect.

"Sit down everyone," called Ted from the small stage. "Plenty of chairs at the back... You lot ready next door...? Turn up the music, Fred... Okay... Send it... the best of bleedin' British and that's just it. Carnaby Street presents the *Jive* collection, so eat your hearts out."

After fifty-seven outfits had been paraded, criticised, torn to pieces and applauded, Ted had a final range of twenty-two.

By eleven-fifteen, the formality at the start of the evening had deteriorated. The food had been eaten and taken away, the dancing had become wild and the volume had been turned up three-fold.

For half an hour Ted had been looking for Roz when he walked into his darkened office and turned on the strip light. The tableau continued for a full, frozen second: Ted at the door with his hand still up to the light switch; Roz lying on the carpet in a compromising position with Fred, the sound engineer.

"Put your clothes on and get out, Fred. Collect your wage packet on Monday."

"She offered it. I'm not the only one."

"So sod off before I kick you into the street. Fuckin' pretty sight and that's no maybe. My bloody bird and my bloody office. How the fuck do you fuckin' well like that...? No, Roz. You stay. You and I'll talk. Ta-ta Fred. You're a jerk. Bugger up a friendship and a good job for a quick lay."

The office door slammed.

"You've been doing that with Mother," said Roz, pulling down her skirt and adjusting her blouse.

"I've been what?"

"Having it off with my mother?"

"Don't talk daft. Your mother and me are in business. Who else 'ave you 'ad?"

"Why should I tell you?"

"'Cause if you don't I'll belt the holy shit out of that plump little arse of yours as I won't have no one what's fucked my bird workin' for me, got it."

"Your English..."

"Charmin', fuckin' charmin', lyin' on your back like a bleedin' whore and you criticise my English. Maybe I should give your mother a go?"

"Don't you dare!"

"Why not? You're jealous of your mother, that's what. Why you started young. Competition. Proving you can pull 'em. Well I'll tell you. A woman with no teeth can pull a drunk if she flashes right.

You got me into this business, so I'm grateful. Strictly business from now on. You can screw who you like."

TOWARDS THE END of each year the Royal Academy of Dramatic Art stages a play to show off what the staff consider to be the year's best talent. Every London director receives an invitation and as quite a few of them have learnt their craft at RADA the turnout is good. That year the principal was particularly pleased to see in the audience Richard D'Altena, a man tipped for a knighthood in the New Year's Honours list and a doyen of British film and theatre, as actor and director. The play was an Ibsen classic that among other things called for a very young, very pretty girl to say nine lines. Her beauty would underline the story far more strongly than the words and the hunt had gone on until it had reached the first-term students and Tammany. Zach was delighted and so was Blake, but imperceptibly the focus of her life had begun to shift from 27 Sunderland Avenue, and the creation of *1066*, to RADA.

Richard D'Altena had known Tammany's mime teacher for twenty-five years and though they had comforted each other they had never made the mistake of marrying so that when the play was over (much to his relief) he suggested to Edith Sanders he take out to supper the male lead, herself and that pretty young girl who came on in the second act but whose name he could not remember.

"NOT POSSIBLE," said Richard D'Altena. "The lady is even prettier off the stage than on."

"Hello, Sir Richard."

"Not yet, Perkins," he said, but he smiled broadly at the suggestion. "Any chance of a corner?"

"Four of you? Hello Mrs Sanders. Nice to have you with us."

"He was at RADA with me," whispered Richard to Tammany when they sat down. "May I suggest the meal? Now, what do you do with your spare time, apart from being taken all over the place by good-looking men?"

"I'm helping to write a musical. We've done the first act and Blake's music is super. Zach writes wonderful dialogue and bits of it are very funny."

"I'd like to hear some of it."

"Would you really? Blake and..."

"Not so fast, young lady. We can't have the whole cast at the first audition. Here's my card with my home number. Give me a ring one evening and bring over the score. I play the piano quite well even if... Well, that's not important. A musical. There hasn't been a smash hit English musical since Noël Coward."

"Would you really mind if...?"

"There's the card," he said, pointing to it.

"You will have nothing to do with that old lecher," said Blake.

"It's an opportunity. Can you imagine what it would do to *1066* if Richard D'Altena agreed to direct? The production money would be thrown at us."

"Don't be naïve, Tammany. That old bugger's after getting into your pants."

"He's a perfect gentleman."

"No such animal."

"My uncle."

"I'll bet he's been up to some tricks that would not be classed as gentlemanly. We've got a creaking old matinee idol who can't get it up with women his own age and has to crank it up with young blood. Now Roz..."

"Don't be so horrible."

"Do you want to be compared to Roz?"

"Not in that department, thank you."

"Well."

"He's nice."

"Why can't I come to his flat?"

"I don't know."

"I do."

"It's a chance, Blake."

"You won't even let me..."

"We've been through that. I don't want to be thought of as a whore or a kept woman or what."

"That's classic. It's you who keeps me most of the time."

"Don't let's make it sordid. I want it beautiful."

"Well, keep away from the old lecher, as he won't have my patience."

She looked at him whimsically. "Do you really want to?"

"Of course, Tams. I love you. Why don't we get married?"

"I'm too young. We want to have fun without risking babies."

"I'll wear..."

"You won't. We'll forget."

"Okay... Do you think Zach's having it...?"

"Of course he isn't. One in the family is enough. Poor Ted. Walking into his own office. And she talks about it."

"She'll grow out of it. She's a nice kid."

"Yes, but she isn't improving her chances by hopping into beds."

"That's what I'm telling you."

"You don't think I'd hop into bed with a man of fifty-six?"

"Phone him and see what I mean."

"I will. I damn well will. He's a nice man. A little lonely because he doesn't have a wife."

"Pass, Tammany."

"BUT YOU LOOK WONDERFUL," Richard D'Altena said to Tammany. "Give me your coat. The evenings have the scent of autumn. A tang of winter. I love the end of October. A touch of three seasons... What's this...? Manuscript... Wonderful. We'll put it on the piano and have a drink first. The servants are out so what would you like? A dry martini? Just a touch of Noilly Prat. Hollywood gave me a lot. Wonderful place. Now tell me, have you had a nice day?"

"I've been looking forward…"

"Splendid. We'll have a wonderful evening. You'll stay to supper? Stewart Granger taught me how to cook."

"Blake said…"

"Your dress is magnificent."

"I borrowed it from the boutique just for…"

"Splendid. Did you see me burn the oil from the lemon rind over the martini? Watch again… Now there we have a dry martini… To your good health and future career. It is so exciting at the beginning. I can remember when I went to RADA how I was determined to get to the top. How do you like my cocktail?"

"Wonderful. This room is so…"

"Come and sit down," he said, and led her to the chair. As Tammany sat, the empty martini glass taken from her, the front of her dress fell open slightly, giving Richard D'Altena a tantalising glimpse. For a fraction of a second he came out of character and forgot to show his immunity.

"Er… Tell me all about yourself. At Quaglino's I did most of the talking. How can people be friends if they know nothing about each other?"

"Oh, there isn't much."

"Lots must have happened. All I know is you train at RADA. Tell me."

"Well," said Tammany. He went to the cocktail cabinet as she talked.

"How does that look? The same twist of lemon. Cheers again."

"Cheers again," said Tammany, warming to her story and the unaccustomed strength of her neat dry gin. "Now Uncle's trade in Asia has picked up, they've moved the big office from Singapore to Hong Kong where Kim-Wok Ho bought lots of land for the company after the Japanese surrender. He was at the surrender representing the Malayan communist guerrillas. What a big-time communist was doing buying property I'm not sure but soon afterwards he became a partner in Uncle's firm. He comes down to

Merry Hall quite often. If he was twenty years younger I would make a big play... Don't look shocked. I'm half Asian. Cheers."

"Cheers."

"Adam and I grew up at Merry Hall with two grandmothers, though only one of them is my real grandmother. Adam's my brother. He's doing his National Service in the RAF. My father went down to live in Cornwall."

Richard D'Altena made himself comfortable and was content to listen to childhood stories of Sarawak days with Adam, but that was after he had plied her with the third martini. He let her talk, prompting her onward, watching the youth and beauty of her: her sultry voice caught up in the excitement of her stories, the long, silky black hair touching her cheeks, the sexuality of the girl.

"Follow me into the kitchen. There is a stool you can sit on while I prepare our supper."

AFTER SUPPER, George Shearing was put to work on the gramophone and the perfect sounds of the blind pianist moulded the mood and softened her resistance. She found herself sitting next to him on an enormous couch quite tiddly but glowing with the excitement of talking about herself to such a famous man who listened so carefully to what she was saying. He sat back on the far side of the couch with his coffee cup and smiled at her from there and she wanted to sit closer to him. After the second cup of coffee she got up onto wobbly legs and managed to make it to the piano and picked up the reason for her being there.

"Maybe tomorrow," he said. "Tonight is too romantic. Would you like to dance?"

"No."

"I see." He had made his first mistake. "Let's have a look," he said, recovering.

"The first six songs," said Tammany, setting the music up on the stand and pulling out the chair before looking back at him hopefully. He gave her the famous smile and told himself the best things took a little longer.

"My goodness! He writes music properly. Has he been trained?" he added, giving a small yawn he had suppressed from the moment she had told him 'no'.

"A music scholarship to his public school."

"Public school. What's his father do?"

"Stockbroker." She turned off the gramophone.

"Let's see how it sounds." He put on his reading glasses and sat himself down at the piano. By now he thoroughly disliked the sheet of music set in front of him but automatically he read the notes and moved his fingers over the keys. "Can you sing it?" he said, using his director's voice.

"I helped write the words."

"Stand a little away over there. Are you ready?"

"Yes." Tammany sang as if her life was in jeopardy.

He jumped to the next song, read through the music and began to play.

"Don't sing this one," he commanded.

She waited tensely, watching the expression on his face, the actor's mask having dropped away.

"Marvellous," he said. "Perfectly marvellous... Now listen," and he played the Norman hunting song without looking at the sheet of music and the song took on a further dimension. "Not quite right," he said, and started again.

"That's it!" said Tammany in excitement. "You've got it. Blake will be..."

"How old is he?"

"Twenty."

"Needs experience, but what the hell. Arranging is technical. Arrangers are two a penny. Where's the book?" He held out his hand, expecting her to give it to him immediately.

"What book?"

"The script. The story."

"Oh! The story. That's in my head and Zach's."

"Who the hell is Zach?"

"Zachariah Booth. He's opening in *I am a Camera* at the Mayfair on Wednesday. He's playing..."

"I don't care what he's doing on Wednesday. Who else is involved?"

"Lorna listens. She's my..."

"So it's three of you."

"I did say that at Quaglino's."

"You probably did but you didn't say it was good."

"Is it?"

"The music, yes, and that normally makes a musical. If the story makes sense, has a beginning, middle and end and the dialogue is as good as these lyrics."

"It's based on my ancestors."

"Kidding?"

"Oh no. A lot of folklore but his tomb is quite clearly in Ashtead Church. You can come and..."

"True story. Good publicity... Do you want some more coffee? Why didn't you make me play this when you arrived?"

"I tried."

"Never mind. How many songs?"

"Six. He's done some background music."

"Splendid... Come and help me with the coffee."

"There's a magician. Sort of Merlin. He gives the family long life. Says the Beaumonts will live at Merry Hall for a thousand years and if my cousin doesn't upset..."

"Love interest?"

"Three of them... Henri came over from France with a childhood friend, he's also buried in Ashtead Church. Quite a well-known rubbing."

"And the other."

"The robber's daughter."

"Robber? Who's he?"

"Sort of Robin Hood. Lives in the forest. Good friend of Sir Henri but not of the other Normans."

"Bit of plagiarism."

"We can change..."

"Not necessary. All stories have been told a hundred times before... We'll use instant coffee... Just depends on how they are told. A good actor can make a bad script worth watching. Good scripts are as rare as musical arrangers are plentiful. Hamlet wasn't original. Plenty of Hamlets in literary history but only one Shakespeare... The coffee is too hot... You sit down over there and I'll play them through. Have a biscuit." Tammany smiled to herself, realising the man had forgotten her as a woman... "Wonderful music. We must all get together. When?"

"Tomorrow."

"Splendid. Where? You can come here if you wish."

"I have a better idea. Merry Hall."

"I'd like to..."

"Grandmother will be pleased. It takes an hour and a half to drive."

"You'd better bring the aunt who designs the..."

"Not to the Hall."

"Why ever not?"

"Aunt Isabel has a bit of..."

"A reputation? Splendid... What's the matter?" he said. She was smiling.

"You'll have to watch out for Granny Beaumont."

"I'll bring her flowers."

"She loves flowers."

"There you are, see. Now you'd better run along. I'll keep the music. We can all go down in my car."

"There's Lorna, she's with..."

"How many?"

"Five."

"We'll take the Bentley."

"Do you know what time it is?" said Blake.

"Not exactly."

"Two o'clock in the morning. I couldn't find his damn address in the book. Where is my music?"

"I left it there."

"He didn't even look at it."

"Don't shout. You'll wake up Mrs S..."

"What were you doing for seven hours?"

"I do believe you're jealous."

"Damn right I am. That man has a reputation worse than your aunt Isabel's. Who else was there?"

"No one."

"How much did you drink?"

"Three martinis, I think, and a glass of wine with supper."

"Where did you go?"

"Nowhere. Richard..."

"So it's Richard, is it?"

"Yes."

"I won't have it, damn it. What did you do for seven hours?"

"Mostly played your music."

"For seven hours. There were only six..."

"He rearranged them. Blake, he's a musician as well as a lot of other things... It worked, you dolt. He's sold on it. Wants to meet us all. He's picking us up at eleven tomorrow to go down to the Hall and one look from Granny Beaumont will put any ideas out of..."

"So he had ideas?"

"He's a man."

"He invited you round for..."

"Probably. That was the risk we took... Not every man attacks a woman and a man like that has a reputation..."

"Damn right he has and I won't..."

"If you will just keep your petty jealousy under control this is the break we..."

"Petty, is it?"

"Yes."

"He's fifty-six."

"That's why he didn't make a fool of himself and even though he has all the charm in the world I still don't…"

"What?"

"Go moonstruck because I was having supper with a movie star who is London's best stage director and I'll tell you something, Blake Emsworth, he's one hell of a fine actor."

"Who's shouting now?"

"You're twenty. You've got a lot to learn. I'm eighteen and so have I but I learnt tonight. A woman has power. He invited me so he could look at my body and I gave him a good look because I wanted something back from him. Now he's more interested in your damn music than me."

"Are you sure?"

"Haven't I been…"

"Did he like them?"

"Yes. He liked them one hell of a lot. Now let's get some sleep. I'm going to my room, as it isn't fair on you."

*B*y three-thirty in the afternoon of Christmas Eve the light was going. Down by the River Mole the banks were white, humped by the undergrowth of old bracken and leafless bushes. An occasional, lazy flake of snow twisted down to extinguish itself in the grey water that moved with cold precision to the Thames and the English Channel. Cows were huddled in the sheds, hot breaths steaming the warm, hay-filled barns.

Merry Hall was white and grey. Outside, only the yellow snow-tinge of the leaden sky broke the silent beauty. All the windows and doors in the Hall were shut and velvet sausages stuffed with sand had been tucked up snugly to keep out the draughts. The curtains in the drawing room had yet to be drawn closed and inside by the big, crackling fire, the grandmothers were enjoying afternoon tea. Apart from the servants, they were alone in the Hall, the rest of the family and guests having gone off tobogganing soon after breakfast.

"Want a crumpet?" said Lady Beaumont.

"Three's enough," said Lady Hensbrook.

"Better not then." She put the plate back on the table as a piece of wood tumbled out of the fire. She picked it up with a pair of tongs and put it back. "Geoffrey should have got some leave from Malaya. That damn war."

"I don't know why Pippa doesn't fly over with the children," said Lady Hensbrook, referring to her daughter in America.

"You'd better go over."

"Never been in an aeroplane."

"Take the boat."

"Seasick."

"There you are, you see. Sure you won't have one? There are only two left and Pavy gets..."

"The Christmas tree looks very nice. What time's Reggie arriving?"

"I've spent a good part of my life waiting for my children..." The fire crackled.

"More tea?" said Lady Hensbrook.

"Thank you, Mary... The grandchildren are a blessing."

"They don't behave the way we used to behave."

"The next generation never does. Come in," she said loudly in answer to the knock, and Pavy pushed open the door and closed it quickly, pushing back the sausage with his foot; he also felt the cold. The telegram was still in its envelope on the small silver tray, ominously alone, addressed to Lady Beaumont, Merry Hall, near Ashtead, England. Her hand was shaking as she took the envelope from Pavy.

"Shall I, madam?"

"Please, Pavy. My fingers..."

Pavy slit the envelope and unfolded the telegram, handing the message to Lady Beaumont. She glanced up at him and then at the telegram.

"Reggie," she said with relief, reading the signature before the message... "Damn! Damnation! Why can't my sons come home for Christmas? Look at this, Mary. Holed up in Kansas City, wherever that is. The plane's not taking off. He is having Christmas with Pippa and Chuck."

"That's something."

"They should be here. Don't you agree, Pavy?"

"Yes, madam... Have you finished with the tea things?"

"Better not," said Lady Beaumont. "I'll have a jolly good talking to him. Thank you, Pavy... And where is Tug? It's getting dark." She got up in her agitation to look out of the window. She could feel the cold penetrating the glass of the window. "Snowing again."

Pavy put more logs on the fire and went out with the silver tray in one hand and the empty envelope in the other. Lady Beaumont followed him across the room and pushed the sausage back against the bottom of the door.

"Better draw the curtains," said Lady Hensbrook. "They should have been back by now."

"When did we last have a white Christmas?"

"'47, I think."

"We've been alone a long time."

"Some old people..."

"Are we old?" said Lady Beaumont.

"I never accepted middle age."

"Do you miss Hensbrook?"

"I live with him a lot. Mostly the years before the war when he was all in one piece. Come and sit down. They'll be back soon."

"Can't toboggan in the dark," Lady Beaumont murmured, and began drawing the curtains, cutting off the outside light. The flickering flames from the fireplace became visible. "I wonder if we will ever be together again?"

"You mean in this life?" She was thinking of her husband, Lord Hensbrook of the family.

"Oh, yes. You can only talk about this life. Don't know enough about the other one."

"All of them. Family's too big. They have their own lives. I don't know half the guests."

"Who's the girl from Rhodesia?"

"Complicated," said Lady Beaumont, sitting down and taking the teacup from Lady Hensbrook. "Geoffrey had a man in the war he took out of the ranks who ended up a captain. Went to Rhodesia. Some relation of this man's wife. The girl's been writing to Raoul for years. They collect stamps... Never thought we'd have Richard D'Altena for Christmas. Do you think he and Isabel...?"

"They've been photographed together. He's more interested in Tammany."

"She's nineteen. I'll have a word with him."

"What would you say?"

"I have no idea," said Lady Beaumont. "That's the phone," she said, getting up to answer. "Hello! Ashtead 101... Hello, Tug. Oh dear... What are you going to do for Christmas? Not much fun spending Christmas on your own... Roads must be terrible. I'll give your love to Tammany and Adam. She looks just like her mother... I will... Same to you. Have a hot drink or something." The phone went dead. "Hello! Hello!... Must be the weather. Poor Tug. He was looking forward to spending Christmas with his children."

"They'll be disappointed... And here they are."

The living room door burst open. "The outside door's open!" said Lady Beaumont in alarm.

"Sorry, Gran," said Adam, "the others... It was super on Box Hill... Any crumpets left?"

"No," said Lady Hensbrook. "Your grandmother just ate the last one."

"I expect Conway will bring some more," said Lady Beaumont. "Mrs Breed baked yesterday so there should be some cake. That coat is covered in snow."

"Sorry, Gran."

"Your father phoned. He got as far as Exeter. The roads..."

"Hey, Gran," said Karen, coming in and backing up to the fire, "I went right down to the bottom of the slope on top of Adam."

"Nearly strangled me she was so..."

"Has Dad arrived?" said Tammany, coming into the room and taking off her balaclava.

"That thing's dripping wet," said Lady Hensbrook.

"Sorry, Gran. Are there any crumpets?"

"Dad got stuck in Exeter," said Adam.

"Oh," said Tammany.

"He may get here tomorrow," said Lady Beaumont. "I ate the last one and you'd better change your clothes before…"

"Has Uncle Reggie arrived?" said Tammany.

"His plane is snowed-up in Kansas City, wherever that is."

"Midwest," said Adam. "Come along, Karen."

"Did you have a nice time, darling?" said Lady Hensbrook.

"It was terrific, Gran."

"Go and change. By the time you come down, tea will be ready."

"Oh, goodie. I am starving."

"Close the door!"

"Why do children always slam doors?"

"Complicates the seating," said Lady Hensbrook, who was not listening.

"What does?"

"Tug and Reggie. Beau will have to sit at the top of the table."

"Adam, Mary."

"Oh, yes, Adam."

"You're not encouraging Beau with his silly…"

"Of course not, Alice. I'd forgotten Adam was home…"

TAMMANY OPENED the door to her bedroom and closed it quickly to keep in the warmth. A well-banked fire had burned through and the flickering coals would have been light enough without the small light on the dressing table. The room was small but warm as toast. It was the one part of Merry Hall that really belonged to her, and she took off her sweater and bra, stretching in front of the mirror.

"What am I going to wear?" she said and began to search through a well-stocked wardrobe looking for something that would enable her to compete with Roz without freezing to death. She sat down at the dressing table and brushed her hair, counting up to a hundred strokes.

'Why is Blake so jealous?' she thought. They had not enjoyed themselves for weeks and she had not changed. If other men looked at her there was nothing she could do about it. Life was so complicated. A movement from her bedside chair caught her attention.

"Blake...? Blake...? You...! What the hell are you doing in my room? How did you get in?"

"Walked in twenty minutes go."

"Get out," she said, trying to cover her breasts with her arms.

"Why?"

"You know perfectly well why... Get your hands off me."

"I've wanted to touch you for a long time," said Beau, looking at her in the mirror. "Quite magnificent. Especially the brown nipples. The East evokes the harem in every man... I wouldn't, Tammany. I deliberately made certain Rosalyn saw me come into your room. If there was going to be any screaming it should have been done already."

"You call yourself a gentleman?"

"Other people do. Tell me, how many affairs are you having at the moment? There's Blake and D'Altena and goodness knows how many up and coming actors. What a good description," he chuckled. "How many, Tammany?"

"None." She had hunched over the dressing table. "Get out of my room. Are you drunk?"

"Not at all. I wanted to look at you."

"Blake will..."

"Blake Emsworth couldn't punch a hole through the top of the rice pudding, and anyway he wouldn't believe you weren't up to something. The man is so jealous of D'Altena he can't eat his food. Now there's a man. How do you find him?"

"Get out!"

"When I'm ready."

"Take your hands off my shoulders."

"Very smooth skin." He jumped back just in time to avoid the hairbrush. "Those breasts of yours are quite magnificent." He walked out of the room, leaving the door open. "See you at supper, Tammany," he said loudly and laughed his way down the corridor.

. . .

"THIS WAS GRANDFATHER'S BUTTERFLY COLLECTION," said Raoul. "Brought back from India. When he told Gran he was showing a friend the collection, he was really going off for a drink. The best brandy and port was kept here. Do you like England?"

"Oh, yes," said Cindy. "It's been fun but don't you get bored being inside so much? We live out of doors in Rhodesia."

"What happens when it rains?"

"It only rains for six months and most of that in January and February. The rainy season... What are you going to do now you've left school?"

"Dad will be furious. The crammer was a waste of time. I won't have passed my school certificate."

"Why?"

"I never listen. You have to be interested. I want to be a farmer."

"Here?"

"I've tried to speak to Uncle Reggie but he's always busy."

"What kind of job would it be?"

"Kind of manager. Bailiff. I'd get a cottage and a small salary."

"Come out to Africa," said Cindy on the spur of the moment. "Dad will give you a job."

"I wouldn't know how to grow tobacco. Do the natives speak English?"

"Very few."

"Not much use if you can't say anything."

"You can pick up enough in three months."

"Learning is not my strong point."

"But if you want to... You'll like Africa, Raoul. Plenty of space. They've just opened a new block about fifty miles from Umvukwes. Crown land. If you can show them you know how to grow tobacco and you have five thousand pounds they give you six thousand acres at seven and sixpence an acre."

"Seven and sixpence?"

"It's not that easy. No roads. No buildings. You have to drill boreholes for water and stump out the lands before you can put in a crop. Pioneer farming. During the rains, you're cut off by the flooding rivers. And it's hot."

"Six thousand acres... I haven't five thousand pounds."

"You start as a learner assistant and work up to manager. A manager's bonus can be five thousand pounds. It's hard work. Lonely for a bachelor. We can go by boat to Beira and catch the train to Salisbury. The fare's a hundred pounds."

"Gran might help."

RICHARD D'ALTENA also heard Beau leave Tammany's room, which caused him to pour himself another tot of whisky. "They are all the same," he said aloud. "You just think they might be different. And does it really matter, D'Altena? Won't Isabel satisfy you just as much and be a lot better company?" He looked at the mirror and drank down the whisky. "Youth is definitely wasted on the young. The Emsworth lad has enormous talent and because he's jealous of every man who looks at her, he's struggling to write a note."

Feeling better from the whisky, and dismissing whatever had happened in Tammany's bedroom from his mind, he put on his green velvet smoking jacket, adjusted his bow tie, the black one with the big white spots, and went down to the library to play the piano.

ROZ TIPTOED DOWN THE CORRIDOR, past Tammany's bedroom, and knocked on the last door.

"Are you changed?" she said.

"Come in," said Blake. "Hello. I thought it was Tammany."

"She won't be ready for a while. She had a visitor." Roz picked up the tie he was planning to wear.

"A visitor?"

"Beau. He stayed for half an hour."

"She can't stand Beau."

"Love? Hate?"

"Are you...?"

"Don't you get frustrated?"

"Beau!"

"Play her own game. Give her some competition."

"I'm not that kind..."

"I'm a woman, Blake. We don't want pliable men. Are you having an affair with Tammany?"

"No. We don't think..."

"Oh dear... Do you wear underpants under those trousers?"

"Of course I do."

"Take them off."

"Please... Don't be silly... Tammany... What if someone...?"

"What's good for the goose... It'll do you good. The music will flow again," she said, using her last card as she pushed her body up against his. "Blake," she said huskily. "I've wanted you for weeks... That's nice isn't it? I can feel you. Oh, Blake, it's so hard."

ADAM WAS STANDING at ease with his back to the drawing room fire. The debris of tea had been long cleared away and everything was back in its place including the velvet sausage in front of the door. The room was silent. Five minutes earlier Adam had been connected to his father's hotel room in snowed up Exeter and received approval for his journey and the promise of funds.

"I'll paint something commercial," Tug told him over the phone.

"Sure you can afford it, Dad?"

"There are some things that have to be afforded. Sorry I didn't make your passing out parade. I was thinking of you. Your mother would have been proud. What did the Air Marshal say?"

"Told me to send his regards to Uncle Reggie," Adam said, laughing.

"Give Reggie my regards."

"Still in America. Didn't Gran..."

"Poor mother. Tell her I'll spend some time in the summer. No point in trying tomorrow."

"Look after yourself."

"Love to Tammany."

"Bye Dad." He had not seen his father since joining the RAF nine months earlier. The door was pushed open and he looked up from his reverie.

"Hi, Adam," said Lorna. "Have you seen Gran?"

"Forty winks. Conway's gone to wake her."

"She's been avoiding me."

"What's the problem?"

"Doesn't matter. I wonder where my father is spending Christmas?"

"Whooping it up in some jungle mess."

"Can you imagine father 'whooping it up'?"

"Sure. All brigadiers whoop it up now and again. They wouldn't be brigadiers if they didn't."

"How does it feel?"

"What?"

"To pass out top."

"Not as fulfilling as the rest of hut eleven passing out with me."

"Why?"

"Haven't you ever wanted to do something for fifteen blokes just because you like them?"

"You bet," she said, smiling. "Do you like Zach?"

"Yes."

"Would I be mad to marry him?"

"Probably not."

"An actor?"

"You want to ask Gran?"

"Yes. Do you think...?"

"Your mother will be the stumbling block, not Granny Beaumont."

"I think it's jealousy. Mother's had a good family life but it's dull. There were a few years before the war."

"Why doesn't she go out and live with your father?"

"Karen's schooling. The heat. Granny Hensbrook needs her.

Maybe the perfect surface marriage with a rotten core. I accept my parents as they are."

"Is the musical really any good?"

"I think so."

"Isn't it Richard D'Altena's excuse? He can't keep his eyes off Tammany."

"Possibly... Zach thinks the music is marvellous but he and Blake are old friends. For the moment Blake's dried up so nothing is happening. What do you think of Blake and Tammany?"

"Seems all right."

"Do you mind her having an affair?"

"She isn't having an affair."

"Who told you?"

"Tammany."

"They spent nights together."

"Not recently."

"No, not recently."

"That was the reason. Tammany didn't think it fair on Blake."

"You two are close."

"What are we having for supper?"

PART II

FEBRUARY 1954

1

———

*T*he BOAC Comet came in first from the sea and smacked the Kai-Tak runway screaming its Rolls-Royce engines in reverse until it stopped and began to turn and taxi, the wind buffeting the aircraft until it came into the lee of the terminus buildings. Adam peered out of the small window at Hong Kong, excitement mingled with fear. As the aircraft turned for the final stop, he caught a glimpse of the runway turning back into the sea.

"You may unfasten your seatbelt," said the air hostess. "Don't forget your hand luggage." She smiled at him. Earlier in the flight from London she had taken him into the cockpit on the captain's instructions.

"Thanks for everything."

"My pleasure. Your book is in the front pocket."

"I nearly forgot."

"Have a nice time in Hong Kong."

"Yes," said Adam, scrabbling under the seat for his grip. When he looked up smiling she was gone down the aisle. Passengers were getting off and he got up to follow them, remembering the description of Kim-Wok Ho as a tall, somewhat fat Chinaman in his early sixties. Passing through customs, he looked around the milling terminus full of noise and movement. The Chinamen all looked the same to him.

"Where you go?" asked the man who had taken control of his luggage cart at customs.

"Don't know. I'm being met."

"Okay."

'Better find a telephone and phone the office,' he thought, wondering what to do with his suitcase.

"I'll take that," said Adam and tried to pick up his case.

"No. Very not," said the porter, who needed the tip to feed his family. They had managed to push through the crowd that was surging forward to meet the London passengers.

"Mr Beaumont?"

"Yes."

"Dan Chang. From the office. Give him two dollars and he'll let you have the case."

"Oh. Thanks. Hello," said Adam, shaking hands with a man his own age. "I was looking for..."

"He sent me in a roundabout way... Come on. Mr Craig wants to meet you in the office and it closes at five... Dan is short for Daniel. My mother wanted me to have the handle of an Englishman. She thought Daniel very British."

"Your mother English?" said Adam with surprise as he followed Dan with the suitcase to the far end of the airport building.

"Plenty of Eurasians in Hong Kong."

"Are there?"

"Oh yes. We'll catch the chopper across to the Island."

"But we are on the Island."

"Not yet. The airport's on Kowloon. New territories. They're building a tunnel, but that will take years. Mr Craig is due at Royal Hong Kong at six... Hi, Mary..." he said to the terminus receptionist. "Ready to go?"

"Go on through, Mr Chang."

"Adam Beaumont," he said, nodding towards Adam.

"Hi, Adam."

"Give me your suitcase," said Dan. They walked out of the building. "Mary's Eurasian. Father's a Scot. Can't talk till we land. Chopper makes a fearful noise." He waved at Mary and ducked into the wind heading towards the helicopter standing on its circle, blades rotating.

"Wind's terrible," said Adam.

"What?" Dan signalled him up the steps. Two Chinese and a European were on board and they waited until the twelfth passenger was strapped in before the pilot took off, flying straight into the wind and landing two minutes later on top of an eighteen-story building on Hong Kong Island. They scrambled out, luggage and all, through a door into the air-conditioned building. "Can you hear?"

"What?" said Adam, his ears blocked as he imitated a yawn. "Sorry. That's better."

"We can take the stairs. Mr Craig's on the next floor."

"Where are we?"

"Union Mining House, Hong Kong. Your uncle opened it. There are Union Mining Houses in London, Johannesburg, Mount Isa and here."

"Where is Mount Isa?"

"Australia."

"Where's the nearest RAF station?" said Adam, changing the subject.

"Only one. At Kai-Tak."

"Must leave my card in the officers' mess."

"Just leave your card if I were you," said Dan, reaching for the glass door with *Beaumont Limited, Hong Kong* lettered on the glass.

"What do you mean?"

"This is Hong Kong. They don't meet so many Eurasians in London."

"Is that a problem?"

"There is always a problem... Brace yourself. You're now about to enter the presence."

"Mr Ho?"

"Mr Craig. He is the Managing Director here in Hong Kong."

"But Mr Ho...?"

"He's never here. In a British colony, the British appear to run everything... This is Mr Beaumont, Miss Ellenbogen. Is Mr Craig free?"

The secretary pressed an intercom button. "Mr Beaumont's arrived," she said into the speaker.

"Send them in." The voice was correct, with an Oxford accent.

Adam was shown into the office with big windows on one side giving a picture of a large part of Hong Kong leading back up the mountains and over to mainland China.

"Craig. First and second name. Father detested confusion. Have a good flight?" He was sitting behind a carved wooden desk.

"Thank you, sir."

"Mr Kim-Wok Ho sends his regards. Please, sit down. A drink? Chang, do the honours. What will you have?"

"A beer, thank you."

"A beer?"

"Yes, thank you."

"I see... Mr Ho wanted to be here to meet you but he is very busy. I don't see him that much myself. How is your uncle?"

"I haven't seen him since last year."

"Oh."

"Very busy," said Adam, accepting the bottle of beer and the glass from Dan. "Thanks, Dan. The family don't see him very much."

"Congratulations," said Craig, getting up and putting his hand out across the desk. Adam shook it without understanding. "Sword of Honour. Very good."

"Oh," said Adam.

"You do play tennis?"

"Oh yes, sir."

"Good. We'll have a game. Are you good?"

"So, so."

"Pity. Chang will show you round tomorrow. We operate on three floors. The rest are let. You'll want to know everything. Sir Reginald's quid pro quo. He wants you to learn all about Beaumont Far East as well as attend to your personal business. Good health. Welcome to Hong Kong. Been here thirty years. Twenty-five with Butterworths before your uncle had a word with me. Jolly good. Beaumonts are now bigger than Butterworths. My boys are at Ampleforth. Know the school? Catholic. Their mother is a Catholic. Doesn't worry me anymore. World's changed since the war. You'll be staying on the Peak. Company flat. Chang will show you... Now, to your business, Adam. I think Adam is more appropriate under the circumstances. I have prepared this dossier. I met your mother in Singapore before the war."

"Did you?" said Adam, brightening and taking the folder.

"Beautiful woman. How is your father?"

"Well. I haven't seen him..."

"The problem is Marshbank, of course. Dr Grantham's easy to find but is rarely sober. Lord Gray is very old. A recluse. His wife died recently. They hadn't spoken for five years. Chang will go with you. Mr Ho has put out the word to his cousin Ping-Lai Ho that you wish to meet Marshbank. Nothing worse than a renegade Englishman. Of course your father knew him when he was a District Commissioner. Master of disguise, they say. The Americans have been looking for him since '46. The power of money. Rich, all right. He and Ping-Lai Ho control the heroin factories in Malaya. Everything's gone when the police raid a factory. Money again. Everyone is corrupt in Asia; apart from the British, of course. Now let me see," he said, pulling his diary forward. "Tomorrow will be fine. One-thirty. I'll have Miss Ellenbogen book a court. Forecast says the wind will drop. Anything I can do? You can ask me questions about my dossier after tennis. Five pounds I win. Three sets."

"Make it five sets," said Adam. 'Damn you,' he thought. 'I might be a half-caste but I'm still a Beaumont.'

"You do have five pounds?"

"Oh yes, sir. They pay us twenty-one shillings a day in the air force."

"I'm going to like you, Adam," he said, smiling for the first time. "Sorry to cut it short, but it takes half an hour to get to the yacht club. Do you sail?"

"My first recollections are of *Windsong* off Kuching. Forty-eight feet. Bermudan rigged."

"Good. You are going to join us when you finish with the RAF?"

"I don't know. Maybe someone will make me an offer?"

"Oh, they will," he said, opening the door. "One-thirty tomorrow. I can lend you a racquet. Young Chang here will arrange the rest... Sword of Honour. Damned impressive," he said, and closed the door without saying goodbye.

In Dan's office on the sixteenth floor, Adam sat down to read the dossier.

Dr Grantham. First name unknown. Successfully practiced medicine in the Strait Settlements for sixteen years. For no apparent reason known to the writer turned to alcohol. Seventy-three years of age and reported to have been a witness at the Beaumont marriage. No visible means of support. Lives in a hut outside Kuching and spends his days drifting from bar to bar talking to anyone who will buy him a drink. Excellent raconteur even when drunk. Holds his alcohol level the right side of coherency. Certain bars will buy him the first drink as he attracts business. Memory highly erratic as is his recognition of faces. The affidavit would have to be accompanied by another stating he was sober. Any barman in Kuching will tell you where to find him. Never married.

Lord Gray. First name Edward. Created Baron Gray of Kuching after the war for services to the Colonial Office and the war effort. Organised guerrilla resistance to the Japanese from behind enemy lines. Headed up the administration of Sarawak under Rajah Brook at time of Tug Beaumont marriage. Well aware of marriage and its implications. It is said his wife caused Tug Beaumont to resign from the Colonial Service and join Beaumont Far East. Gray is very old for his seventy-eight years and not expected to live much longer. Lives in retirement in the house previously occupied by Tug Beaumont. Wife dead. Had not spoken for five years. Never leaves the house. Memory inconsistent.

Peregrine Marshbank. District Commissioner of Rejang District in Sarawak at time of Beaumont marriage and reported to have been best man at the wedding. Educated Cranleigh School, Surrey as a day boy. Left Colonial Service soon after Tug Beaumont, having sided with him against the Sarawak government's snubbing of Tammany Beaumont snr. Joined Beaumont Far East as a manager. Reggie Beaumont brought him back to England and fired him. The rumour has it that Tug Beaumont was introduced to opium by the subject. Rumour also has it that Tammany Beaumont snr was the cause of the rift between the previously good friends. Mr Kim-Wok Ho will not verify the latter but concurs with the former.

Soon after leaving Beaumonts, subject joined Ping-Lai Ho, cousin of Mr Kim-Wok Ho our Chinese associate, and broke into the American drug traffic. Listed by the FBI as a major supplier. Nothing is known about the man's whereabouts and indications are that it will be extremely dangerous to make contact. On this, the writer concurs. The man has not been seen for ten years though he is thought to be very much alive by the growth of the Malayan trade into the United States.

His partner Ping-Lai Ho is reported to live in an air-conditioned luxury home up on the Thai border but the local sultan refuses to allow his residents to be investigated by foreign police. Anyway, the jungle areas are controlled by the communist guerrillas. It is through these guerrillas resulting from Mr Kim-Wok Ho's wartime activities that Mr Ho expects to make contact with his cousin. Your itinerary has been communicated to Marshbank together with your reason for journeying. Marshbank dislikes the British system. It is highly unlikely he will help you to establish your inheritance. The

man is a rogue poisoning millions of people across America and
Europe.

Adam put down the report and turned to Dan. "Have you
read it?"

"Won't one affidavit be sufficient?"

"The College of Heralds require two in the event of a missing
birth certificate."

"Marshbank won't come out of cover."

"He was my father's best man. Dad never understood the
change of direction."

"Drugs kill people."

"The Japs used bullets. So do the communists. The British kill
in their own turn. You have proof of your birth. I don't."

"I don't even know the name of my father."

"What!"

"Kim-Wok Ho brought me up. Does it matter?"

"Certainly."

"Being alive is more important."

"Wouldn't you like to know?"

"Yes."

"In England the antagonism..."

"Is far worse in Hong Kong," said Dan, finishing his sentence.
"I'm amazed he offered to play you at tennis. You'll be the first
Eurasian. Are you really any good?"

"Not bad, actually."

"Beat him," said Dan emphatically.

"I'll try... I'm going to Sarawak alone."

"You don't know where to start."

"I was born there."

"The instruction came from Kim-Wok Ho and your uncle.
Marshbank can just sit back and do nothing."

"Gray's affidavit with Grantham's might be enough."

Dan stood up and put his hand on Adam's shoulder. "I've got

some people coming round tonight," he said. "Play some jazz. Show you a good Chinese restaurant. You do eat Chinese food?" he said with a grin.

"Oh yes."

"They all want to meet the Asian line of the Beaumonts."

"It's the main line, Dan. I'm heir to the title."

"It's the system, Adam. You are bucking the system, as they taught me in America. Eurasians don't become British baronets."

"This one will."

"Why?"

"To take those sly grins off their faces. To prove my mother was not a whore. To make me feel right. And that's another thing on this trip, I want to meet my maternal grandfather."

"I certainly wouldn't do that," said Dan quickly.

"Why ever not? I'm part of his blood."

"A part he doesn't recognise."

"You must be kidding. He'll be proud of me."

"You've lived too long away from the problem."

"What the hell does that mean?"

"The half-castes are rarely wanted, whichever side of the family. Come on. Life goes on." He looked at his watch. "In half an hour I'm going to introduce you to the prettiest Eurasian in the Far East."

"A girl?"

"You bet she's a girl."

"I've never met a Eurasian girl apart from my sister."

"Why didn't you bring her?"

"Studying drama. Royal Academy."

"My word."

"How did you get your American accent?"

"Went to school there. Kim-Wok Ho paid the fees."

"Is he your father?"

"I don't know."

RUBY WHITE WAS A WHORE, though she would not have looked at it

that way. Her family had not been a part of any particular tribe for
three hundred years and had drifted around Asia doing their best to
survive. The pretty girls became whores but the men often did not
make it; drifters have very few friends. Ruby's ancestry was as
complex as Asia and the nearest bloodline to anything normal was
through Grandfather White, who had set Ruby's grandmother up in
rooms near the Shanghai railway station while he helped build
China's railways. His contract was for three years and then he had
gone back to England, leaving Ruby's father behind as a permanent
reminder of his stay. The railway engineer had sent money for the
boy but not for the mother, assuming rightly she would find
someone else to give her support. He had never written, and none
of the Asian members of his family had ever seen a photograph of
the man. But in their genes he worked and the quarter share of an
Englishman mixed with the tribes of Asia, honed by decades of
hard living, had made something of Ruby. When Dan Chang
described her as the most beautiful Eurasian in the Far East he was
not exaggerating.

AT THE END of December 1953, a meeting had taken place in London
between Sir Reginald Beaumont and Kim-Wok Ho to discuss,
among a varied list of business, future and past, the case of Adam
Beaumont.

"I have been looking for a wife for years," said Reggie, his feet
up on a pouffe in his flat. "Trouble is, you never know if they love
you for you or your business. My kind of money changes people.
Even the thoroughly nice girl wakes up to the possibility of being
rich; it never improves them. I don't care which of the boys inherits
the Hall provided they don't squabble over it. What is important is
their happiness. Can you see Adam as squire of Merry Hall? The
locals would never think it right. Beau could do the job if he wasn't
such an insufferable prig. Funny that. People who have reason to be
conceited don't normally have the problem. There's a bad streak in
the boy. I've a mind to have those affidavits forged and set him hard

on his arse. If he was my son I'd have given him a good backhander early on in the piece but brother Geoffrey thinks the sun shines out of his arse because he can hit a cricket ball. Adam's too good to let him go out of the business but where do we fit him in? That streak of having to prove he's better because he looks different will be a winner in business, but not in the City of London."

"Hong Kong, but not as managing director," answered Kim-Wok Ho.

"Won't that change in twenty years?"

"Probably, but he won't feel any more comfortable. Eurasians only feel at home among Eurasians."

"Are you sure?"

"Put him under Craig's wing."

"How do we convince him?"

"Offer him a job and find him a woman. The combination works. Show him something tangible to come back to."

"Do you think that Sword of Honour was political?" asked Reggie.

"Probably. The best among the best is difficult to determine. Britain's had enough of empire."

"You think so?"

"Costing instead of making money. Get out but keep trading. China will have to trade with the West sooner or later. Once the peasant has been properly fed he will want the next stage. Get Adam to Hong Kong on this pretext and I'll have him meet a girl that will bring him back again. He can have my job when I'm too old to function. Peking have asked twice. Who is to be the go-between if I join my ancestors? They might accept a half-half. Oh, and they want some jet engines. About fifty of the type in the Comet."

"I'll have a word with Rolls. We can sell them to you through Jordan. Hussein's getting some to frighten the Jews. Just keep invoicing the same box of four."

"Do they come in one box?"

"Haven't the faintest idea... Will Adam have to join the Party?"

"Of course. And believe in it," said Kim-Wok Ho.

"And Marshbank?"

"He won't come out from cover but I will lean on Ping-Lai Ho nonetheless."

"There's a Polish restaurant in Chelsea I want to show you. Genuine Polish vodka. Marvellous stuff. What's going to happen in Malaya?"

"Does it matter?" said Kim-Wok Ho.

"Not particularly," said Reggie, thinking he had better not say that to his brother Geoffrey.

RUBY WHITE HAD GIVEN considerable thought as to how to seduce Adam Beaumont and keep him seduced. The instruction had reached her from Kim-Wok Ho through Dan and her salary was more than she expected. Her problem was time. A quick come-here-lie-down-and-give-me-a-bang was temporary, unsatisfactory and unlikely to hold the young man's attention for very long. There were more ways to a man's brain than through his manhood, she had decided early on in her career. A slow, don't-touch-me-yet seduction was usually the easiest, provided the final climax was highly memorable. Ruby had two nights and one day to fix her body in Adam's mind so as to bring him back again, and those two nights had to last him a year with regular boosts from well-written letters that Dan would help her to write. Dan had been no help at all, claiming he only knew a little about the import/export business. Her salary would continue for as long as a good and brisk correspondence lasted with Adam and for six months after he arrived back in Hong Kong at the end of his National Service.

When Adam walked into the Beaumont apartment on the Peak, she was pleasantly surprised and the broad, oriental smile she gave him was genuine. She had not been told he was Eurasian, only that he was heir to an English baronetcy, which had conjured up in her mind a fat, slug-like man with an accent pitched too high. 'I'd do it for free,' she thought to herself, warming to the pleasures of her job.

Dan gave her a wink over Adam's shoulder; he had also been worried until he had met Adam at the airport, though he had known more of the background. Unfortunately, people described by others are rarely as advertised.

"You'd better have a White Lady," said Dan.

"Beer, thanks." Then Adam was introduced to the other five people in the room, three of them young women and all Eurasians of varying mix, one man with an Oxford accent, two of the girls with pretty American twangs similar to Dan's and the others Australian of the more fruity New South Wales variety that Adam had never heard before. All four girls were pretty, but Ruby had the power in her eyes. The first look and smile had given Adam a nice jolt in the pit of his stomach.

Ruby was tall among Asians, having taken something from engineer White. Wearing a green sheath, slit from her throat to her navel and showing the start of firm, creamy breasts, her bottom cheeks behind were as tight as rubber and brushed the silky dress without the need of panties. Ruby was a one garment girl when working.

"This is Asia, Mr Beaumont," she said prettily. "I will pour you a drink. You don't know Hong Kong do you? Well, let me tell you a secret. The beer is terrible. Something to do with the bad water the communists pump over to us when they feel like it. But Ruby's cocktails are the best in China. Come." She took his hand. "I'll show you how to make them. It's basically good old Beefeater gin, a dash of Cointreau, lemon juice and crushed ice."

"I would prefer a beer."

"Nonsense. You don't want me to be upset on our first meeting." She looked at him sideways, expertly flashing her left breast and tickling the palm of his hand at the same time. Adam's acquiescence made Ruby smile happily as she got to work. Ruby believed in her props and this one in particular would make the evening easier and her subject more pliable and biddable. The gin bottle was spiked with liquid Dexedrine. Its first action was to create a strong bond of attraction between the persons drinking it together; it made them tremendously friendly from a short beginning. The second action was to make them horny with a determined wish to share. Only Ruby and Dan had drunk the stuff before. The rest were new and Ruby was watching their tell-tale reactions with care (dry mouths, garrulousness, smoking more) to keep them just at the perfect level. The second bottle of Beefeater was pure water.

In fact, Ruby did not have to go to all the trouble, as Adam, starved of female company at boarding school and then again in the RAF, was infatuated. No female had ever tickled the palm of his hand before.

"How's that?" she said. "Something light and fresh, something cool and something oh-so-very-good. There. Take it. Welcome to Hong Kong." She raised a glass and looked into his eyes. "Happy days."

"Thank you."

Ruby put her soft, red lips expertly round her little straw and sucked. "Joss sticks," she said, putting her drink on the sideboard.

"Allow me," said Dan, taking the box of Swan Vesta matches. "We won't worry about the dossier until the day after tomorrow," he said to Adam.

"But I'm in a hurry."

"Always look carefully first. Mr Kim-Wok Ho's instructions."

"What dossier?" asked Ruby.

"Adam's mother was killed by the Japs. He wants to find her grave," he said, cutting the enquiry. Ruby's job was to bring Adam back to the East and not worry about his inheritance.

'Damn men,' thought Ruby. 'They pay you but never say why.'

"I think we should have this drink and go down to the restaurant," said Dan. "Are you hungry, Adam?"

"Starving."

"So am I," said Ruby, who found a light, Chinese meal tuned in perfectly with Dexedrine and alcohol. "Come and look at the view." She took Adam to the bay window, which looked out over Hong Kong. "You'd never think the whole of China was out there. What was your mother?"

"Malay. From Sarawak."

"Hong Kong's beautiful," she said, accidentally brushing her silky breast against his arm.

BY THE TIME they left the restaurant, the 'speed' had worked through Adam's bloodstream and his balls were making more sperm than they could handle. Thoughts of Perry Marshbank and Merry Hall had left him completely. A very dry French white wine had been drunk with the duck, accentuating the dry, hyperactive quality of the Dexedrine. Ruby's manners had been perfect, eating her food delicately with chopsticks and drawing everyone into the centre of her conversation. For the eight of them, high as kites with only two of them knowing why, the other diners in the restaurant did not exist and Adam knew he had never enjoyed himself more in his life. Even his attempts at humour had been received with gales of laughter, and the others' jokes were funnier than any he had heard in the air force. The camaraderie of strangers was remarkable in its intensity.

"My place," Ruby had said after Dan had paid the bill with the other three men unsuccessfully clamouring to pay their share.

They set off in two taxis, taking only minutes to reach Ruby's flat. Hong Kong was small but Dan and Ruby had planned a short journey and given the company a chance to pair off nicely. Dan arrived first with his choice of girl, one with a well-pronounced backside, who he had touched up in the back seat without any resistance while the other pair shared the front seat. In the back seat of the second taxi, Ruby was all decorum, which was more than could be said for the other couple up front. Fortunately, the taxi driver had to watch the constant flow of Hong Kong traffic.

Upstairs, the drinks came out again, but Ruby served an alcohol-free punch, telling them it was as lethal as hell as she knew they would not come down for a couple of hours. More joss sticks were burnt, which was important, and the lights were kept high enough to see what was happening. Soft music followed the columns of incense curling up to the ceiling, but the evening had come down to the individual intensity of couples waiting for sex. Ruby was more than satisfied with her work and Adam thought he was in heaven as he tried to sneak his hand around Ruby's shoulder to get at her left breast from the other side, snuggled up as she was on his lap.

The flat had three bedrooms, as Ruby shared it with two other girls, one of whom was out on a job in New York and the other with a communist Chinaman in Taipei. Each bedroom was bugged in and out with one-way mirrors from the central lounge. Ruby had found that certain old men required a little more and though she did not indulge herself, as old men did not turn her on, she laid on the goodies when necessary. One by one the couples made for the bedrooms until Adam and Ruby were left on their own in the lounge, with Adam not knowing how to make the final approach despite his excruciating need. After five minutes of groping, he found that breasts, bottom and anything closely surrounding them were out of bounds and the kisses were merely increasing his need.

"Have you ever seen it?" asked Ruby in his ear.

"What?" said Adam stupidly.

"You know," she giggled, and he tried again for the gap between her thighs, without success. "Come and look." She giggled again as if she were tipsy. "I've had too much to drink," she said, and tongued the inside of his ear. "A wealthy bachelor owns the flat. I rent it from him. You can see into the bedrooms without being seen. Shall we peep?"

"Oh no," said Adam, who was still the RAF officer under his sexual excitement.

"It's very sexy," she said, giving him the impression it would turn her on – which it did – and that anything could happen.

Uncomfortably, Adam got up and walked soundlessly across the carpet with music still moaning from the radiogram. Deftly, Ruby turned up another volume knob and bedroom sounds from three separate couples filled the room.

"What's that?" said Adam in alarm.

"You don't know?" said Ruby in genuine surprise. "Come and look." She took him to the one-way mirror. Adam gasped in shock and excitement.

"Now it's your turn, darling, as I can't wait any longer... Go slowly... Plenty of time." And she marvelled at the ability of the Dexedrine to bring the sexual need to a frenzy.

2

---

*P*ing-Lai Ho did regular business with one million Americans and fifty thousand other assorted nationalities every week and was content with the arrangement. He was the growers' connection in the hills of Burma and Thailand where the farmers made their living out of poppy seeds. They harvested them like any other crop and delivered them for cash to the market. The police only rarely interfered, since it was the only way the farmers could make a living, other crops being too bulky to transport over the mountains.

The farmers never saw the transformation that took place in the Malayan jungle factories owned jointly by Perry Marshbank and Ping-Lai Ho. Marshbank was the buyers' connection. Conducting weekly business with one million Americans, he became rich and with that wealth Ping-Lai Ho had purchased his own Sultan, in a manner of speaking, living high in the hills without a care in the world. From his colonial-style veranda he could see the distant tea gardens of more legitimate husbandry, but these were British owned, very efficient and made the correct eight per cent on capital. Of late the British had been having trouble with the communists. Ping-Lai Ho smiled at the irony of legitimate business.

The veranda was inlaid with marble. Pillars, taking the weight of the roof, were of carved teak, showing snakes sliding upwards to the heavens. Good cane furniture of the type favoured by two generations of British rubber planters decorated the cool centre of the veranda. Banks of flowers were everywhere (Ping-Lai Ho being a keen gardener), the fragrances mingling with a gentle mountain breeze that just stopped perspiration forming on Ping-Lai Ho's upper lip. From the middle of his lower lip a tuft of black hair grew down to the blue-dragoned silk gown that covered his well-pampered body. On a marble table by his side, a bowl of many fruits rested alongside a crystal vase of jasmine blossom. At a distance from his high perch on the hill and far across the valley came the sound of angry gunfire, causing Ping-Lai Ho to lift his glass of ice-cold guava juice to his lips, sipping it through a straw.

'Why do people wish to kill themselves?' he thought. 'World wars. Minor wars. Drugs until they wither away... Death wish. So what's the problem? At least my clients think they are enjoying themselves... Beautiful evening...'

He looked out over the green vista, pinked by evening clouds where here and there the fire smoke of suppers rose gently. He ignored the gunfire. His Chinese cook came out onto the long veranda and offered him the evening menu, which he studied with care before choosing a five course meal and a good bottle of claret. Tuesday's girl would help him drink the bottle and maybe early the next morning she would manage to get it up for him and he would have a little sex. At sixty-three it did not really matter. It was the contentment and the near proximity of youth that concerned him most. The female chef, nineteen years old and very sexy, took the order back to the kitchen. Male servants were not allowed in his house or even in the garden.

The contrast of the white roll of rice paper and the small petals of the jasmine caught Ping-Lai Ho's attention immediately and made him stretch out a plump hand to remove the eyesore, not realising at first what it was. He began to read with alarm at the breach of his security.

Dear cousin,

When you die, I will piss on your grave, but for the moment I require your assistance and don't start ranting at the very lovely member of your staff, as it will be of no avail. Your new chef (pretty isn't she, I thought you would like her) is a dedicated communist and will remain in your employ since, with your remarkable relationship with the sultan (and on this I never break another man's rice bowl), who in turn has an excellent relationship with the British, she will be safe. She will also transmit on the wavelength you use for your business. By now you will have heard a firefight with British soldiers who are proving remarkably good after their successes in Burma against the Japanese. The Japs have gone with the help of the British, and now the British must go. The East is for China, as you know. Quite a difficult one with the British as we will wish to go on trading with them when we have kicked them out, as their scientists are far in advance of our own.

But I digress, dear cousin. I wish to get in touch with your partner who for the past ten years has cleverly avoided arrest. Adam Beaumont, Tug's son by Tammany, wishes to clear his mind about his parentage. There is some problem with the inheritance of Merry Hall as Reggie still hasn't married but I do not think that that is the crux of young Adam's problem. People, especially when they are nineteen, do not like being in this world without proper roots. I require you to arrange a meeting for Adam with Marshbank so that the boy can hear from his father's best man that his mother and father were properly married. As I grow older I cannot see that it really matters, but the boy's pride and confidence are at stake. A letter (easily forged) will not be enough for the boy himself. I don't think he gives a jot about the inheritance but misses his mother. Tug and I went through a lot together in the war and I owe him this much. The daughter, by the way, is prettier than her mother if that were possible.

Your chef will arrange the meeting anywhere in the world, and this is not a police trap. If people wish to inject themselves to death it is one of the advantages of their free market, free choice system. You may have to be persuasive with Marshbank, as the man will be loath to break his cover. So far, the guerrillas have not attacked civilian targets but the thought of all those lovely girls of yours could change their minds and you would just be in the way.

For this personal favour (your safety) there is a quid pro quo which I am afraid you will have to pay, but think pragmatically. You are paying the sultan already, so another million pounds a year will not be too much. It gave my Party friends a sense of justice when I pointed out that the American man in the street would be helping with their efforts. In retrospect, you would have been far better off staying in partnership with me and joining the Communist Party. The thing I enjoy about them most is their pragmatism. They are aware of the need for Hong Kong and Singapore in their plan of things. Even the old emperors allowed the Europeans to trade with the Middle Kingdom in a roundabout way. Trading at a distance is the byword in Peking, which suits me very nicely. Business is very good but then I understand you are also doing well.

A meeting please with Marshbank within thirty days and don't try and screw your chef or she will slit your belly with a blunt knife.

Have a nice day.

The note was signed by Kim-Wok Ho .

Ping-Lai Ho was breathless for a short while, until he saw the advantage of his new position, which caused him to laugh with great guffaws that dislodged his round reading spectacles from the end of his nose. Then he stopped laughing abruptly. Marshbank had grown powerful and he had no idea where to find the damn man. No one did.

Gunfire broke out again from the distant hill. First he saw the puffs and then two seconds later the distant crunch of the mortar bombs and it made him think.

.   .   .

BRIGADE HEADQUARTERS for the province of northern Malaya was situated deep in the jungle, in the house and compound of a rubber planter who had been attacked by communist guerrillas the previous year. The planter had beaten off the attack but had decided an office job in Brighton was better than a lonely grave in the Malayan jungle; his dreams of wealth and a solid foundation for the future of his family had been left behind along with the spirit of the man. The brigade consisted of the Royal Surrey Foresters, into which Geoffrey Beaumont had originally been commissioned from Sandhurst, the Queen's own 8th Regiment of Gurkhas, and the Special Air Force of the Rhodesian Army. The planter's bungalow had been converted into the officers' mess and brigade headquarters. The manager's house had been given over to the sergeants and the 'lines' had been allocated to the troops. The area around the compound had been cleared of undergrowth and the planter's once-precious rubber trees cut down to give a good arc of fire and a clear sweep for the searchlight. A parade ground had been established, with a flagpole to keep up the Union Jack, and everyone felt reasonably safe.

Brigadier-General Geoffrey Beaumont was monitoring the contact his patrol was radioing back to him, well satisfied with the method of 'seek and destroy' which the British Army had developed as the war progressed. The mess orderly had left him alone in his office (previously the planter's bedroom) with the mail from home, most of which were bills, one in the sloping hand of Georgina, which he put aside to read when he had fewer problems on his mind. Military problems he could handle, private ones he could not. He looked up at the punkah that was barely turning above his head and willed it to go faster. The colonel of the Rhodesian SAS let himself into the room and saluted.

"Guerrillas have broken contact," he said.

"Hunt them one by one," said Geoffrey.

He saluted and left Geoffrey alone with his mail.

Geoffrey Beaumont had learnt early on in the war that conventional means were useless against guerrillas, that tanks and artillery were unserviceable and aircraft only valuable as transport. War in a jungle was man-to-man and Geoffrey had trained his men accordingly and proved the guerrillas could be beaten. He had also denied them food, decreeing that rice could only be sold when cooked. After twenty-four hours in the sweaty, rotten jungle, cooked rice was poisonous. The guerrillas had been forced out of their hides and were unable to intimidate the local population.

Geoffrey picked up the letter from his wife, slit open the envelope and sat back in his chair to read.

Thank goodness I can tell you. That man has gone to America. Something about a film with Richard D'Altena. Anyway, he has gone. Lorna is sharing the family flat with Tammany and I just hope she has no other friends like that one. Geoffrey, you have no idea what he looked like even after he shaved off his beard. Your mother thought he was contemptible. An actor! Presented at court and she goes out with an actor. At least Tammany's boyfriend has gone into his father's firm of stockbrokers, though I don't think they see too much of each other anymore. I want to see Lorna married off properly before the end of the season. Please write her a letter.

Mother has been sick with a dreadful cold. This house is impossible in winter. Reggie should have the whole place centrally heated.

Beau is doing well in the army and everyone likes him. I met the commanding officer at Aldershot. Charming man. Very pleased with Beau. Thought he met you during the war. Everyone is certain our son will play cricket for the army and emulate his father.

I did not want to tell you before but Raoul is the complete opposite of darling Beau. All that money we spent on his crammer was wasted. Failed his school certificate miserably so I have let him do what he wanted. Cindy Escort was staying with us over Christmas and her father has offered Raoul a job on his tobacco farm in Rhodesia and the two of them have gone out on the boat together. I mean, the boy would never have got his commission, and a brigadier's son in the ranks would have been just too embarrassing. Oh, Reggie lent him the hundred pounds and gave him another fifty to spend on the boat. They sailed last week.

Karen is impossible and received a terrible —

Geoffrey dropped the letter quickly as an explosion shook the building, followed by two more in close succession.

"Mortars," he said, his eyes sparkling. "We've got 'em sergeant," he bellowed through the door as he picked up his Sterling and slung it comfortably over his shoulder. Outside, simulated panic was spreading around the camp as the anti-terrorist units went smoothly into operation. Geoffrey arrived at his tunnel at the same time as the Rhodesian lieutenant-colonel.

"Escort will lead," said Colonel Jones, referring to his senior lieutenant.

"Nonsense," said Geoffrey.

"If you will excuse me, sir. Brigadiers don't lead platoons."

"I never lead anyone from behind, colonel. Right," he said to his nine men and Lieutenant Peter Escort. "We have three hours of daylight. Track individually. I thought the target would look too juicy for them to ignore." He led them into the tunnel, a beret having replaced his peaked hat. Geoffrey Beaumont was out to enjoy himself and his excitement was infectious. "Silly buggers, mortaring an armed camp," he said. Simultaneously, three similar patrols had gone underground to break out into the thick jungle. The communists would have been wiser to withdraw as fast as possible but their commander was watching the main and only gate to the compound, which was shut fast, the British having jumped into foxholes to defend themselves. The man was enjoying himself directing mortar fire at the planter's bungalow up till the moment a Gurkha's knife slit his throat. The firefight was over in twenty minutes. The British had come at them from behind out of the jungle. Silence returned to the distant tea gardens and the far distant bungalow set up on its hill.

. . .

THERE WERE good and bad bars. The 'Whistling Sailor,' situated at the worst end of The Gut near the tired and seldom used 'B' wharf of Kuching Harbour, was the pits. The barman was of indeterminate race, thin with a row of malnutrition ribs and a black moustache too big for his face that matched the colour of his deep-set eyes. He wore a filthy pair of trousers and an old pair of sandals to keep his horny feet out of the broken glass. He stank of body odour, which mingled with the other smells: stale liquor, fag ends and vomit. The one window pane that was meant to look out over the harbour and give the customers a pleasant view of the ships could not be seen through, due to several layers of dirt and the seething mass of buzzing flies that were attracted by the light to the hope of freedom. The shirtless barman sat on his side of the bar at one end and Doctor Grantham at the other.

The doctor had finally reached the bottom of his career and was unsuccessfully bumming booze off the locals. His small, pink eyes stared at the bottles while withdrawal symptoms screamed through his emaciated body. The hair that hung down to his shoulders would have been white had it been washed but now resembled a well-used dish cloth. He was, however, one up on the barman as he had on a shirt, admittedly button-less but one that thankfully covered the shame of his old, debased body, which gave the barman's a good run for stink, capping it with the smell of piss, a problem of old men who can no longer hold onto their water. There was one thought in his mind as he stared at the bottles. When the outside door was pushed open, he straightened his back and turned with a glimmer of hope in his drink-soaked eyes and quickly looked back at the bottles. Images of his past had been playing tricks on him lately. Quite often he found himself hallucinating. The barman scratched under his armpit but otherwise did nothing.

"Dr Grantham?" said Adam, but the old man on the bar kept his eyes fixed on the bottles. "My name is Adam Beaumont. You knew my father, Tug Beaumont." There was no reaction, Adam might have not spoken. Dan tried to catch the barman's attention.

"Mr Barman!" The black eyes looked up from the study of the butt ends on the floor. "You speak English?"

"What you want? Better go hotel in town."

"This is Dr Grantham?" asked Adam.

"Sure."

"Is he all right?"

"Probably not."

"Can we talk?"

"Sure."

"What does he drink?" asked Dan.

"Anything."

Adam and Dan brought barstools to either side of the motionless old man and Dan pointed at the bottles. "You have any whisky?" he called to the barman.

"No."

"Beer?"

"Sure."

"Three beers. No glasses." The only glasses he could see were trying to dry next to a bowl of scummy liquid and when the surprisingly cold beers came he wiped the necks carefully with his handkerchief before putting one in front of Grantham and sliding the other left-handed down the bar to Adam. The doctor's eyes followed Adam's beer.

"Cheers," said Adam, picking up his bottle and hiding his disappointment. He had never seen a man at such a low before and wondered if his affidavit would be worth the trouble. Adam put the cold beer in the old man's right hand; as the frosty beer touched the palm the fingers closed on the bottle and the hand came off the bar counter, bringing the bottle straight to the doctor's mouth, where it stayed until the bottle was empty. Dan ordered him a replacement.

"Money first," said the barman, and Dan handed him an English pound note.

"Hey, Doc," he said. "Wake up. These lads have money. Real

money... Pops. Wake up!" Which caused Grantham to shake his head. Dan flinched involuntarily.

"I am sorry," said Grantham in his best British accent. "Dr Grantham. We have not had the pleasure." He put out an emaciated right hand to Dan, the left having taken hold of the second bottle of beer.

"Daniel Chang. Hong Kong."

"Delighted." He turned to Adam with a look of inquiry.

"Adam Beaumont. You were witness at my parents' wedding."

"There were plenty of those in the old days. Wonderful things, weddings. You could drink as much as you liked on the bridegroom's father. Don't get invited anymore. Went to hundreds of weddings in the old days. Your most excellent good health. My eyes are not what they were. You sound British, young man, and your friend American. Lovely little bar, isn't it?"

"Yes," said Dan, who was being overpowered by the smell.

"I was born in England," said Grantham, reciting his patter by rote. "Guy's Hospital. One of the best, of course. They wanted me to specialise. Played rugby for them."

"Did you?" said Adam, trying to visualise the skeleton playing rugby.

"Fly-half," said Grantham. "Very fast. My scrum-half played for England. Now, what was his name? One of the problems of getting older, young man. You forget things. Frightfully inconvenient. Whereabouts in England?" he asked, a smile brightening his face.

"Surrey. Merry Hall. My father may have..."

"There were many friends in the old days," he said, clutching Adam's wrist.

"You don't remember my father?"

"I don't think so. Could I have a brandy with my beer?"

"Of course," said Adam.

"Here," said Dan to the barman, standing up. "Look after him. That ten shillings is for you. The pound for the doctor."

"Thank you."

"Nice meeting you," said Grantham.

"Goodbye," said Adam, putting his hand on the old man's shoulder. "Look after yourself."

"I will, young man. Thank you for the drinks. Give my regards to your father."

"I will," said Adam as he followed Dan out of the bar.

"Sorry, Adam," said Dan outside. "I was going to hurl."

"Poor old bugger."

"It's the East. In the old days it was malaria or booze."

"Do you think he played for Guy's?"

"Probably."

"What makes a man sink so low?"

"Want to go back and ask him?"

"He wouldn't be able to remember," said Adam, getting into the driver's seat of their hired car.

"Now this is a pleasant surprise," said Lord Gray. "Please, sit down. Can I get you something? No servants. British pension. No perks when you retire. Boring. Now where was I? Sit down. How is your grandmother?" he said, looking at Dan.

"Excuse me, sir?"

"Are you Adam? Well, there you are. Sit down. How is Lady Beaumont," he asked, this time looking at Adam.

"Very well, sir."

"Good. Excellent. Don't look so surprised. Victory Ball '46. Merry Hall. Your grandfather kindly invited us. Marvellous party. My wife was alive in those days. Can I pour you a gin? There must be some gin somewhere. Can't afford to drink much. Terrible thing living on a British pension. All goes in tax. They make you Lord Gray with one hand and slice your pension with the other. Nine and six pence in the pound because they call it unearned income. Titles cost them nothing. There you are, you see. Your grandmother wrote to me. How can I help?"

"My mother and father..." began Adam.

"Charming people. They came to supper. Rebecca was alive in those days. Wonderful woman," he said, forgetting they had not spoken to each other for years. "I miss her, you know. We were very happy."

"I lived here as a child," said Adam.

"Did you?" said Gray in surprise. "Then you know my house. How extraordinary. I would never have thought anyone else would have known the place. Long way from anywhere. You did find it all right? You won't get lost going home? Maybe tea?" he said hopefully.

"That would be perfect," said Adam, meaning it. Everyone else in the East made him drink alcohol. "Were my mother and father married?"

"Married? I should think so. There was a lot of talk about it. Rebecca would have known more about that kind of thing." He winked.

"You don't think they were married?"

"I wouldn't say that."

"As administrator, didn't you see the marriage certificate?"

"No."

"They were married in a church. Where would they have registered the marriage?" asked Adam.

"With the DC."

"My birth and my sister's?"

"The DC. What year were you born? Would you put the kettle on?" he asked Dan. "You know how to use gas? Beautiful view isn't it," he said, turning back to Adam and nodding at the lagoon. "I love palm trees. Saw a picture of one as a small boy. Brought me out to the East. Pensions are not everything. Even a centrally heated flat in Ealing wouldn't compensate. Gin isn't everything, is it? The natives bring me fish."

"1934. Who was DC in 1934?"

"Now let me see… Marshbank. Dreadful man. Discharged from the service."

"Who would have a copy of my birth certificate?"

"No one, I should think. The Japs razed the DC's house and their parish records, so to speak."

"Weren't copies kept anywhere?"

"Meant to. Never did. Enough bumph. Your father will have a copy."

"He doesn't have. In the hurry to leave Singapore…"

"There you are, you see."

"Were you able to contact my uncles?" said Adam, referring to his grandmother's letter, which he'd read before leaving England.

"That I did. Most uncooperative. Your mother's family did not recognise the marriage. Your father insisted on a British marriage, you see. The custom here is…"

"Then they were married?"

"I think so. You don't really know, do you, unless you are there? I believe Grantham was a witness."

"He can't remember."

"Not surprised, poor fella. Shocking state of affairs. And an Englishman. Rebecca said something should have been done about him. Drink, they tell me. How's the kettle doing? You don't take milk, do you?"

"Well…"

"Thank goodness. There is a fridge but it never works. There's only me, you see."

"Is my grandfather alive?"

"Yes."

"Did the uncles explain about me?"

"Yes."

"Can I meet him?"

"Not really. Better not, I mean. Bad form. No English. Bit primitive. Long house. Just one. Whole family in one room, so to speak, and there are thirty-seven of 'em. Cramped. No room for another."

"I don't wish to live with them."

"Two of the uncles are in Singapore. They went to the mission school like your mother. They speak English."

"Can they vouch for the British wedding?"

"Probably not. Because your parents were not married according to Sarawak custom, their marriage was taboo. So are you, for that matter. There you are, you see. Bit of a problem... There's the tea. Three cups and two saucers, isn't that a bit of luck? You always need a bit of luck now and again, don't you?" he said, smiling up at Adam.

"It's as though I don't exist," said Adam, walking with Dan on the beach in front of the bungalow where he was born, Lord Gray having gone off for a nap soon after his tea.

"It's not just the title?"

"Oh no. I want to belong. Gran's great but Tammany and I are different. This is why we're different," he said, sweeping his hand.

"I know... I'm also half-half."

"Should I go and see them?" he said, referring to his relatives. "It's only half an hour."

"Do you want my advice?"

"That's why I asked."

"Leave them alone. Don't upset their lives. They live differently, Adam. The livestock lives under the house. This is Sarawak. Your mother changed but they have remained the same. There are two worlds. You and I were born from half of each but we grew up to think with the one. Those people half an hour away are your ancestors. Very old ancestors. Your mother took a shortcut into the modern world."

"But they should be brought into the modern world. I have young cousins. What about them? What about their education?"

"Who will pay for them?"

"I will, of course."

"How are they going to learn?"

"At school."

"They can't speak English."

"They will learn."

"And having learnt English, they must get themselves an education."

"There must be teachers who speak their language."

"But their language is inadequate. Their words relate to the jungle and day-to-day living, not to the laws of relativity. And when your cousins learn English they will learn words that will have no meaning to them, as there will be no comparison. And even if they learn our language and learn a little of our education, what will they do with it? They will be agitated, dissatisfied. More than seventy-five per cent of the world is like them, the uneducated masses, but they go through life with periods of happiness. In their lifestyles are pleasures we have forgotten to appreciate. The task of education is too great even for the mass of Chinese and they've been civilised for five thousand years. Better we find this Marshbank and go back to Hong Kong." They walked back down the beach in silence. "We better say goodbye to Gray," said Dan.

"It's very beautiful."

"Paradise. Your relatives have a lot to be thankful for."

"The RAF seems so far away from here."

"That is exactly what I'm trying to tell you," said Dan. "Imagine trying to explain to your relatives what you do for a living."

3

*D*awn Westcott put two more pieces of driftwood on the roaring fire, dusted the mantelpiece and went back to her bar to dust the counter. She was thinking, something she was not prone to do, and her thoughts were unhappy. At twenty-seven she was not married and so far as she could see she was 'on the shelf' and would go on pulling pints in the Barley Oats for the rest of her life. Every summer she had had an affair, sometimes two, except for last year and this had set her worrying.

At a quarter past six the outside door opened and let in a gust of bitterly cold air.

"Evening, Dawn. Fire looks nice."

"Get yourself warm. Pint, Mr Beaumont?"

"Please. Have one yourself."

"I'll take a half," said Dawn, forgetting her diet in her surprise. For five years Tug Beaumont had never offered anyone a drink, making his pint last as long as possible before walking the half mile out of the village to his cottage up on the cliff above Shingle Cove.

"Don't look so surprised," said Tug. "Painters sometimes get paid for their work."

"You sold a painting?"

"Four."

"Well, that's wonderful. I thought…"

"Seascapes. Local. Nothing to do with the East. Adam needed the money."

"Adam?" asked Dawn in surprise. As a long-standing barmaid in Penzance, she was meant to know everything about the locals, including rumours, scandals and those about to happen.

"My son. Didn't I tell you? Probably not. I haven't said much to people for a long time. I was married, you know. Son in the RAF and a daughter at the Royal Academy of Dramatic Art. She's really something. Just like her mother. Pretty as paint."

"And your wife?" Dawn had fully recovered her wits and was out to glean as much information as possible.

"Killed by the Japs."

"I'm sorry."

"She was a native."

"Of Cornwall?"

"Sarawak." Dawn looked blank. "Part of Borneo… Far East. Have you heard of Singapore?"

"Oh yes," said Dawn. "That was the place the Japs took when they shouldn't have."

"Same area."

"You mean she was dark?"

"And beautiful."

"Well I never. Cheers. Good luck… Well I never."

"You've lost a lot of weight," said Tug politely.

"Have I?" Pleased with the remark, Dawn turned to have another look at herself in the mirror behind the gin bottle. Involuntarily, she pushed out her chest.

Tug smiled into his pint of bitter before drinking. "How old are you, Dawn?"

"Twenty-seven, but you know it's not right to ask a lady her age."

"Sorry," he said, but he was still smiling.

"Four pictures… Get a lot for 'em?"

"Three thousand pounds." He was so chuffed that he had come

straight from the phone booth into the bar after calling the gallery in Exeter.

"Three thousand quid. Blimey! Four pictures."

"Paintings."

"I always thought you didn't have a penny."

"I didn't except for the Gauguins."

"What's them?" said Dawn suspiciously.

"Art. Quite valuable."

"Oh. You sold someone else's pictures. Now I've got it."

"No you haven't. This time they were mine. My son needed money to go out East to prove to himself I was married to his mother."

"You was married to her?"

"Certainly. Do I look the type who would live in sin?" He was still smiling.

"Suppose not. Never can tell these days. Three thousand quid. How long did they take?"

"Six weeks."

"Three thousand quid in six weeks!"

"Yes."

"How old are you, Mr Beaumont?" she asked, giving him a queer look.

"Tug... Now that is something you should never ask a gentleman. Give us the same again."

"Do you know I think I will... Is that cottage of yours draughty?"

"Why?"

"Just askin'," she said, trying to figure out what he would look like without the full growth of beard and with a decent set of clothes. "Where are you from? Originally, I mean?"

"If I said I was heir to a baronetcy, you wouldn't believe me, now would you?"

"No, I would not."

"Well, I am, see." He patted her hand on the bar. "And you?"

"London. Well, Clapham. Down the Waterloo line a bit. Nothing much. Went into bar trade when I was twenty-one. Mum didn't think it was proper before then. Left school at fifteen. Legal age, you know. Most of us did. Me, I was boy crazy. Boys, boys, boys. Didn't like them books. Pity, really. Never learnt much."

"And your dad?"

"Never met 'im. I'm a bastard and proud of it."

"Does it worry you not knowing who your father was?"

"Whatever for! Probably want to borrow some of me wages to go boozing. Men's like that. Mum never married. Said no one was going to 'ave 'er scrubbing floors for nothing. She had seen it, my mum. Her mum told 'er. Good and proper... Want some crisps? I like Smith's crisps... Seeing like you bought the beers. Why don't you and I have a little party? Been a long winter."

"Yes it has," said Tug, thinking of a long line of winters since the war. "I like Smith's crisps."

"Well, isn't that lucky? Can't see no one else comin' in on a night like this. Wind like that can cut you in 'alf. How you walk up the hill I don't know. Why not give the fire a poke."

"Why not... Come and sit round the fire. The gaffer never comes in on Monday. Are you often here on your own?"

"Not often."

"I've known a lot of barmaids from the waist up."

"How do you mean?"

"From my side you only see the top."

"Not bad, is it?"

"Neither is the bottom." He was smiling again.

"You are saucy." She wiggled her bottom down onto the bench. "Not too hot? No one knows nothing about you round here."

"I'm a recluse. Maybe not... Painted twenty-seven pictures of my wife. It was fading... I always tried to put her back where I remembered her. Had a bungalow right on the beach thirty miles out of Kuching. That was the capital. Joke really. Wasn't much to be capital of. Sarawak is one of his majesty's smaller colonies. They are trying to give it back to someone or other at the moment... Had to go back to the earlier paintings to remind myself and now I only see her face as a painting. Why do memories fade? It's like people dying all over again. I suppose it can't be helped and I can't go on moping for the rest of my life. I killed the Jap who did it. Kim-Wok Ho and I went in on a commando raid. Kim-Wok Ho was the leader of the communists fighting the Japs in Malaya. Now they're fighting us. Silly, isn't it, trying to kill yesterday's friends. My brother's out there. A brigadier. Good soldier. Sandhurst. That kind of thing... I'm rambling."

"Go on while I pull another pint," she said, not understanding the gist. It was a barmaid's job to listen when a customer wanted to talk. It was why they came into pubs, the customers.

"That'll be nice," said Tug.

"Don't stop."

"Put a full magazine into the little sadist. Tammany was monitoring Jap shipping for the allies."

"That's a lovely name."

"Yes. Everything was lovely about my Tammany. But killing the killer doesn't help... Maybe time does... Thanks, Dawn. Aren't you having another?"

"Don't you remember I was fatter last year?"

"I didn't look."

"Now, I suppose you didn't."

"I was DO," went on Tug. "District Officer. Adam and Tammany Junior were born in that bungalow. We were so happy and I never thought anything would... But it did. There is always something. The Colonial Service didn't like me being married to a native, so I left. Joined my brother, Reggie. We were traders. Now, if you think three thousand pounds is a lot of money you should have been in Singapore. Cornered the rubber market. Bought and bought and refused to sell. War didn't come to the East until the end of '41. Filled go-down after go-down and then shifted to America. Too dangerous to go to England. U-boats... Made a fortune. Probably wrong from a war but the Japs were trying to buy it up as well. Someone has to make money. Take Reggie. He only has to glance at something and it begins to look like a cash register."

"Is he very rich?"

"Stinking. Sir Reginald Beaumont has a finger in just about…"

"I've heard of 'im. Wasn't he a Spitfire pilot?"

"And a Mosquito."

"Well I never, and him your brother. Wait till I tell my mum you came in my bar. Does he ever come down to Penzance?"

"Not even once, I am afraid."

"I'm glad no one else came in tonight."

"So am I. Time I talked to someone. My poor children. Never see me. Adam took the Sword of Honour in the RAF and I couldn't even face his passing-out parade. And Tammany's been in a play I haven't seen. Maybe I'm over my wife. Took too long, but she wouldn't like me moping all my life."

"Frightens me 'ow as some people can love each other and so many of us can't. What's it like being in love?"

"Haven't you been in love?"

"No."

"That's sad."

"Yes."

"You're young. Plenty of time to fall in love."

"You think I will?"

"Everyone does. You'll just have to wait. The most exciting things in life come as surprises. I mean, I phoned that gallery to tell them to send my paintings back and they had been trying to contact me. I didn't think I was good enough to sell. Now they want more. I haven't been as excited since the day I stepped off the boat in the East. And if it wasn't for Adam I would never have exhibited but he needed the money. Life is strange, isn't it… We'd better put some more wood on the fire."

"How old is your daughter?"

"Nineteen. You will never believe it but she and two of her friends are writing a musical about the first member of our family who arrived with the conqueror. They're calling it *1066*. Tammany says Richard D'Altena is interested in producing it on Broadway but you can't believe everything the children say."

"Richard D'Altena? The movie star? Your daughter knows Richard D'Altena?"

"That's the bit I don't like so much. He is much older."

"Much older. You mean she and him?"

"I don't exactly know what I mean. Daughters don't tell fathers everything. She had a boyfriend but he seems to have faded out a bit. Finished writing the music for the play and went into stockbroking. Doesn't sound right to me if his stuff is going on Broadway. My mother tipped me off and I must have a word with Tammany. D'Altena is using the musical as an excuse. He's in his fifties."

"Sounds like her boyfriend found out."

"You could be right. Adam says there's nothing in it, and he and Tammany are very close."

"Why don't you get her down here for a weekend?"

"I suppose I could now I've got some money. She reminds me so much of her mother, I was afraid..."

"You really are a queer one. All these people you know and they're famous."

THE HEAD OFFICE staff of Sigram Incorporated were running around like ants in a well-disturbed nest. Their chairman of the board, who was also a seventy per cent shareholder, was arriving on his six-monthly inspection and the office that was permanently kept ready for his exclusive use was receiving its more than usual daily cleaning. No one was ever sure when Montague Heron would arrive. Three years earlier, he'd conducted a savage inspection, and while everyone from the president through six vice presidents and downwards had been relaxing and congratulating each other on a successful deliverance, Mr Montague Heron had come back and started all over again, extracting the true stories from those that had been concocted for his ears and forgotten the moment the chairman went down in the elevator.

He knew that frightened men always told the truth, be the news good or bad. He said the irregularity of his visits compensated for the rental of the wasted floor space when he was not in town. Unbeknown to the Sigram staff, there were eleven such suites of offices in New York all belonging to a non-executive chairman with the same habits but different names. Sigram Incorporated was quoted on all the major stock exchanges. The company made plastic bottles, approximately one billion of them a day, and there were many smaller products extruded by the factories across the United States, Europe, the Middle East and Southern Africa. For years, they had been trying to break into the Asian market but the Japanese had prevented anything but token sales and were keeping it that way.

Montague Heron had given the company president half an hour's warning of his arrival, which would coincide with a meeting set aside for the British industrialist and mining magnate, Sir Reginald Beaumont. It was not the president's habit to chop and change his appointments. Being the man he was, the business of making profits came before running around after his chairman, despite the fact that his three hundred thousand dollars a year salary was held in fief by Montague Heron.

So the chairman was joining the meeting, which made everybody happy, in particular Heron, who intentionally came up in the same elevator as Reggie. Reggie always looked at everyone in an elevator and gave Heron a good look without recognising the man he had last seen when he had fired him in London before the war. The office Heron had left as Stratton three hours earlier would not have recognised him either. Montague Heron, alias Tobias Stratton and ten other names, appeared in America's Who's Who. He was a master of disguise and a resident of Kansas would have vouched for his mid-west accent despite his British birth. The man called Heron could imitate all forms of the spoken English language and could have made a fortune on the stage. Two of his twelve corporations had extensive film, TV and live theatre interests purely by request of the chairman.

"After you," said Heron in his mid-west accent when they

reached the top floor and Reggie stepped out onto good carpeting and walked to reception.

"Mr Radley, please," said Reggie, but the pretty receptionist was paying him little attention. "I have an appointment," tried Reggie again. "Beaumont of Beaumont Limited."

"I'll take you along," said the man behind him, and Reggie turned to face the man from the elevator, never surprised at the American way of doing business.

"Heron's the name. Don't often get in on the detail stuff... Montague Heron," he said again as Reggie looked at him curiously.

"There's a rumour in London that you don't exist," he said with a smile. "Glad to meet you." He put out his hand.

"No umbrella and bowler?"

"Not in New York."

"You don't mind my sitting in?"

"Not at all. We can get a decision today."

"Radley calls the shots."

"And you call Radley if he makes a mistake."

"Will you have dinner with me tonight?"

"I have tickets for a show."

"You like theatre?"

"I have a niece who's got me interested."

Heron knocked on the president's door and opened it for Reggie to go inside.

"Came up the elevator together. Hal Radley. Reggie Beaumont." They shook hands.

"The meeting is about a joint venture in Hong Kong," said Radley. "Reggie has an entrée into the Chinese mainland."

"You two carry on," said Heron and sat back to watch.

At forty-seven, Reggie Beaumont did not have a grey hair on his head. Heron looked hard for signs of a rinse and found nothing. The charcoal grey, Savile Row suit was immaculate on the five feet eleven inch frame that showed no signs of wrongly placed bulges. There were small lines at the corner of his eyes and the face was developing a craggy look to it but the brown and green eyes were alert with youth and the pleasure of being alive. The light brown hair was parted perfectly on the left side but showed no sign of lotions. A slight indentation at the parting indicated the passage of years. Above all, the man was abundantly healthy and enjoying himself.

'Still a confident sod,' thought Heron as he followed them into the board room, where the vice presidents of finance and marketing were already waiting, pushing back their chairs from the long table to get up as the newcomers entered the room.

"Sir Reginald Beaumont..." began Radley.

"Reggie Beaumont," said Reggie. "We're in America." He put out his hand to the vice presidents in turn before putting his briefcase on the table in front of a chair, indicating Heron should take the head of the table.

'Bastard still runs everything,' thought Heron and made the best of sitting in his chair.

"Anybody got any coffee?" asked Reggie. "Best coffee in the world comes from America." And before they could talk business, the president of the company was out of the door ordering coffee, a trick Reggie had used before in different guises to enable strangers to relax with each other on their first meeting. Reggie had found that getting somebody important to do something menial for him brought everyone down to size and when the coffee arrived he was the one to get up and pour, dismissing the secretary with a delicious smile that caused an immediate reaction in her sexual organs.

"We can pass the sugar and milk around the table," he said and sat back in his chair, stirring his steaming cup of black coffee while he smiled around at everybody.

"Now let's get down to this joint venture in Hong Kong," said Radley, thinking it was going to be a pushover, the English being renowned for no longer being able to resist American business techniques. "John, you have the plan and the figures," he said to his finance man. "Everything worked out, Reggie. We take fifty-one per cent as the manufacturer with all the know-how and you pick up forty-nine per cent for your knowledge of the market and how to sell into the commie Chinese."

"What joint venture?" asked Reggie innocently.

"You kidding?"

"I never said anything about a joint company and even if I had, the question of majority shareholding would have been sorted out in the first letter."

"You mean you want fifty-one per cent in a company selling our product with our name on it?"

"Let me try and explain, Mr Radley. Until ten minutes ago none of us knew each other from a bar of soap. Certainly we had heard of each other's reputations and banks were able to tell us how much we are worth." He smiled again at everyone around the table. "Partnerships are very delicate affairs."

"Oh, we're Catholics," interrupted Radley. "Once we get married we never get divorced."

"Not according to my records," said Reggie. "Your joint venture in Mexico was very Catholic but came to an impasse."

"Those Mexicans were impossible," said Radley. "They wanted half the profit just to allow us into their country. No capital, no expertise, no nothing."

"And what happened?"

"We pulled out, naturally."

"And dissolved the partnership."

"It had not gone very far."

"But if it had and you had felt in ten years' time they were not supporting their shareholding in proportion to the number of shares, what then?"

"I don't quite get your point," said Radley.

"Divorce," said Reggie. "Nasty, messy, expensive. What I want from you gentlemen is a licence to manufacture your products in Hong Kong. All the risk is mine. You receive one per cent of the net sales for providing the knowledge. No capital. No management. No problems. Each month you will receive a cheque for one per cent of sales and your auditors are welcome to look at my books. A very simple franchise agreement, gentlemen. One we can all live with and not haggle over in years to come."

"And what's to stop you varying the product slightly once you have our expertise and then cutting us out?" asked the marketing man.

"What is to stop a major client of yours manufacturing your products?"

"Lack of the same knowledge you are after?"

"Not really. Anyone can extrude plastic."

"Why franchise?"

"Because your methods of operating are tested. New machines come on the market and you test them. You have a name. For one per cent of sales I buy a product that works. Good for me and good for you."

"Why is it good for us?" asked the marketing man.

"Because without us you do not get the Chinese market. I am offering you revenue without expenditure from a source you could never penetrate."

"Why?"

"You don't know the right people. The old saying. 'Not what you know but who you know.'"

"And who do you know?" asked Heron, knowing perfectly well.

"That's my business," snapped Reggie.

"I didn't mean to be rude."

"Next time I'm going to bring a couple of my partners to the meetings in America. Four against one is barely cricket."

"You have partners, Mr Beaumont?"

"Certainly. If in a few years we all come to trust each other then we can talk of joint ventures. But for now, treat me as a new client who wants to buy your product but in a slightly roundabout way."

"There is merit," said the finance man, and the haggling went on for half an hour.

"One per cent," said Reggie, and handed round copies of a report that he and Chuck Everly had prepared in depth. "Here's how we see projected sales as you would from a fifty-fifty joint company, and I've checked the figures myself. We can both make the same amount of money without being married to each other." He began to pack his papers back into his briefcase.

"When do you require an answer?" asked Radley.

"Seven days enough?"

They all stood up.

"Dinner tonight?" asked Radley.

"How about tomorrow?" said Reggie. Everyone wanted to take him out to dinner. "Tonight I have a date at the theatre and on Wednesday I fly to Hong Kong."

"You will go ahead with plastics irrespective?" said Radley.

"Oh yes. In Hong Kong, if the Chinese want something, you make it quickly one way or the other."

REGGIE ALWAYS TRAVELLED on the airline of the country to which he was flying; it was only in the return leg that he flew BOAC or BEA. He had flown from London to New York by Pan-American in slacks and a sports jacket, tourist class, as was his custom. First class passengers he normally found boring. Being absorbed in a number of business problems, he had taken no notice of his fellow passengers and even while the aeroplane was taxiing along Heathrow runway he had pulled out Leslie Charteris's *Saint Errant* and was quickly into his story, sensibly leaving behind the problems he could no longer do anything about. The pilot talked to the passengers about height and speed and wind direction but Reggie was not listening and it was only when the coffee trolley came round and he was lightly touched on the arm that he saw the pair of legs that had been sitting next to him unnoticed for half an hour. The calf length dress, with a long slit, was unable to hide anything as the legs were too long for an average aeroplane seat and had been forced to rest against the seat in front at an angle of sixty degrees. They were visible in all their glory.

The girl repeated, "Coffee?" to him in an enquiring American accent.

"Sorry. Deep in the book. Thank you."

"Milk?" said the air hostess from the aisle.

"Black. No sugar." Reggie almost spilt some of the scalding liquid over the legs as he tried to get a better look at them while taking the coffee cup at the same time.

"Are you English?" she asked, and they looked at each other for the first time and smiled.

"You are American?"

"Yes," she said and then laughed. "I'm Lee Tuchino. Dancer. Twenty-two years old. Windmill Theatre for six months and going home. And I am definitely going home."

"You didn't like England?"

"Not really."

"You saw the wrong side of England... Reggie Beaumont. I'm in business."

"You sell?"

"Everybody sells."

"What are you doing tomorrow night?" she asked.

"I heard you American girls were forward but..."

"Party. Homecoming. Theatre people. Old friends. You're welcome."

"I might just..."

"Come over. Give me a pen and I'll write down the address. Casual gear. Bring a bottle. Nine o'clock or whenever. They'll rave all night."

"Do you know how old I am?" asked Reggie.

"What the hell's that got to do with the price of cheese?"

AFTER THE THEATRE, Reggie took himself to supper and ate a large fillet steak with a full bottle of French red wine before calling himself a cab. He arrived at the address just before midnight, hoping he wouldn't fail to recognise the girl from the aeroplane, whose legs he'd seen more of than her face. When he got out of the cab in front of a block of flats, he could hear the music. The confidence generated by several glasses of good wine saw him enter the elevator and ringing a doorbell with a bottle of Scotch under his arm. The noise and cigarette smoke hit him forcibly.

"Hi! Come in. Glasses and ice in the kitchen."

The lights were dim and people crowded the passageway, spilling into the rooms. Most of the guests were high or happily drunk and Reggie felt twenty years younger. In the kitchen he found a dirty glass, washed it in the sink and poured himself a Scotch, adding water from the tap.

"One of those," he said to himself, and hid his bottle deep in the rubbish bin; if there was any other liquor around it was also hidden, and as Reggie had to wait until Wednesday for his flight, he was counting tonight as a holiday. He'd find an excuse to avoid dining with Radley. Business entertaining with elderly wives was not his idea of fun; the wives always looked at him with disapproval or lust when he told them he was single. In Reggie's life, business was done in an office and not over brandy and cigars in a restaurant. He loathed cigars anyway. Slowly, sipping his whisky, he moved towards the main room, looking at the girls. From just inside the room he watched the dancing until his eyes focused on a very tight backside supported by legs that went on forever.

"Found her," he said out loud, which did not matter as no one could hear him above the music. The girl was wearing the latest cropped trousers from London, accentuating the full length of her dancer's legs. A pair of red pointy pumps matched the red and white vertical striped trousers and the cropped white sweater above. The girl's face was oval, olive skinned; a short haircut created a long face to go with the length of her body. As she turned nearer to where he was standing, he was pleased to recognise the *Jive* label on her pants. Lee was the centre of attention and Reggie realised why he was making so much money out of his investment. He made a mental note to tell Ted to get his arse over to New York and start selling, as the girl made the other dancers look drab. She stopped when she saw him and broke away from her partner.

"You made it," she shouted.

"You asked me," he said.

"What?" She took him by the arm and led him back into the kitchen. "Wow! Isn't music great?"

"Loud."

"I'll get my coat."

"Where are we going?"

"I'll show you, lover."

"You're high."

"It'll go on all night."

Reggie started scratching around in the rubbish bin and came up with his bottle of whisky. "Pass it around," he said to the nearest man, and followed 'the legs' into the passageway.

"There's a new guy, Earl Grant," she said. "Not known much, but he's playing in Harlem. You like jazz?"

"Now you're talking."

"Too many people. Bottle parties are a place to get out of when you've found what you want. Got enough money to buy me supper?"

"I think so," said Reggie as Lee covered herself with a full length coat and led him out of the party.

"They always have a party on Mondays," she said. "Show business. Most are out of work."

"You said it was a homecoming."

"So? I couldn't exactly ask you to take me out."

THE OUTFIT CAUSED a sensation and Reggie smiled at what certain people would say if they could see him jiving with the best of them with Lee's long legs flashing all over the small dance floor. They finally sank back at a table well away from the band. The beer was cold and her hamburger hot and the noise level such he could hear himself talk.

"You like the gear?" she asked.

"Smashin'," said Reggie, imitating Ted Cornwell.

"Carnaby Street. It will sweep America if they bring it out here."

"I'm sure they're working on it," said Reggie complacently.

"You can jive."

"Thanks."

"What do you sell, Reggie? That accent is so cute. You'll do well in America. How goes the selling?"

"So-so."

"How long in the States?"

"I fly out Wednesday."

"Just my luck. Anything I fancy flies away."

"Have you got a job?"

"You kidding?"

"Come with me to Hong Kong for a week."

"No money."

"I'll pay. Have you any more Carnaby outfits?"

"All my money goes on clothes."

"Wear them and I'll find a way for the British taxpayer to foot the bills."

"What are you talking about?"

"Doesn't matter. Are you coming?"

"Sure. Why not?" Lee was always one to make up her mind on the spur of the moment.

"You may have to work in Hong Kong."

"Hey! I'm not a hooker, even if the Windmill is a girlie show."

"Modelling. Straight modelling, Lee. I own the company that makes your clothes and Hong Kong is a cheap place to manufacture."

"Are you pulling my leg?"

"Actually I am not." He pulled from his wallet the card showing him to be chairman of *Jive*. "You can match the logo with one of your pants."

"Hong Kong here I come," said Lee, and Reggie was glad the card only read Reggie Beaumont, Chairman. He could hear Ted's words. 'You can't have a baronet as chairman of a jazzed up company like *Jive*.'

. . .

As THE BOAC flight from New York carrying Reggie and Lee landed at Kai-Tak airport, another aircraft carrying Tobias Stratton was preparing to land at Singapore airport, and even if Hal Radley of Sigram Incorporated had been on the plane he would not have recognised his chairman. Tobias Stratton of American Wires and Cables Incorporated had a distinct stoop, which made him look like a short sexagenarian with a back problem. His blue eyes were rheumy with approaching old age. The accent through customs and immigration was classy New York. A car was waiting for him outside the terminal building and he was soon swallowed up in the afternoon traffic.

*S*itting at the Long Bar of Singapore's Raffles Hotel, Adam was bored. Three days earlier, he had been contacted in Kuching and told to wait in his hotel room at Singapore before returning to Hong Kong. He was further told to sit at the Long Bar between five and seven every evening. The voice, which suggested a slight Australian accent, told him his friend was not required in Singapore and Dan had flown back to Hong Kong with a string of messages and a Chinese silk scarf for Ruby. Every time Adam thought of her, his hormones jumped, and on more than one occasion he had to concentrate on his quest to eliminate the ominous bulge in his trousers.

Adam had had a haircut and bought himself a new suit that he could not afford, but he wished to look his best when he returned to Hong Kong just as soon as he had the proof of his parents' marriage. The Singapore beer was not to his taste and he had gone onto the gin slings, not realising how quickly and permanently the East changed people and their habits. For three evenings he had religiously sat at the bar by himself as instructed and this was his fourth wait.

Staring well past the barman into his memory, he did not take any notice of the British gentleman who took up the bar-stool next to his, despite numerous empty seats down the bar. If Adam had been concentrating on anything other than Ruby he might have noticed the incongruity of an Englishman seeking a seat next to someone when privacy was plentiful. The man, who was sitting ramrod straight, had a sharp military moustache, and was wearing his regimental tie and a well-cut blazer, the badge of which was emblazoned with 'Malta Cricket 1949' above a Maltese Cross. The grey flannels were slightly baggy, as they should be, and the accent when he ordered his gin and tonic from the bored barman was plummy.

Adam took no notice. There were plenty of the same type in British Malaya and there was a war going on. Adam had taken a quick glance to make sure it was no one he knew, as he had no wish to meet under the circumstances, and had gone back to his gin sling and erotic reveries. After the effort of conjuring Ruby back into his mind's eye again, he was irritated when the man spoke.

"Army?"

"No, sir," he said, turning and recognising the superior rank. "RAF."

"Butterworth?" Which was the main RAF base in Malaya.

"No, sir. I'm on leave."

"Regular?"

"No, sir. National Service."

"You do hold a commission, I presume?"

"Yes, sir. Pilot Officer Beaumont."

"Fought in the war myself. Not this one. Just a skirmish. The real war. Japs. Behind the lines. Lucky to be alive. Have a gin?"

"Well..."

"Two gin and tonics or is that a sling?"

"Gin sling."

The man just nodded at the barman. "You on your own?" he asked Adam.

"My friend flew back to Hong Kong."

"What are you doing here?"

"Waiting for a friend."

"People are always late."

"Seems to be, sir."

"Here we go. Bottoms up... That's better. Good old English gin. I knew a Beaumont during the war."

"My father was in the jungle."

"Your father would be Tug? Of course. His wife was from Sarawak. Lovely lady. Brave. Japs got her. Sorry, sonny. Of course. Your mother. Lovely lady."

"You knew my parents?"

"Extremely well."

"Maybe you can help me. After the Japs overran Sarawak all the records of Rejang district were lost, among them my birth certificate and that of my parents' marriage. Some people say they were not married at all."

"They were married."

"Are you sure, sir."

"I'm sure. I was there."

"But..."

"Come and have dinner with me and I will tell you all I know. It is a quarter to seven? Good food. I insist. Tammany was her name."

"Are you...?" Adam was immediately on guard.

"Careful, young man. It is bad manners to ask your elders questions. The best way to learn in life is to listen."

"THE MAN you want to see ate here with your mother and father."

"Please tell me..."

"What is a name? That name, the only one you wish to hear spoken, has meaning to certain authorities. My name is Guy Faulkner."

"But I..."

"Do you wish to see my papers? My passport?"

"Of course not, sir. But I thought..."

"What you think is dead. Buried in the past. Normally it would be left there, but the past sometimes comes back to haunt us."

"Won't they recognise..."

"Even your father could have dinner with Guy Faulkner and be none the wiser. However, word has reached me, whichever me I am, and a person by the name of Faulkner has responded, not under threat from anybody, but because he wished to."

"Why?" asked Adam suspiciously. After the days of waiting, he had not expected a meeting.

"Even in the hardest of us is a wistful streak. A 'what might have been'. Even in the most rotten of us rests a spark of good. But before I go on, I will give you a warning. Should you try and connect the person you wish to talk to with Guy Faulkner I will deny our conversation and I will retain your breach of trust in my memory, which will not be good for your career, which is going to be difficult enough as it is.

"But to return to your question. Why? Many years ago, the establishment jailed a man for borrowing money to give the man you seek an English public school education. He was a bank manager but so poorly paid that he borrowed from his own bank without permission. Foolish? Certainly. But the desire of this man and his wife to see the man you seek uplifted in society was so strong that he borrowed. When he had served his time to a just society he and his wife committed suicide because the man was unable to obtain any kind of work. His fellow man had rejected him.

"Prior to this, the man you have come to find was content in the Colonial Service. But the tentacles of society's revenge are long and word was passed to the administrator's wife that one of her husband's District Commissioners was the son of a jail-bird. Mrs Gray was a particularly venomous woman, as your mother and father found out to their cost.

"And then came your uncle Reggie and they all moved out of the Colonial Service, much to the administrator's relief, and went into commerce. Mrs Gray tried to drive them out of the East, but your uncle had too much money for that one. The man you seek learnt his final lesson. Only afterwards did that man start his highly successful career. If society tars a man with feathers, he should wear them. But I digress again, and here comes the food. I always eat a good curry in Raffles. One of the best in the East. The side dishes are superb... Thank you, waiter... And a light German or Danish lager? Do you drink beer, Adam? Thank you, waiter. Two Carlsbergs will be fine. How is Tug?"

"A recluse. Paints pictures and lives by himself in a cottage overlooking the sea. Ever since my mother died he's withdrawn into himself."

"Your sister?"

"Drama school. She is very beautiful. She has become the protégé of Richard D'Altena the actor-director. She writes as well. Fact is, they have a musical D'Altena wants to produce on Broadway but I don't know if he will find the theatre or the money." Adam went back to addressing his curry.

"Is the musical good?"

"The music is catchy and original but I'm not much of a judge. People who know say it's good."

"Could you send me the book and a record of the music?"

"I wouldn't know where to send it, now, would I?" Adam smiled.

"I will have you contacted in England."

"Why?"

"Always why. I like the theatre. I have friends in the theatre. And you?"

"RAF for another year and then I want to come out East. Hong Kong. Work for Uncle Reggie. Trading."

"You knew your father's best man could never give you written proof?"

"Yes. I suppose so. My temper with Beau has subsided. I wanted to know my mother was good. Maybe that is all I need."

"That she was." Faulkner smiled wryly. "The problem was the best man who also loved the bride. Do you understand why Faulkner is here?"

"And my mother?"

"Loved your father. Eventually she despised the best man, but the best man still has memories. Forget about Merry Hall, it will only give you pain. You have an impediment in your birth that no certificate or title will change. If society can find a chink in a man's armour..."

"They called me 'The Chink' at school."

"You are different, or so you look to them. Their society will never accept you. To your face they will give you smiles but when you turn your back... They are cruel. They create a web of hurt around you that isn't visible. There are other societies than theirs. I am part of one. Extreme wealth. A little subterfuge and I laugh at them. Genuinely. To see them self-destruct. They poison themselves. Isn't that a classic?"

"But drugs are terrible," said Adam, who had no idea that Ruby had used one on him to draw out his sexual excitement.

"In twenty years, half of adult America will be using heroin or cocaine. Then they will change the law. Can you imagine locking up Oscar Wilde for being a queer in this day and age?"

"No... I can't. But mainline drugs kill. Do terrible things to people."

"So does alcohol. Cigarettes give cancer. A whore can give you VD. People want to escape. Decadent society. Too much free time. The rich buy cocaine and heroin. Don't think of little girls dying in attics. A few, maybe, but it's the rich who want kicks. In Roman times it was gladiators and orgies. Drugs provide the orgies in their minds. The sellers do not create the demand, as society would let you believe. They don't go out looking for custom. It comes to them. Crawls to them. The demand is far higher than the supply and hence the price and the huge profits. Take away the people and the traffickers don't have a business. It's like prostitution. Lock up every man that has paid a whore and every woman who has taken from a man and you can put the whole lot away. Why blame the prostitutes? Society's double standards! Democracy! If a man or a woman wants to self-destruct I can't stop him, nor can you, and neither can the lovely society you belong to. If they could find the man I refer to they would hound him to his grave in a hysterical screech of righteous indignation, but take away the fun thing he gives them and they will tear each other to pieces. Illegal drugs are no different to illegal booze during prohibition. Sure, drugs hit harder, but so does the atomic bomb."

"You believe that, don't you?"

"Yes. A strong man will not be an addict, otherwise the American economy would have fallen apart. A man who has a job to do will have a fling on Saturday and then go back to work with a clear head on Monday morning. The weak who junk all day or sit in bars all day are worthless. Governments like the booze and cigarette way. Tax drugs and the same governments will whitewash the habit in six months."

"Would you swear before God that my mother and father were married in accordance with the rites of the Catholic Church?"

"I would, but I can't write it down."

"Thank you. I won't break your trust. I don't agree with drugs. Everyone is likely to become an addict. Very few people who drink alcohol become alcoholics."

"Talk to me in thirty years' time."

Adam put down his napkin and pushed back his chair.

"Don't go yet," the Englishman said. "I travelled a long way at your request."

"I'm sorry."

"Another beer?"

"Yes, another beer." Adam was distinctly uncomfortable.

"So it is to be Hong Kong."

"I think so. There's a large population of Eurasians."

"And the Hong Kong British will accept you?"

"I hope so. The RAF..."

"There, you're just one fish in a big pond. They'll put up with you there out of curiosity. What you need to counter your impediment is power, and for that you need wealth. Reggie is rich, but the moment he dies his business empire will be torn apart by death duties. A grateful government applauding his lifetime's work. Look what they did to poor Gray. Living in your house. A DO's house. Poor as a church mouse. High and dry on the banks of forty-five years of faithful service... You think I'm bitter. So what? It's true. They brainwash you to conform and then they suck your blood... You came out here looking for your inheritance. Merry Hall. The baronetcy. What made you come?" He held up his hand to stop Adam from speaking. "Antagonism... Those looks... The 'you're not one of us'. You have a colour problem, but whatever we did was not and will not be accepted by those people. They laughed at the day boy at school. I said to hell with them. Why don't you? What have they done for you? Has anyone put out a hand to help you on your way?"

"Uncle Reggie."

"Possible. He may have reasons. At school?"

"No."

"Air force? You won, but you fought. At home with the family? You and Tammany against the others."

"Granny Beaumont..."

"Yes, there's always one or two, but they sink back when the majority get going. You can't live in a house that hates you."

"Oh, it's not that bad."

"They despise you. Tolerate you at the best."

"You make it sound..."

"As it is. I know. I've been there." The man made up his mind. "You came for an inheritance and I am going to offer you one. I never married. Never had children. I would never ask you to be involved in drugs, which is why the legitimate side of my business has been meticulously kept apart. I need an heir far more than Reggie Beaumont."

"I don't believe it. Are you offering...?" Adam laughed, picking up his beer. "The money was made from people's suffering."

"So was America."

"No. I could never... You don't really think I would even...?"

"When the jibes really hurt you I'll get in touch. I will make myself known to you. Within ten minutes of leaving this room, Guy Faulkner will be dead... Millions, Adam and all the power. No one will dare to call you a 'chink'. If you can't join them, beat them. There's always another way in this wonderful life of ours. And we only have one of them to live."

5

Despite Dan's warning, the officers' mess at Royal Air Force Hong Kong had welcomed Adam with enthusiasm. Each of the officers had been through an Officer Cadet training course and none of them had won the Sword of Honour. They were impressed. Being men doing what they wanted in life, there were no chips on their shoulders. After Adam had left his card on the silver tray on the mahogany table at the entrance to the mess, the Station Commander had instructed his adjutant to contact Pilot Officer Beaumont and invite him to the following Monday's dining-in night. In uniform, Adam had introduced himself to the mess president for the evening and no one had turned up an eyebrow at his oriental appearance.

He was made an honorary member of the mess for his stay in Hong Kong, which gave him access to the tennis courts. There were four weeks left of his leave and though his quest had been inconclusive he had remained in the city. Dan had given up his flat for the lovers and Craig had put Adam through a crash introduction to the workings of Beaumont Limited despite the office being in a turmoil following the arrival of Reggie Beaumont. Adam had won his five pounds from Craig in three straight sets. A mute silence pervaded the Beaumont office at the mention of tennis. Even Reggie had smiled.

A small crowd of off-duty officers and airmen had gathered around the tennis court. Adam and Dan were two sets all and going into the fifth and final set with Dan taking the fourth set eleven to nine. The final set followed service and reached six games all before Dan broke Adam's service and everyone around the court thought the match was over. Dan stood on the back line to serve for the match. Moving two feet nearer the net, Adam returned serve with the ball still rising fast. His eye was seeing a double-sized ball and the first two cross-court returns left Dan flat on his feet. The third one annoyed Dan, and he served two aces in a row but lost the game in his over-excitement to two double faults that broke his concentration and lost him the next two games and the match. Both of them were surprised to hear the round of applause from the spectators.

"Three matches all," said Dan with his arm over Adam's shoulder as they walked off the court. "Shit, I've missed a good game of tennis since leaving college."

"Beer," said Adam. "I'm dehydrated." He took his friend for a large shandy in the officers' mess, where both of them now felt quite at home.

"I'm going to enjoy working with you," said Dan.

"This is my kind of city," said Adam. "Everything about it. Fast business. Plenty to do."

"And Ruby."

"Cheers," said Adam, smiling.

"I'll beat you tomorrow," said Dan.

A WHORE's first rule is to collect the money before she drops her drawers. The second is to have no feelings. Being able to rationalise with the best of them, Ruby had told herself that although she was being paid to sleep with Adam, he knew nothing about the arrangement. Two weeks of living together had given Ruby a sense of belonging she had never enjoyed before and as the sexual drive was like opium to Adam, so the feeling of home was to Ruby.

She had laid the table on the small balcony that overlooked the teeming harbour with its constant movement and multitude of contrasting smells. A snow-white tablecloth had gone over the bamboo table and on it were the silver, crystal plates, salt and pepper set in carved ivory, a bowl of pink lilies from the new territories and, scattered where space allowed, the big flowers of the hibiscus she had picked from the tree that grew outside Dan's block of flats. Not a breath of air swept the twelfth floor balcony and the block being built in a crescent prevented neighbours looking onto them; the whole feeling was of space in front, of room to fly out and join with the seagulls.

One of the things Ruby liked most about Adam was his punctuality, his regard for other people. He would have finished work at three, played his tennis, had a beer in the mess and would be on his way home. Her joy in waiting was boundless. Everything was set out in the kitchen. Her rice would be cooked with blue cheese added at the last moment. Large Australian prawns lay on their sides in an oval dish waiting for the quick dip into the hot fat in the wok. The salad dressing was mixed and ready for the crisp green leaves sitting on the second shelf in the fridge. At the bottom of the fridge were two dozen slipper oysters, brought in from China by fishing boats that morning and sold in the fish market where Ruby had found them herself. Half an hour earlier, she had opened the big shells, the size of a woman's slipper, pushing the sharp knife in at the clockwise position of half past seven and cutting the muscle inside cleanly to release the top of the shell and reveal the succulent oyster in its bed of mother-of-pearl.

The red dress and white earrings, along with the white, high-heeled shoes, were all new and the ultimate pleasure from her morning's shopping.

"Ruby White," she said to herself as the key slotted into the lock and her stomach flipped with excitement, "there is nothing more stupid than a whore falling in love, so sorry."

. . .

LEE TUCHINO HAD ALWAYS BEEN quick on the uptake. She had recognised Reggie Beaumont the moment she sat down in the aeroplane and had positioned her legs to attract the maximum attention. After half an hour of watching Reggie reading *The Saint* from the corner of her eye she had been rewarded by Reggie's reaction when he had finally looked up at the coffee trolley. The slightly shaking hand that had hovered the cup over her bare thigh had been indication enough of her bull's eye with the legs.

Lee had been an Anglophile from the age of ten, when she had read the stories of King Arthur and the Knights of the Round Table. Castles and forests (enchanted, preferably) with the King's deer captivated her mind and the romance had remained, making her take up a career in show business and embark on the subsequent trip to the Windmill Theatre in England. Dreams are dreams, but she kept her fantasies topped up by avidly reading the *Tatler*, *London Illustrated News* and anything else that smacked of English gentry, which was how she had first come to read about Reggie. She had seen pictures of Merry Hall. She knew about his air force career and his business empire. She had read about his quirk of always travelling tourist class. But above all she knew he was single. In the back of Lee's slightly more practical brain, and after six months of flashing a leg in London, she had realised the only slim, very slim chance of finding her dreams was to marry them, and so, cool as a cucumber, she had asked him to a party and there he was, her Arthur. The *Jive* pants coincidence had been blind luck, as had the number of her seat on the aeroplane, but everyone had luck of sorts and the trick was to make the best of it.

The image of the second generation American Italian now on her way to Hong Kong had been beyond her practical dreams. She had been worried he would think her a whore or an opportunist (which she was, but would never admit to herself), but after the first week in Hong Kong and two very lively dinner parties for two she knew a lot more about his mind and the kind of person he was, which was charming, but the damn man had still not made a pass and how could a girl turn down a pass if it was never made? He had had her modelling his clothes to prospective local buyers, and he had been very attentive, but far too much in the way a father would be to his daughter.

Finally, she had concluded that Reggie must be queer and shrugged her luck away from looking at the man to looking at the job opportunity. Dancing in girly shows was out, so what else could she do? Life was far too frustrating and what a waste of a hunk, even if the hunk was a bit too old and craggy. Or advanced, as Reggie had told her, never old. "You never get old in this life, Lee," he'd said, "just a little more advanced."

It was only in the second week of their stay that she found out the man was anything but queer. The damn man had a Chinese girlfriend, and after looking into the matter further, Lee found he'd had her for years. After that, she wasn't sure if she preferred the queer Reggie of her mind to the real Reggie with a Chinese mistress. And then he had asked her to go to England and model for *Jive* full-time and her plane trip had gone right round in a circle. One thing she knew for certain: when she landed back at Heathrow airport, she was more frustrated than when she left, and the looks she'd received from Reggie on the plane hadn't helped. Reggie had caught her staring at him and she could not work out the meaning of the wink he'd given her but had the horrible suspicion it was the one that said 'two can play this game'. If he had made a pass at her that night, she would willingly have given in to him, but he had done nothing of the sort. He had put her up in the family flat with his nieces.

Lee Tuchino was not impressed.

"Did you see him?" Kim-Wok Ho had asked Adam two weeks earlier.

"Yes, sir."

"And?"

"He wouldn't give me a sworn statement."

"Are you sure it was Marshbank?"

"Yes."

"Would you recognise him again?"

"No. He said the Faulkner disguise would never be used again."

"Pity."

"I gave him my word."

"You will give a lot of people your word. You will even try to keep it some of the time. Very difficult. Grantham?"

"Wreck of a man. Couldn't remember. I felt sorry for him."

"Why? He did it himself. He was a good doctor by all reports. Gray?"

"Not a great deal of help. Still a civil servant at heart. He doesn't have the right piece of paper to prove the marriage. He might give a guarded affidavit that would be worse than nothing. Was he really head of the Sarawak government?"

"Yes," said Kim-Wok Ho. "Never judge a man from his final years of old age. Where do you go from here?"

"Home. I didn't need the compassionate leave. My annual leave would have been enough."

"Better stay. Craig wants to show you the ropes. You owe that one to your uncle. And I have a favour."

"Of course."

"I want you to come to Peking with me."

Adam had stared at him before speaking. "Well, I mean that isn't possible," he began. "Serving officers are not allowed into communist countries."

"No one will know. I wish you to visit the Chinese side of our business. The only one, really. Without Chinese trade, Hong Kong would not exist."

"The Chinese would not allow me into the country."

"They will. I've already asked them. They are going to give you Chinese papers for the journey."

"Why?"

"I've told them you may be taking over from me."

"I haven't even thought about a career. I'd like to come back to Hong Kong. Maybe when Mr Craig retires I could take over his..."

"Craig is English. You are Eurasian."

"Wouldn't Dan be more suitable? He is half Chinese. I am half..."

"Two people decide my successor. Myself and Reggie. Provided the Chinese agree, that is."

"Uncle Reggie is trying to get rid of me, by the sound of it."

"Trying to make you happy, more likely. All that matters in life... Happiness."

"Don't you have any children?"

"Not really. I never married. My ancestors will be furious. Must seem so pointless after thousands of years to come to an abrupt end. Lots of families disappear."

"Does my uncle know you want me to go into China?"

"Oh yes. He thinks it is the solution to your problem."

"If the RAF found out, they'd court-martial me."

"They won't find out. How do you like Hong Kong?"

"I think it is the most wonderful place in the world."

"Good."

"Don't the British suspect you of something?" asked Adam.

"Probably. But they want the trade. The British always want to make money. You will like China. It will open your eyes. The place is never what the other man tells you. Especially if he's biased."

KIM-WOK HO GAVE the Chinese border guard his pass and the boom came up across the road and the car moved smoothly into gear and drove forward into China. Beside him, in a black wig and a people's black shirt that fitted roundly to his neck, sat a confused Adam, his conflicting loyalties providing him with insurmountable problems. He had asked a favour, been given it and was now paying the price. They drove into China for half an hour, well-tended fields on either side of the Rover.

"Looks much the same, doesn't it?" said Kim-Wok Ho.

"Yes... All those people in the fields are communists?"

"Chinese first. Communist second."

"You are communist?" asked Adam, thinking he understood.

"In China, yes."

"In Hong Kong?"

"A thorough capitalist."

"How can that be? How can you be two things at once?"

"Communism works in China. Capitalism never has. There are six hundred million Chinese and most of them were starving ten years ago. They have to be told what to do for their own good. There must be stability if so many people are to have enough food. Before it was always war. The peasant grew a crop and the war-lord burnt it or stole it. Constant insecurity. You could never plan a season ahead. We now have five and ten-year plans and we know for certain that nothing will interfere with the programme. A man wants peace, food and shelter. When everyone has that in abundance they can think of the luxury of democracy, but they probably won't want it. A man only needs so much wealth. It is only under constantly changing governments that he needs more than he can use for fear of losing the bit he requires to survive. Take away the fear of not losing his wealth and he will say he doesn't require very much at all. Stability. That's all we need. The chance to live in peace and quiet. What else is there?"

"A man needs a goal. He can't just see the rest of his life slotting in. There has to be a challenge."

"Trying to feed a family when you are poor is quite a challenge. I saw the old China. My father was a war-lord and changed his mind. Went on the long march with Mao. The Chinese people deserved more than they were getting."

"Why don't you live in China?"

"To build wealth for China it is necessary to stop the people seeing others who have, for the moment, more than themselves. We have to close our borders. We have to say that everything in the Western world is wrong, which we know is not true. We have to guide the people but at the same time we must have access to

Western technology. Hence Hong Kong, Macau, Singapore and people like me. It is not so strange if you think about it carefully. Maybe one day the world ideologies will meld into one and all this nonsense will not be necessary. When you deal with people there has to be a lot of subterfuge for their own good. We have already doubled food production."

"Good."

"No one goes hungry. Everyone works."

"Good."

"I hope you will see that clearly in the years to come," said Kim-Wok Ho, taking his eyes off the road to look at Adam.

They drove on into China.

PART III

SEPTEMBER TO DECEMBER
1954

t evening time on Santa Carolina, an island off the coast of Mozambique known to Rhodesians as Paradise Island, upwards of six big-game fish boats would sit in a small bay guarded by its coral reef. Onshore, hanging by their tails from scaffolds, were blue marlin and hammerhead sharks, the joy of any fisherman. Along the shore away from the dead fish were palm trees; under one, at the tip of the island, Peter Escort was fast asleep. The boats had come ashore unbeknown to him an hour before, the deep chug-chug of the diesel engines dropping as they came in one by one through the gap in the coral. By the time he stirred, the big fish had been weighed and photographed alongside their human killers. The blue that day weighed eight hundred and seventy-two pounds.

The ship had brought them back from Malaya to Beira, but Peter had needed time to adjust to his homecoming after two years of jungle warfare. He had taken leave of the Rhodesian Special Air Service at the docks and started his three months' leave by hiving off to the island to think and mend his mental wounds; he was not a man who enjoyed the killing. The air was balmy and he luxuriated in the feel of it before fitting the goggles over his face. He crossed the soft sand and ever so gently lowered himself into the water, gripping the air piece with his teeth so that he could breathe with his face in the water, looking down at the myriad of small, tropical fish. He had been on the island a week and he was almost ready to go home, unlike his great-uncle Gerald, who had never made it back after his commandos' failed assassination attempt on Rommel in '41.

CLAY HUNTER WAS the manager of Greswold Estates, its three sections each growing eighty acres of Virginia tobacco. At thirty-two he was the youngest manager in the Umvukwes and needed two more good seasons to have enough money to go out on his own. Next to him in bed, Sybil Crane was thinking, something she rarely did; being the only pretty unmarried girl in the Umvukwes, she did not have to marry.

Clay got up and went to the bathroom for his early morning piss, wishing he had drunk a little less beer at the club the previous night. Along with an assortment of other fellows, he had been screwing Sybil for six months, and was wondering where in heaven he was going to find a replacement.

"Peter is coming back this week," he called from the bathroom, watching her reaction in the bathroom mirror; he never closed the door when he went for a piss.

"I know," she said after a while.

"Well?"

"He was meant to be back last week."

"Well?"

"I don't want to get married, Clay. Can you imagine sleeping with the same woman for the rest of your life?"

"I suppose so."

"Do you want to get married?"

He came back into the bedroom smiling, with only one thing on his mind.

. . .

IN THE COTTAGE three hundred yards downriver, Raoul Beaumont heard Sybil loud and clear, which caused his frustration level to peak. As he was only an assistant, Sybil would not look at him, and Cindy would not let him touch her, which was quite right if his intention was honourable, which it was. If only Sybil had not flashed it at him in the club the previous evening and would stop shouting her climaxes for the entire bush to hear, his sexual needs would remain under control. He was aroused to the extreme just listening to her from three hundred yards away.

UP AT THE BIG HOUSE, Jake Escort was cleaning his shotgun with loving care, having dispatched four guinea fowl at first light as they came out of the gum trees by the dam. Unlike Clay, who was nicknamed for his ability to hit clay pigeons with a shotgun from any angle and distance, Jake had missed two birds that had dropped low over the main stubble. Unlocking the barrel from the hand carved stock, he slotted the pieces into the leather case and put it under the bed. His wife was still asleep. He got off the bed carefully so as not to wake her and walked across the polished wooden floor to the big bay window and looked out over the croquet lawn to the tennis court and the bush that went on and on to the Urungwe range, shimmering in the heat haze of distance. For the beginning of September it was going to be a hot day.

SIXTEEN FANS WERE SLOWLY TURNING high above the coffee tables in the lounge of Meikles Hotel. The tobacco floors had been open three weeks. The farmers who had sold that morning were drifting into Salisbury's premier meeting place, the men distinctive in white baggy shorts and with faces mottled red by the sun and imported whisky. Wives wore print dresses as a standard uniform.

Outside, in Cecil Square, a perfect blue sky, cloudless for weeks. Groups of people, black and white, lay on the grass and looked up at it through the bright green leaves of the coral trees, which were getting ready to bloom red.

A fat-bellied, red-fezzed African with the marked distinctions of great weight and a grey moustache put the silver tea tray down in front of Isabel Beaumont and went off with the one and three pence. Isabel and Lorna had left England on a Union Castle boat sailing from Southampton to Beira.

"Three from Zach," said Lorna, looking at the American stamps and shuffling them into date order carefully before putting down the first letter and picking up the second. "He didn't get that part." Zach wrote most to her when he was out of work.

"What does Ted want?" said Isabel, ripping open the envelope from Ted Cornwell. She had told him only to write in emergencies. "What a lot of mail in six weeks." She started to read.

Lorna poured cups of tea and put in the right amount of milk and sugar before opening Zach's third letter. Lorna was barely conscious of the man at the next table sitting on his own. He had tried to catch her eye between the first and second letters but the fleeting eye contact had been too brief to have any meaning.

"Ted is trying to force Reggie into giving him a twenty per cent shareholding," said Isabel. "Why are men always greedy? Wants my support. Mandy's given him hers but they've been sleeping together for months."

"I didn't know that," said Lorna, putting down her letter.

"Ted has an affair with any woman my daughter comes in contact with. Sort of revenge. Childish, but they aren't much older than children." She turned back to the letter. "Ted will burn his fingers with Reggie."

"Maybe not. He's pretty astute."

"You as well?"

"Not me, Aunty, though he's tried. My pride would be hurt if he hadn't." She went back to Zach's letter, smiling to herself, while Isabel finished her business letter and picked up one from Roz.

"Aunty, they've done it."

"What?"

"*1066*. They've found a backer."

"Who is he?"

"A man called Montague Heron. American. Big industrialist. Well known as an angel on Broadway. Does films as well, according to Zach."

"Richard didn't tell me."

"You haven't opened his letter, Aunty dear," said Lorna, picking Richard D'Altena's letter out of the pile and offering it to Isabel.

"Roz wants to open a nightclub."

"I hope it's nothing like Uncle Reggie's Bretts."

"What do you know about Bretts?" she said, looking up again. She was sensitive on the subject of Bretts: Carl Preisler's face came back to her quite vividly.

"No more than anyone else in the family. Granny Beaumont said she thought it was a knock shop, whatever that is. Probably Roz wants the nightclub to meet men. I just don't know where she gets the energy."

"Neither do I," said Isabel with sincerity.

"Here's the catch," said Lorna. "This Montague Heron insists Tammany plays the lead. That's another man she's pulled from the other side of the footlights."

"Richard has never made a pass at Tammany."

"They're trying to get Blake as musical director at Tammany's request. Must still be in love with him."

"What happened there?"

"Don't you know? Roz seduced Blake. Told him she saw Beau coming out of Tammany's bedroom. Rebound. Tammany won't talk about Beau."

"She hates his guts."

"Love-hate. Who knows...? Reggie is trying to get Lee Tuchino a part in *1066* as a dancer."

"She has plenty of leg and you can never have enough of that in a musical."

"The age difference is quite ridiculous," said Lorna.

Isabel kept quiet as they went on reading their accumulation of letters. The man at the next table was still trying to catch Lorna's eye, and Isabel gave him a brief smile of sympathy.

"Dad's been posted to Germany," said Lorna. "Wow! They've made him a major general. How did Zach hear before me?"

"He reads the newspapers. There's a letter from Georgina somewhere in the pile. Geoffrey is a good soldier."

"I only wish mother appreciated him more."

Again, Isabel was silent.

"You must be Lorna Beaumont," said the man from the next table, who had got up and was now standing looking down at Lorna reading her letter.

"Yes," she said, looking up in surprise.

"I'm sorry. I was listening. Very rude," he said, causing Isabel to put her tongue into the lower part of her cheek. "Granny Beaumont, you see. New major general. Your brother works for my father. I'm Peter Escort. What are you doing in Africa?"

"Visiting your father," said Isabel. "Lorna's aunt."

"I would never have believed it," said Peter Escort.

"That could either mean Lorna looks a lot older than she is or I look a lot younger."

"Younger, of course," he said, liking the woman.

"Sit down," said Isabel.

"Thank you. Why aren't you on the farm?"

"We arrived this morning," said Lorna. "Breather on our own."

"I know what you mean. I just took a week off on Paradise Island. Talked to the palm trees."

"Where's Paradise Island? Sounds inviting."

"It is. Off the coast of Mozambique."

"What are you doing here all on your own?" asked Isabel.

"Waiting for the farm manager." He was talking to Isabel but looking at Lorna, who finished Zach's letter and put it down, Peter's eyes following her hands in search of the non-existent ring.

"The boyfriend," said Lorna, seeing his line of thought. "America. Out of work actor."

"I'm sorry," said Peter.

"It was his choice."

"How long are you staying in Greswold?"

"A week. Then Raoul is taking us to the Victoria Falls and the Zambezi Valley."

"Can I get you a drink?" said Peter, looking from one to the other. "It's past twelve."

"Best idea this morning," said Isabel, perking up as Peter waved his hand to attract a waiter and Clay Hunter and Sybil Crane worked their way towards them between the tables.

"I timed it perfectly," said Clay, shaking Peter's hand. "Mine is a Lion Lager. What will you have, Sybil?"

"Hello, Peter," she said. "I'm sure Peter remembers."

"You haven't changed," said Peter.

"Mrs Beaumont and Lorna. Clay Hunter. Sybil Crane."

Sybil turned to see the competition.

"I'm Raoul's sister," said Lorna. "Have you met my brother?"

"Of course. How was your war, Peter?" she said, turning her back to Lorna.

"Why don't we all drive up to the farm together?" said Clay. "It'll save me a journey tomorrow. Your dad thought the Beaumonts were arriving tomorrow."

"That's how things go," said Peter, wondering what Sybil was doing with Clay. "How are mum and dad?"

"Never better. You look good, Peter."

"Good to be back."

"Welcome home," said Sybil.

CLAY HUNTER DROVE the lead Land Rover down the trail the elephant had made for him to the great Zambezi River below. It was one of the last parts of real Africa, rugged to an extreme, peaceful and totally unspoiled. Dropping down a ten mile trail, Peter Escort followed in the second Land Rover, watching for the first sight of the great, bulbous baobab trees.

They arrived at the banks of the big river at four o'clock in the afternoon of the second day, making camp on the same site that Clay Hunter had used for nine years. Clay sent Peter among the trees to bring in fallen branches for the fire that would burn strong flames all night to keep off the wild animals. When dusk was setting, Raoul went down to the water with Lorna to catch river bream, while Clay went inland with the .22 rifle to shoot guinea fowl, which would be baked all night underneath the hot fire and eaten for breakfast.

"Not quite like Merry Hall," said Raoul. "You've got one, sis... Hey, now that's a big one!"

"Help me! It's going to fall off," shouted Lorna in her excitement, and Raoul put the landing net deftly under the two pound fish and landed it on the riverbank. "I've never caught anything that big before," she said, as he put another worm on her hook.

"Just dangle it in the water," he said. "You can see them coming up as the worm goes down... Have you spoken to Beau recently?"

"He's too busy being a 'debs delight'. He doesn't mind who he escorts as long as their father's rich. I can't see when he ever does any work for the army. He's very popular. Far too high and mighty for me now he's going to inherit the Hall. Young, good-looking man with old houses and titles are much sought after. Even though Uncle Reggie won't leave him any money, he's not worried..."

"He's worried, all right... Pull it in, Lorna! Just wind. That's got him!"

"Raoul, they're so big..." The fish was a good pound and a half. "What do you mean, he's worried?"

"The word has gone round the debutante set that Beau Beaumont is *not* going to inherit the Hall, after all."

"Reggie isn't getting *married*, is he?"

"Not that I know of. Beau wrote to me. Adam's trip to the East convinced him his parents were properly married. That was all he wanted. He's left for the East now that he's out of the RAF. He has little interest in the Hall. But Uncle Reggie has put the facts to the College of Heralds. England is changing. The empire we were born to is being given away. The College of Heralds will accept Adam without question, provided Beau doesn't stick his oar in. Anyway, the rich heiresses aren't interested in any of that. They want to buy certain titles and there are more titles than money in England these days.

"He's a great pragmatist, my brother," he went on, "and a great opportunist. I used to hero worship him, but not anymore. When he leaves the army in five months' time, Uncle Reggie is lending him a hundred thousand pound sterling at three per cent interest to get him out of England. Beau wants to come out here. Before I knew his problem, I was boasting in letters about the chances of making it big in Rhodesia. He's done a lot of follow-up work and agrees with me. It's the land, Lorna, it's so cheap, and there are so many miles and miles of it going begging. When the rains fall, you just have to stand back quickly and watch the tobacco grow."

"You'd better take the hook out of the fish," Lorna said matter-of-factly. "So brother Beau is going to do some work for the first time in his life."

"I don't think he's even going to do that. He's made the deal. He's got the hundred thousand pounds and that's a fearful lot of money out here. He's going to employ people to do the work for him. He wants me as his personal assistant, as he wants someone with the local knowledge to check on his managers. Managers, plural, Lorna. Our brother never does anything in half measures."

"It can't be definite. Dad knows nothing."

"Dad's been away. He's away again and mother agrees to anything Beau comes up with. He's been to Rhodesia House and applied for a resident's permit."

"What's in it for you, Raoul?"

"Probably nothing." He stood up with the fish.

"Come up, you two," called Clay, who was back with five birds. "Have you caught any fish?"

"Plenty."

"That's my lad. You always did learn quickly."

"Not 'til I came to Africa," he said to his sister. "Come on, I'll show you how to fillet them. Clay taught me."

"Clay taught you a lot," she said, looking up at the campsite, the fire bright and throwing shadows into the new dusk.

"He's taught me everything. He may be ten years older and my immediate boss but he's also my best friend. And as I know him well, sis, keep away from him. With women he's dynamite."

"That's big talk, little brother."

"Not so little anymore... How is Karen?"

"That one's going to be the beauty of the family and the scourge of men."

"Good. I'd like to see you and Tammany with some competition."

THE NIGHT CAME SWIFTLY. Dusk had turned to blackness in ten minutes. They could look up into the heavens and see the gentle dusting of the Milky Way, the night sky a myriad of stars that went further than their minds could comprehend. There were three layers of the heavens, an awesome vision of infinity. Their world had come down to the patch of firelight, flickering a short way up into the witch-like branches of the fever tree.

Clay had cut a stick from a wild fig tree and whittled away the end into a sharp, sap-wet point, which he was now poking into the fire in order to retrieve the baked potatoes without scorching himself. A separate fire was frying Zambezi bream in a huge, cast-iron pan. Clay had cut the fish on each side, sprinkling them with a mixture of salt and coarsely ground pepper.

"This is the most beautiful place in the world," said Isabel.

"You're right," answered Clay, lightly touching her arm with the tips of his fingers.

DAWN FOUND Isabel stiff despite the hollow Clay had dug for her hip and filled with dry leaves and grass, but she had at least slept through the night. She pulled back the mosquito net. Fish eagles were plummeting down into the water for food and a small herd of impala were drinking. The smell of fresh coffee had woken her; Clay was crouched at the fire ladling it into cups from an open pot hung on a tripod over the flames.

"Sleep well?" he asked.

"I did, thanks. I could build a hut and stay here forever."

"Could you live in Africa?"

"Yes."

"But you've been here such a short while."

"Could you go back to England?"

"No... Not even if the family allowed me to."

"Family?"

"Mother, father. The establishment. I didn't fit in."

"Neither do I."

"Dress designing must be stimulating."

"You have to live life as well."

"Your husband? What happened?"

"Killed in the war, poor Henry. We were miles apart before then. I wanted the Manor House, not Henry. People are cruel to each other. They take for the wrong reasons. I wanted to marry his brother well before Reggie became rich, but he saw through me like a pane of glass. Wouldn't look at me on principle."

"Why ever not?"

"I'm not a very nice person, full stop."

"No one is nasty through and through. There's good in all of us. There may even be some good in me though father never found any. The remittance man. I've been back a few times and lived it up in London 'til my money ran out. They did me a favour. I would have been a rake in England."

"By reports you don't do badly out here." She nodded at Sybil struggling out of her mosquito net.

"She's Peter's girl. He was cracked on her."

"Is he still?"

"War changes people. Lust and love are totally blind. He's a good man. Now, Lorna..."

"She would never live in Africa. Chased after by every man in London. She will enjoy her safari but nothing more."

"Poor Peter."

"You think he...?"

"Oh yes. Don't you?"

"He's been attentive, but we're guests in his father's house... Very nice boy," she added, looking across at him speculatively. "Why the army?"

"I've never quite worked that one out. He loves the bush. The farm. Make a good farmer. Maybe he intends to retire after twenty years' service and then run Greswold. That's probably it. I asked him once but he said that five years hence was one hell of a long time."

"When looking forward from youth, I agree with him."

"How was your coffee?"

"The best. Are those birds ready? I'm starving."

"Let's test." He went to the main fire, swept the fire away from the ashes with the largest log, and prodded gently for the guinea fowl buried underneath.

"It's still got its feathers on."

"They come away with the clay. Soft inside. Look at that. The brown flesh is falling off the drumstick."

"Can I have a piece?"

"Not until it cools," said Clay, laughing.

"Smells good," she said, accidentally touching his bare shoulder with her breast as she leant forward to have a better look.

"So was that," said Clay, and Isabel blushed like a schoolgirl.

"I'm old enough to be your mother."

"Nonsense."

"Stop playing games, Clay Hunter."

"It's cool enough," he said, touching the bird with the back of his hand and then tearing off pieces of the drumstick. "Open your mouth... How's that?"

"Orgasmic," said Isabel with her eyes shut.

"I told you so."

"Are you going to share that bird?" said Peter, coming across to them.

"Have some coffee first," said Isabel, stretching out her long fingers to pluck a piece from the carcase and putting the meat into her mouth, sucking it in slowly and chewing well. "Beats pheasant any day."

"My aunt is going bush happy," said Lorna, joining the party.

"What a lovely way to go," said Isabel.

RAOUL WALKED with a .375 rifle tucked comfortably under his right arm. He and Cindy had travelled half a mile upriver from the camp and the sun was hot on their backs. As they moved up the bank away from the river a flock of green pigeons burst out of the wild fig tree. Raoul propped his rifle against the tree and they sat down with their backs to the trunk. They did not speak, comfortable with each other's silence, as together they watched the river flowing down in front of them heavy with the weight of long-carried water. Around them, the bush was crackling with the heat of the day.

"I'm going to Cape Town," said Cindy.

"How long for?"

"Four years. Maybe six if I take an honours."

They were silent for a long time.

"I've got to do something. I can't sit around waiting to get married and screw my brains out like Sybil." Raoul said nothing. "I'm too young to get married. I know I got you out here, but you came for a job. We were pen friends, remember? You told me all about Merry Hall and I wrote about Africa... I've got to do something with my life... A farmer's wife is limited. She can help in the dispensary. Help with the books. Help in the store. But it's always helping, Raoul."

"When are you going?" he asked flatly.

"Next week. I was going..."

"I'll miss you."

"Oh, Raoul. Give me a kiss?"

"I don't think I could right now."

"Try to understand me."

"I'm trying."

"Don't you see what we've done to Africa? It's time we give something back."

"What are you going to read?"

"Soil erosion. Conservation. I want to help Africa. I was born here. So was Dad. We're Africans. All the foreign aid in the world isn't going to help. Give a man food for a year and he'll expect to be fed for a lifetime. But showing him how to grow a better crop, how to stop his topsoil flowing down the river to Beira, and he'll grow himself something worthwhile and be proud to be a man. All right, I read a lot of this, but it makes sense. If we don't give something positive back to Africa, we might as well get out and leave the poor sods to starve."

"I hear you, Cindy."

"But do you understand?"

"Maybe I'm just selfish."

"Why don't you come to UCT?"

"That's a laugh. Me at university. I couldn't even pass my school certificate. You know it's why I'm out here."

"You didn't pass your school certificate because the subjects didn't interest you."

"Possibly."

"But what I'm talking about does interest you. We've talked about these problems for hours."

"Maybe I've talked a hole in front of me."

"Maybe not. You also want the knowledge. We've been writing to each other since we were twelve. Instead of writing letters, I'm going to send you my papers and notes. You'll have a copy of all the books and I'll be your eyes at lectures. The vacs are long and then we can really argue it out together. And that's a whole lot better than me coming home with a lot of new ideas and you telling me about the new grading shed... It's the best idea I ever had."

.   .   .

SOMETIME LATER, Peter had walked a hundred yards upriver and was sitting on the rock that jutted out, the campsite obscured by a bend in the river. The pain had reached his fingertips. Everything he had thought of for the future included Sybil.

"How can you say such a thing?" he'd shouted at Cindy.

"Because it's true, Peter. I'm sorry, but it's true. If you were married to her with children I would probably have kept my mouth shut. Maybe Raoul shouldn't have mentioned it, but he did, giggling about it, not knowing. That's when I knew it was true. She was screaming so loudly Raoul could hear from his cottage."

2

Zachariah Booth's room on the East Side of New York was similar in many ways to Holland Park. One of the small differences was the row of hats, with and without feathers, hung from a pole across one corner of the room. Zach owed six weeks' rent. His circumstances had come full circle. Sitting with his long legs, booted but not socked, stuck up on the small table, he was waiting for an old friend. The fact that he was out of America if he did not find himself an acting job within two weeks did not worry him a jot. He would solve the problem of the six weeks' rent and start a fresh slate of credit with Mrs Preston. George, his English agent, was sure to have a part for him.

For the reunion, he had carefully chosen a green hat with two chicken feathers. Both feathers unfortunately needed replacing, but Zach had been unable to find an unplucked chicken in New York at short notice. He had had two jobs with Richard D'Altena and that had been it. Zach liked an audience when he was performing and a whole bunch of people running around with cameras did not constitute an audience to Zach. Accordingly, Richard had lost interest in him and after he had been unable to finance *1066* they had lost contact. Though that had now changed there was, according to Richard, no part for him in the musical he had helped to create. He took his hand-carved pipe out of his mouth and let out a good chuckle at the thought of it, the smile lines at the corners of his eyes creasing happily.

BLAKE EMSWORTH ENJOYED the ride on the subway. He had grown accustomed to his black bowler hat and rolled umbrella, so he was unable to see what the gentleman next to him was getting at.

"You an actor, buddy?"

Blake gave him the Englishman's look of horror at being spoken to by a stranger and failed to see the incongruity of the guitar balanced on his knee. The American tried to outstare him without success before reverting to silence.

At the prescribed station on the East Side, Blake walked off with dignity and ran into another problem when he asked the first policeman he encountered where he could find an off-licence.

"What you say?"

"An off-licence. You know, old chap, a place you can buy the old hooligan juice."

"Hooligan juice?"

"Booze."

"You want a drugstore? Straight down there and on the next corner. Where you from?"

"England."

"That explains everything."

"Drugstore," Blake went off muttering. "That's a place you buy medicine." Nevertheless, he managed to find an assortment of booze and made his way to the address he had been given. Reaching into a less and less salubrious area, he began to whistle.

"YOU LOOK BLOODY RIDICULOUS," Zach said to Blake. "Short back and sides and a gent." He threw the bowler hat and umbrella onto the divan and rummaged in the carrier bag.

"Nice little place you've got," said Blake sarcastically.

"Home from home."

"Open the Scotch. At least that's the same in America."

"Try bourbon. Great." They looked at each other for a moment before Zach gave Blake a bear hug. "It's not very British, but it's good to see you."

"Better pour a drink or you'll have us both blubbering."

Zach poured neat Scotch into tumblers. "Cheers."

"Good health."

"How's the stock exchange?"

"I don't know."

"Sounds interesting. Why the gear?"

"Purely to see the expression on your face. Absolute picture. From now on the hair can grow."

"How is Roz?"

"Roz? You must be joking. We split up weeks after I joined the pater's firm. If Tammany hadn't gone with Beau..."

"Maybe she didn't."

"He was in her room. You don't have to see the knickers coming down to put it together. Being in her room was enough."

"They're cousins."

"I got the message from Beau over dinner that night. He gave me that look of 'I can do what you can't'. Roz did me some kind of favour, though one of them wasn't joining the stock exchange. I tried. The family appreciate it. I took out all the right girls and even grew fond of one of them but it wasn't what I wanted. Mother was actually quite excited when Richard phoned from New York and said he found a backer for 1066. He's registered our copyright. I've asked for a ten thousand dollar advance and a contract. He's talking to Heron right now."

"Can you get me a part...?"

"No, Zach. Richard's adamant. He wants you involved with the script."

"That's bloody nonsense. I'm an actor, not a writer. I did that writing as a joke. Something to amuse the three of us. It was fun. None of it was meant to be taken seriously, and if Richard hadn't lusted over Tammany... I'm sorry, Blake, but that's how it was. Heron is the same. They want Tammany, not 1066."

"It's going to cost Heron a fortune if it flops and neither of them are going to get Tammany. I know her."

"Are you certain?"

"Almost."

"People change, Blake. The biggest aphrodisiac in a woman's life is money and Heron's loaded. And he's quite a bit younger than Richard. Probably in his late forties, stinking rich, and he wants her. Now, if that isn't a combination."

"Then why put on a musical if he has that much power with women? Take a suite at the Dorchester and sit it out in London 'til he's got what he wants. Damn sight cheaper. Businessmen don't waste money, Zach, no matter how much they've got. I just spent two years at the stock exchange."

"You think we'll get it?"

"What?"

"The ten thousand dollars."

"No. As Richard said, this is America. He's asked for fifty thousand, with you and me on payroll from the start of rehearsals."

"When's that?"

"Two weeks."

"They don't play around in America."

"That's why they're rich, buddy," he said, and they both laughed.

"Have you seen Lorna?"

"She's in Africa."

"What the hell is she doing there?"

"Visiting friends with Aunt Isabel."

"You are slow with the drinks tonight, Mr Emsworth."

"My apologies, Mr Booth."

THE FRENCH WINDOWS were wide open to the sea and the lapping waves down below. Not a breath of wind. The shutters were up and sun streamed into the studio, lighting up the canvas where Tug was at work with his back to the sea. It was a big canvas of Merry Hall set up on its hill with horsemen in armour outside the Gothic doors. The commission had come from the Stately Homes of England Society and would be used in their campaign to attract visitors. There were to be ten different great houses going through the ages and though Merry Hall was the only one not open to the public, Tug had insisted his home be one of them. Surprisingly, he'd enjoyed the research, and was confident that the clothes and manners of his people through the ages were authentic, as were the structures of the houses. Tug had been mildly surprised when he found there to be so little difference between the early painting of the Hall and the present structure. The windows were fewer and smaller and the grounds surrounding it less formal; the large courtyard and gravel road leading up to the house were little more than a path and an open patch of ground.

"Hi, Dad," came a voice at his back, causing him to jump, having been absorbed so completely in his painting.

"Tammany!" He dropped his brush back on the stand with his palette. "What are you doing in Penzance?"

"Come to see you."

"Why aren't you at school?" They hugged each other. "You look good."

"And you, Dad. You're smiling. Your eyes, I mean. What's this?"

"The Hall at the time of the first Charles."

"I like it," she said, and her eyes swept round the studio, which she'd never seen before without encountering rows of portraits of her mother. There were upwards of forty new, finished canvases. "Dad, you can paint!"

"Has it taken you all your life to find that out?"

"Yes."

"One-man exhibition at the end of the year," said Tug, looking at the quantity. "In between commissions."

"So much work."

"Twelve hours a day. I've installed spotlights to help at night."

"Don't you get tired?"

"No... You look exactly like your mother."

"Does that worry you, Dad?" There was the old touch of worry in her voice.

"Not any more. I've come out of my shell a bit. A young lady who served in the local pub gave me a lot of help. She's getting married now, but I owe her a lot. She says it was the other way around."

"I'm glad."

"So am I... You like them?"

"Dad they're brilliant... I've left RADA."

"You didn't fail? You were doing so well."

"I wanted to finish. I spoke to our mime teacher. She's always been a good friend of Richard D'Altena's."

"You're not getting married?"

"No. Don't jump ahead too fast. Sit down and I'll tell you all... You can spare ten minutes," she said, smiling at him, amazed how young and fit he looked and so much of the sorrow washed away. He just smiled at her happily. "She must have been some barmaid," she said.

"She was."

"You remember me writing about *1066*? They're putting it on Broadway and want me to play the female lead. The girl was seventeen, you see. Saxon. She married the first Sir Henri. I have the contract in my bag and Mrs Saunders said chances like this don't come twice in a career and my last year at RADA was less important. I haven't signed it yet. I wanted your advice. Daddy, I'm so worried these men want me and not the musical."

"Who is this Heron man?" he asked after she'd filled him in on the details of the production.

"A rich American. It's all I know. Even Uncle Reggie does business with him. He's met him."

"You've talked to Reggie?"

"Yes. He says keep their hands out of my pants and nothing can go wrong."

"He always was a bit crude," said Tug, smiling at the memories.

"Come on, I'm not painting anymore. You can sleep on the couch for as long as you like. I'll take you down to the Barley Oats for a glass of beer. You do drink beer?"

"Only in half pints," said Tammany, and her face clouded.

"Anything wrong?"

"No," she said, shaking herself. "Someone just ran over my grave."

THREE WEEKS before Roz's seventeenth birthday, she screwed her hundredth man and went home to check her diaries. Each man, even if she did not know his name, which happened at parties, received a mention. Every week she subtotalled in pencil and every month in red ink. The first years of her sexual life had been best but lately she had lost interest. Even the group sex and gang bangs had left her sexually unsatisfied. There had been one exception, when one of the girls had got hold of her and turned her on.

For kicks, she had tried drugs, but found drugs and the people who took them boring. She had thought of starting a nightclub but discarded the idea as boring. She had thought of travelling around the world but could not see the point. She was a successful ramp model and saleswoman and for a year she had done exactly what she wanted. She'd been to jazz clubs, nightclubs, restaurants, theatres, Ascot, Henley, and even watched cousin Beau play cricket for the army against the air force. Approaching seventeen, she had tried many things and found all but one to be wanting.

With a flash of insight and a smile on her face, she picked up the phone and called Ted's girlfriend, licking her lips in anticipation. At six on a Friday evening, Ted would still be at the office. Mandy answered the phone in Ted's flat.

"Hi! It's Roz. Why don't you come over to mum's flat? She's away somewhere in Africa and I thought we could get together alone for a change. There's plenty of whisky. If you don't want to go home you can stay over for the night. Give Ted a ring and he'll get himself a date for the evening."

"He's done that already. The new typist at the ad agency."

"Come on over. It'll be fun."

"I'm coming right now," said Mandy, and the phone clicked.

"That's lucky," said Roz to herself, and went inside to dress as sexily as possible.

When Mandy arrived half an hour later, they looked at each other dressed in their sexiest clothes from *Jive* and sensed there was more in the air than whisky and conversation, but neither was sure of the other's motives. Roz had the hi-fi playing soft music and the ice and soda water were out and ready to go.

"You look good tonight," said Roz, deliberately looking at the girl's bosom.

"You don't look bad yourself, Roz," said Mandy, and the look she gave Roz convinced her she was not mistaken in thinking the previous looks in the office had been sexual. "A Scotch for me," Mandy went on, "and make it a good one. That Ted thinks he's God. He treats you oh-so-good when he wants to and then turns off when something else comes along. He wants a bigger share in the company and I agreed before he dated tonight's bird. Right in front of me. Wants to see if she'd make a *Jive* model. Bullshit. He wants a screw and that's exactly how he looks at it. Ted Cornwell never makes love. He fucks. Men make you sick."

"I agree. Here's your drink. It'll do him good not to find you at home."

Two hours and half a bottle of Scotch later, Mandy asked Roz if she was really staying the night. Both of them very nicely sozzled and having verbally torn apart every male they knew in common.

"Don't you want to?" asked Roz, sitting across from her and letting her legs fall apart to reveal a lack of panties. Mandy's eyes were riveted, and she licked her lips before quickly taking a drink. Roz kept her legs open and waited for Mandy's eyes to come back to her.

"Have you ever had a woman?" asked Roz.

"No... Have you?"

"Do you want to?"

"I don't know. I always thought men…"

"Let's go into the bedroom and try. If we don't like it, we don't have to try again."

"How do we do it?"

"I'm sure we'll find out."

"Beautiful," she said, and she meant it.

DAN CHANG HAD DECIDED the worst thing that had happened to his career was Adam not staying in England, but it was the best thing to have happened to his social life. They were inseparable. The tennis score was twenty-four matches to twenty-three in favour of Dan. Adam was still besotted with Ruby and Dan stayed awake at night worrying whether he should tell Adam that the whole thing had been a set-up. He finally decided he would tell Adam the truth if there was any mention of marriage, but his limited experience of life left him safe on this one as he had never heard of any of his friends marrying their mistresses. Many had married and carried on the original affair, but that was different. Maybe the business side could be sorted out and they would eventually run Hong Kong together, but he was not so sure on this point.

That evening, Adam was throwing a housewarming party in his new flat on the Peak. Dan and all of their friends had been told to behave themselves, as there was going to be a surprise, the request for good behaviour being a surprise in itself. 'Especially you, Dan Chang,' Adam had admonished. They'd been told to wear dinner jackets, owned, borrowed or hired, and the girls were all to be in long dresses. Sounded more like the stuff at Government House, but because it was Adam everyone was humouring the man. Craig Craig indicated the dress was quite correct. The boy was learning. Both Sir Reginald and Mr Kim-Wok Ho were right. The boy was good. Excellent, in fact. Some of the praise had originated from the boy thrashing Craig at tennis but never bringing it up thereafter. There were some things an Englishman did not brag about.

Dan was halfway across the lounge to where Adam was

dispensing drinks to his long-dressed and dinner-jacketed guests when his jaw dropped and his pace slackened to a halt. Their eyes had met and the chemistry was instantaneous; beyond any luck in Dan's previous life, the girl was Eurasian.

Adam followed Tammany's gaze and smiled. "That's Dan," he said.

"I don't believe it."

"Neither does Dan by the look on his face," said Adam, raising his voice above the throng. "Come and meet someone, you old dog, and I hope she puts you off your tennis tomorrow. Daniel Chang, I would like you to meet my sister, Tammany Beaumont. Tammany, meet Dan."

"Do they shake hands in Hong Kong?" asked Tammany.

"Give him a kiss," said Adam. "He's my best friend. Sort of family... Come on, Dan, she won't bite."

"You didn't say your sister..."

"This was the surprise and why all you lot have to behave yourselves."

"What nonsense," said Tammany. "No one behaves at RADA."

"You can go back to normal behaviour," shouted Adam. "The good behaviour is off. Everyone, this is my sister, Tammany, the famous actress. Or she will be. After visiting the plebs in Hong Kong she's off to New York to star on Broadway."

"Adam, you'll make me blush."

"Isn't she gorgeous?" said Adam.

"So that's why you were in such a hurry to finish the flat," said Dan, regaining his self-confidence. "On behalf of Hong Kong, welcome," he said to Tammany, then kissed her full on the mouth.

"Hey Dan, not even family do that," said Adam.

"I'm not family," said Dan smugly. "How long are you with us, Tammany?"

"A week."

"Marvellous. Plenty of time to show you around... The game's off tomorrow, Adam. We're going to show your sister every good part of Hong Kong."

· · ·

THE PARTY WAS over and the last guest, including a reluctant Dan, had gone home. Tammany had made coffee for herself and Adam and taken it out onto the small veranda where Adam had installed a comfortable two-seater couch. Sitting down in front of the coffee table, they watched a junk beating up against a light wind with small lights aft and forward. The moon made the sea look black and oily and the wind from the water was warm and faintly salty. Adam sipped his coffee and smiled at the beauty he saw in the sea.

"Did you like her?" he asked.

"Oh yes."

"What's that meant to mean?"

"No one ever wants someone's opinion unless it agrees with their own, but I'm going to give it nonetheless. She's beautiful. She's charming. She's probably in love with you. But she does everything too right. As if she had been trained for the job. She's just too good, Adam. She appears well read and informed but she never allows the conversation to go deeper than superficial. I had the impression she was quoting remembered headlines, someone else's words. Everything she has is on the surface, including herself. Now, that isn't necessarily bad, but it doesn't ring true. What do you know about her background? Have you met her family?"

"No. I've asked. They're dead."

"Brothers and sisters?"

"She didn't have any."

"I'm sorry. I'm lightheaded and seeing things that aren't there. Too much flying and then a beautiful party. Your friends are lovely."

"Dan has taken a shine to you."

"Do you think so? I like him. He makes me feel comfortable."

"He didn't affect you in any other way?" said Adam, smiling at his sister. "Have you got over Blake?"

"No, and I never will. A first love like that is so good. Not sullied. Not dirty. Just beautiful. Maybe that's how it should have been. A memory. I don't know. Maybe I act in too many plays."

"And New York with Blake directing the music?"

"We'll have to see."

"Do you hate Roz?"

"No, Adam. I just feel sorry for her... I'm glad Blake has gone back to his music. That was a beautiful life in Holland Park, writing music just for the fun of it. We had no money at all, but we lived like kings. My favourite dish is vegetable stew. We were so happy. Even Lorna was happy caught up in the excitement of life. I would do anything to go back in time with them into the Earl of Buckingham and hear Barney greeting us through the crowd and the odd tourist gawping at Zach and Blake. We often sang together, Blake and I, that is. Zach had a voice like an out of tune barrel organ... A summer's night sitting out on the roof with Blake playing the guitar softly. The smell of hops. Baxter sniffing among the hops. At peace. We loved everything and everybody... Do you understand?"

"Not really. I never had that experience."

"Then you're unlucky."

"I was in the air force, you remember. There's nothing very romantic about Corporal Penny marching you up and down a parade ground all morning... But there were compensations. I made some friends."

"Isn't that moon on the water beautiful?"

"Yes." They watched quietly for some time. "How are the family?" asked Adam.

"Dad has come back to the land of the living. He's painting so well it broke my heart. Did you ever think Dad was a real painter and not just using it to run away from everything?"

"I'm no judge... I'm glad he's good. Is he happy?"

"I think so. Content, anyway."

"Poor father. He must really have loved our mother."

"The grans are super. Even Granny Hensbrook is developing a sense of humour. She made Karen an apple-pie bed the other day."

"She didn't!"

"There's one problem at Merry Hall. Aunt Georgina. She's drinking. I mean, not just in the evening. All day. Starts at nine o'clock in the morning. Uncle Geoffrey doesn't come home even now he's in Germany. Fighting a war in Malaya was one thing, but Germany is only two hours by plane. They can't seem to talk to each other and now with Beau in the army, Lorna in London and Raoul in Africa she has nothing to do and Karen goes back to boarding school next month. Poor woman. At nearly forty, she thinks her useful life has come to an end. What do people like that do with the rest of their lives? Oh, do you want to hear a bit of scandal? Charles Ainsworth got a girl pregnant and is being forced to marry her. Can you imagine that little rake as a father...? Adam, it's been wonderful being with you again. Do you have any idea how much I miss you?"

"I miss you too, sis. We've had a difficult life so far but we are going to win. Can you imagine having your sister's name in lights on Broadway?"

"Let's hope it comes off and there isn't some terrible catch. This one's just been too good to be true."

THERE WERE WEEPING willow trees all over the garden dipping their long fingers into the lily ponds. Perfectly placed rocks guarded the pools and carp were swimming among the flat leaves where the frog sat. Little rock-sided streams joined with the ponds through a series of miniature waterfalls so that once the fish was in one pond there he was forever. Building up from the streams and ponds were rocks of all sizes, holding pockets of earth in which the flowers grew. All the flowers were small, delicate in colour and shape.

Overlooking the rock garden and tucked pleasurably among a group of willow trees stood a semi-circular arbour with a comfortable bench that fitted the shape of the creepers covering the arbour frame so that should it rain a little, the occupants would stay dry and safe. Honeysuckle was the main creeper, twined with an evergreen so that even in the winter sun there was plenty of shade to be had and peace to be found.

Behind the arbour was the house, small but comfortable and furnished with exquisite taste. Fifty miles away was the capital of the People's Republic of China, Peking, steeped in all its history. Adam knew the house well, having spent three weeks there as a guest of his Chinese mentor, and the tension he had felt at first entering Communist China with Kim-Wok Ho was now completely gone and with it his preconceived ideas of a cold and colourless lifestyle behind the bamboo curtain. As his mentor, Kwang Ho, a cousin of Kim-Wok Ho and Ping-Lai Ho's, had told him, "Everyone is really the same. They just look different."

Now, Adam sat alone in the arbour, seeing nothing of the beauty laid out with such painstaking care in front of him. He was thinking deeply about what he had learnt and was trying to relate it to the way he had been taught.

"Oh, so we want a government," Kwang had told him. "That is good. No man can live in a state of anarchy. What kind shall we have? There are plenty of them and all tried by man as he invented them with many tears and not a little blood. You came to me thinking your English way of governing was the very opposite of ours but let's look objectively at what we have. First, there has been a history of unity and peace in Britain for hundreds of years. In China, the war only stopped in 1949 and before that and back into our middle history there has always been warring among the people. Until now there has never been real unity in China, and without stability no nation can prosper."

"This I understand, but Britain did not require communist dictatorship to find harmony."

"Dictatorship, Adam? No. China is not ruled by a dictator. It is ruled by a party, to be a member of which is a privilege, a privilege that has to be worked for and earned. A man must earn the right to govern his country and not demand the vote because he is there. People must contribute to society before they can tell the society how it should be run. In Britain they go on the dole and still vote."

"The man has fallen on hard times."

"Not all of them. In China, if a man falls upon hard times he is looked after by the state, but if he is hale and hearty he is put to work. A man must work to feed himself and a society that allows him to do otherwise is unjust."

"People take advantage," said Adam.

"Certainly. If the system allows. But it is wrong to say that just because everyone in a country has an equal vote that that country is ruled by the people, for the people. It is ruled for the benefit of the average man by the average man. In China, the best people are involved in government, not the average. A good government is one that gets the most out of its people by showing them the right way to work. A man directed correctly is productive."

"A man must have incentive."

"To achieve what?"

"As much as he is capable of achieving."

"Materially?"

"That as well."

"But why does a man require two cars and a house with twenty bedrooms? Is it just to impress his fellow man? All he achieves is a reduction in his quality of life as he is worrying all the time about protecting his assets. You can't sleep in all those beds at once. What a waste." Adam had a vision of Merry Hall, fully occupied only during the short periods of Christmas time and the Epsom races. "Man needs enough. Too much can make him just as unhappy as too little. Your Western wealth, channelled correctly, would achieve utopia; there are always surpluses or factories working half-time. Why not use them? This is our communism, another coined word that has as many meanings as man. Look at us, Adam. What are we? The cream of Chinese brains are in the Party and the Party rules. Surely this is better than Mr fifty-one per cent. But your world is frightened of us and the Russians even more, and we are frightened of the Russians too. We have no wish to change your method of government."

"But then you have contradicted yourself."

"Have I, Adam? An opportunity seen is not necessarily won. An opportunity achieved is often only good for one reason. Certainly reward is necessary to man, but should not be given at the expense of others."

"We will never agree."

"What I have been saying in the last weeks is that there is some good in your system – technology, freedom of speech, the ability of a man to choose his own job at random, which is good for him but not for the community, and many other values – and there is good in our system – harmony, no wars, a better justice, government by the party rather than a sweet-talking politician. What I have been saying is these two systems must draw together to become one, discarding the bad in both. Through Hong Kong we can draw from the West what we want without upsetting the serenity of our people. And that is why you are here, a man of the East and West in one person. If you can see and appreciate both sides of the story then maybe the world can work together. Don't say any more. Come up to the house for lunch. No intelligent mind can understand the opposite of what he has been taught all his life. You are not frightened of us anymore?"

"No one could be frightened of a really good man."

"Thank you, Adam."

"There are just some principles at stake," he said, and Kwang Ho had smiled and led him back from the arbour to the house.

After four more hours of solitary thought, Adam was no nearer to an understanding of that which was right as opposed to that which was wrong; but he was beginning to realise there were two good sides to every story.

RUBY WHITE WAS the first rich member of her family present or past. From the day her virginity had been sold for a useful sum, she had saved, only spending money on her small apartment and clothes to attract the right kind of customers. She had made up her mind that a good whore was also a rich whore and the trick in life was to hold onto wealth, however limited, and make it grow.

First, she had put the money on deposit with a bank and earned a modest interest, placing half her earnings into the account every day. If she was short of rent or clothes money she worked harder and the harder she worked the quicker her wealth accumulated. She was as worldly wise as an alley cat and never missed an opportunity. Hong Kong was booming after the short stay of the Japanese. Property prices had skyrocketed and companies were tumbling into Hong Kong faster than into a whore's bed. When the land surface ran out, the buildings climbed higher, and to Ruby's mind there was no limit to the sky.

Her first instinct was to own a roof over her head, one from which she could never be evicted, but this required more capital than at first she had possessed. The alternative was the Hong Kong stock exchange, and from her first entry she had the uncanny art of buying at the bottom of the downward swing and selling on the top of the upward. If her stockbroker, who thought he knew everything there was to know about stocks and shares, had followed suit he would have been a multi-millionaire in pounds sterling but whoever thought of taking financial advice from a whore? He was quite well aware of her profession.

Having found her way around the ups and downs, she took a gamble. She pledged her share certificates to the bank and went into overdraft to the tune of eighty per cent of their value, buying more shares and repeating the exercise. By the end of a year, Ruby had pushed her overdraft to a million Hong Kong dollars. She had then had an attack of nerves and sold everything, putting the money into a block of flats, which became hers without bond or partners.

If it weren't for the fact she enjoyed her job as a whore, she would have stopped there; but she did not and thanked any God she could think of for her luck. The fact the money from Kim-Wok Ho had stopped worried her not at all, provided Adam let her stay in his flat – which, ironically, was in the block owned by Ruby herself via her bank as nominee. Even whores knew that wealth was better kept to themselves. She had told Adam when he was in England that she worked at the stockbrokerage, and when Adam had called, her broker had happily participated in the subterfuge, tickled pink by her financial success.

Her problem now was how to tell Adam she was rich; she could never match his heritage, but she could certainly match his wealth. So far, she had sat a prisoner in her own flat worried stiff that she did not have enough to hold him down even as his mistress. She knew too much of men. They liked variety. Something new always turned them on or why would so many respectable and happily married men have paid so much for her services in the past? And that usually worked in a burst and tailed off until they were giving their whore-money to someone else. That was fine by Ruby. In those days, she was in the lending business, but not anymore. Or rather she had no intention of lending Adam to anyone. Her real hope was that Adam would lose his job, go broke, and then she could come forward and offer him help. Once she got her financial claws into him, that should be enough for marriage.

3

*I*t was obligatory for an officer in the Brigade of Guards to wear a bowler hat and carry a rolled umbrella when dressed in civilian clothes. The suit should be dark, preferably with pin-stripes delicately threading the best English cloth, and with it was worn either an old school or Brigade of Guard's tie. Emerging from Bank underground station and passing the steps of the Royal Exchange without looking up at its impressive colonnades, Beau Beaumont vaguely whistled the first two bars of a tune he had heard at Corals the night before. His expression, however, was sombre, in keeping with his journey along Threadneedle Street and in deference to the serious business that went on in the City of London. A perfectly dressed gentleman of sixty passing in the other direction and dressed identically to Beau thought it strange that the young man was twirling his umbrella. Recognising Beau's old Harrovian tie, the gentleman let him pass without raising an eyebrow, and put the twirling down to that day's unseasonably good weather.

Beau was happy as a sandboy for reasons other than the weather. Inside his breast pocket was a typed list of all the Rhodesian tobacco farms owned by absentee landlords and the scheme Beau had put into operation was working better than his wildest dreams. Most of the land he was looking at had been given out to companies by Cecil Rhodes or inherited, and as the place was so far from England the recipients rarely took much interest. Three companies Beau had approached earlier in the week were unaware of the large tracts of land they owned in Mashonaland.

Having made Raoul do his homework, Beau was aware that these lands had never been farmed: virgin soil. Moreover, the companies had never received income from their land holdings, because the money and energy it would have taken to fence, stump out the trees, build contours, dam the rivers, build barns and grade sheds, and worse, find management and labour, was too much for them to bear. Which was where Beau's ideas were fitting in so well with the scheme of things.

Catching the eye of a pretty typist in her summer frock, he turned into the building he had been looking for, ignored the rickety lift and the equally rickety pensioner who was tending it, and took the stairs up to the third floor two at a time, checking his watch to be sure he was arriving punctually for his appointment. The corridor was dark and musty, and smelt of old money. Beau found the suite of offices he was looking for at the end and read the legend, Shangani Mining and Exploration Company Ltd on the list of companies.

He had to push the door hard to get it open. The reception area was just big enough for two chairs and a coffee table. The whole impression was one of a company about to go out of business, but Beau knew otherwise. As a quick rule of thumb in the City of London, he had worked out that a company's wealth was in inverse proportion to the shabbiness of their offices.

"That door always sticks," said the fifty-year-old spinster tending the outside office.

"Bit of oil, maybe," said Beau, hanging his umbrella by its handle on the reception counter and placing his unworn gloves in his bowler hat alongside it. He smiled at the receptionist. "Mr Shead?"

"Do you have an appointment?"

"Of course." Beau passed her his engraved visiting card. Apart from his name, it noted his association with the 'Brigade of Guards', and gave his club as The Cavalry in Piccadilly and his home as Merry Hall. The lady was duly impressed, giving him a new look of respect before going off into the inner sanctum.

"Come this way Mr Beaumont," she said, returning a moment later to lead him through to the manager's office.

"Morning, sir," said Beau.

"Ah, Beaumont. Take a seat. Thank you, Miss Powell. What can we do for you, young man? Army officers don't usually venture into Threadneedle Street."

"Spot of leave, at present. My uncle encourages us to take an interest in business as soon as possible. We have a programme on the go in Rhodesia that we think will be of interest to you."

"Is your uncle Sir Reginald Beaumont?"

"Yes."

"Merry Hall. I see that on your card, but there's no mention of Beaumont Limited..."

"I'm still a serving officer," said Beau, who had got round that one on previous occasions. "Shangani Mining and Exploration owns twelve thousand acres in the Umvukwes which it has never farmed."

"Probably, old chap. Trouble is, these things get written down to nothing in the balance sheet and we lose track of them. Could well be twelve thousand acres hiding in a file somewhere in the office. Where is this Umvukwes?"

"Mashonaland."

"Where's that?"

"Rhodesia."

"That's somewhere in Africa, isn't it?"

"New Federation of Central Africa."

"Read about it somewhere. Isn't that the place they have an ex-engine driver from the railways as Prime Minister?"

"Sir Roy Welensky."

"They knighted him! Whatever is the country coming to?"

"Quite."

"Assuming we own this twelve thousand acres..."

"You do. My research is correct."

"I'm not sure how we'll find it in the files."

"You will, Mr Shead. Now, let me explain."

"Is your uncle involved?"

"He's my partner." Which he was, in a way, if the origin of the one hundred thousand pounds was taken into account. They smiled at each other. "That land is worthless to you at present."

"Certainly seems so."

"I have put together a management team to develop unused farmland in that area and so far I have committed myself to turning fifty thousand acres into something of real value, producing real income for shareholders. Your farm is in excellent tobacco country and should be worth ten pounds an acre. But before that price can be obtained, the land must be opened up. In exchange for turning your farm into a productive unit I need a ten year lease for one pound a year. In exchange, we'll clear the lands, build roads, dams, barns, houses, a compound, workshops and grading sheds. At the end of ten years, they'll be your property. By then, the price should be fifty pounds an acre.

"We have a capital base of one hundred thousand pounds, which will be used to develop your farm, but in addition we require you to guarantee a twenty thousand pound facility at the Standard Bank in Salisbury..." The man looked bewildered. "That's the capital of the Central African Federation," Beau explained. "We, of course, will give you a counter-guarantee for the same amount so you will have turned nothing into six hundred thousand pounds in ten years without spending a penny. You put in the land and we put in the development. Our profit will be ten years' crops less expenses, and out of that profit we have to write off our development costs... This is a full report, Mr Shead." Beau took an envelope from his pocket and put it on the man's desk. "Sir Reginald has vast interests in Africa. Now, don't let me take up any more of your time. Until you have read our report and talked to your directors, you won't be able to give me an answer."

"This really is something out of the blue."

"Literally, Mr Shead. They say the sky in Rhodesia is permanently blue in the dry season."

THERE ARE few things more restful than an autumn afternoon in the English countryside, and after his first two weeks of extensive business, Beau was ready to go home for the weekend and have a rest. He had taken the train from Waterloo with the intention of walking from Ashtead station to Merry Hall, and he was planning to keep well away from his grandmothers. He did not care if his mother had started on the gin bottle at nine o'clock in the morning, and even Karen was not going to upset his peace.

The army seemed a long way away as he walked past the gates and faced the long driveway winding past the oak and elm trees to the Hall on its hill. He was enjoying the feel of his shorts and open-necked shirt. As he came up over the lawns, having taken a short cut through the trees, the last thing he expected to see parked on the gravel in front of the great, gothic front doors was Uncle Reggie's Lagonda. The pre-war car, sitting as if it was ready to take off on its own, shone in the late sun, and Beau knew the engine would be tuned to perfection. From the thirty acre, he heard the banshee noise of an aero-engine followed by the sounds of taxiing, and stopped to watch the patch of sky he knew Matilda would soon appear in over the woods.

"Must have a lady friend with him," Beau said to himself with a smile as the single engine biplane came hurtling over the trees and did a barrel-roll ten feet above the branches. The red plane went into a steep climb and made for the blue sky, growing smaller and smaller until it was lost to the naked eye.

Skirting the house, Beau went in at the tradesmen's entrance. Sensibly, he stopped in the kitchen to purloin two of Doris Breed's homemade Cornish pasties before taking the back stairs up to his room. He ate his lunch sitting on the window seat overlooking the west side of the Hall, watching a flock of sheep grazing in the field beyond the kitchen garden. The Hall and its grounds were soaked by the sun and the scent of flowers and new mown grass were strong.

"It's so damned easy if you work it out," he said to himself. "No one wants to do any work."

Shead had come back to him within forty-eight hours and now he had all the land he wanted and all within a sixty mile radius. He lay down on his bed to digest the food and dozed off, to be woken by Matilda coming in to land at the thirty acre. The engine was misfiring, which did not sound so good, and the pilot was opening and closing the throttle to clear the blockage. Beau went back to sleep.

Hunger woke him, and, feeling refreshed, he dressed in a clean shirt and flannels and went down to see what he could find. Reggie and Lee were out on the terrace overlooking the tennis court, Reggie drinking a beer and Lee drinking an American cocktail she had fixed for herself. Beau hesitated to join them, but his uncle looked up and saw him standing in the French windows. The grandmothers had gone to bed early and his mother was probably in her bedroom with a bottle of brandy. Alcoholism was one subject Beau would never understand.

"I'm glad you're here," said Reggie. "I want to talk to you."

"Oh yes?" said Beau. "Hello Lee. What about, Uncle?"

"You know damn well. I have received seven phone calls in two weeks. I am not your business partner."

"In a way you are."

"I receive no benefit from this venture."

"But you do, Uncle. You get me out of your way. Remittance man. If the scheme's successful I'll be away a long time."

"You are using my name."

"Not really. In fact, not at all. My name is the only one on the letterhead. I can't help your being my uncle, and when they ask me where I got the one hundred thousand pounds from, I say Uncle

Reggie, of course. What they read into that is their business... I was expecting you to call. I have a full report for you on progress and prospects if you'd like to know what I'm doing with your money."

"Tomorrow," said Reggie, having to laugh at his brazenness. "Get yourself a drink. Pavy's bringing out a cold supper in twenty minutes. How's the army?"

"Haven't seen much of it for two weeks. Your engine's misfiring."

"Fuel blockage. We cured it once. Loops and barrel-rolls cause the blockages. If Tug were here, he'd fix it."

"How is Uncle Tug?"

"Painting, I believe... Lee's going back to America. I've got her a part in *1066*."

"Is it good?" Beau asked Lee. "The musical?"

"Richard D'Altena doesn't have a problem. The trick is having a descendant playing the lady lead. I like the music. Catchy... Had a letter from your sister. The flat's lonely."

"How is Lorna?"

"Reading between the lines, I'd say Zach is going to have himself a problem."

"Who's the latest?"

"A Rhodesian Army officer, Cindy's brother."

"Peter? I'll be meeting him soon, though he won't like me. I'm pinching two of his managers."

"When do you go out?" asked Reggie.

"The day after discharge. The war office have given me permission to leave the country during my terminal leave."

ADAM LOOKED up from his desk at the framed photograph of a Hawker Hunter fighter aircraft flying over the patterned green fields of England, the pilot's helmeted face turned to the camera, and put down his pen on the report he'd been writing. His mind was not on the job. Opposite the pilot, who would go on flying forever in his glass prison on the wall, was a communist photograph of a section of the Great Wall of China, one of the seven ancient wonders of the world. It showed the wall climbing over hills and dales to a greater distance than the camera could see.

Adam looked from one photograph to the other and finally got up. He put his hands in his pockets and turned to look out of the window, at Hong Kong bustling below, and further, to the great mass of China that housed its millions upon millions of people, a quarter of mankind. The draw was physical. 'And I'm not even half Chinese,' he thought to himself. 'I'm half Asian, and maybe China is the father of us all. So many questions I want to ask, and even then, the answers they give, are they right?

'Freedom! They all want freedom. And what is freedom in England? Is it the ability to behave within the law? And what are the laws? Who made them? Is the law always right? An Englishman is free to vote, but does the vote of one man make the slightest bit of difference? So what is his freedom? What is justice in China? The right to work? The right to have a home and food, however meagre? England's justice gives the Englishman welfare and a queue to collect his money and the right to drink it in the pub because there's no work; his fellow men don't need him, so they toss him enough to salve their consciences. Or *is* it that? Is it not good to give? Is it not better for a man to choose his occupation rather than to be told? Or *do* we choose?'

He smiled to himself, realising that as at that moment he had thought of himself as an Englishman. 'But am I not English?' he went on thinking. 'Certainly, but only part of me is, otherwise the other half of me would not be staring out at China this way... And government? Are the politicians in Westminster the best brains in the country, or are they just popularity-seekers who've captured the common vote with persuasive words?'

The more he thought, the more confusion tumbled in his mind. And right now he had to write a report on how to con people into thinking how wonderful they would look in *Jive* jeans. Or was it conning? He thought of all those delicious wiggling bums, for starters. He picked up the pen at the same time as the knock came at his door.

"Mr Craig wants to see you, Adam."

"I'll be right there." 'And what does lord and master want today?' he thought as he walked across the thinly carpeted floor of his office, down the slightly thicker carpet in the corridor and into the thick pile of the holy of holies. "Good morning, sir."

"Morning, Adam. Have you got enough work to do?"

"Plenty, sir."

"Good. Because here's some more. This is another consignment of jet engines arriving from Jordan without having been to that country. I want you to produce a false set of documents. Bill of Lading, Certified Invoice of Origin, Packing List. They must please our communist friends and prevent anyone pointing a finger at Beaumonts for selling British technology to the Chinese. If you need help, ask Dan... Who's winning?"

"He is, sir. Twenty-four matches to twenty-three." Craig Craig went back to the papers on his desk with a smile. Adam let himself out of the office and closed the door.

TAMMANY WAS STRETCHED out on the foredeck, her eyes shut against the sun and her legs slightly apart. Her heavy breasts were softly spread over her chest, held in position by the bikini top. The sun had mottled her skin, giving it the texture of apricot. Long, black hair spread around her face on the wooden deck. Dan had been watching her for ten minutes, sitting on the rail of his twenty-two-foot sloop, which had taken every cent of his savings, the repayments feeding hungrily off his salary. Pulling his eyes away from the most beautiful girl he had ever seen, he looked up at the tall mast and the burgee at the top: it was barely moving. The sails were furled, tied neatly with white rope, and the only movement was caused by the swell that rocked the sloop as she lay at anchor.

While Dan's mind dwelt on the beauty of his boat and its passenger, Tammany was thinking, warmed by the hot sun and the knowledge that Dan was watching over her. She felt safe, had done so ever since arriving in Hong Kong.

"Is Hong Kong always so peaceful?" she asked, without opening her eyes.

"Mostly. Sometimes the Triads kill people. The communists started riots a year back, but they fizzled out. Everyone is far too busy making money."

He had a strong urge to kneel down and stroke the soft flesh of the inside of her thighs just below the mound held tightly by the bikini, but he was still unable to overcome his awe. To sexually touch the girl was, to him, to break the perfection. And tomorrow there would be a blank on the deck and the past week would be plucked from his sight as if it had never existed. She was going to New York. To be a star. To be run after by more money than there was in the whole colony of Hong Kong. Who was he but the twenty-one-year-old best friend of the brother, showing her the sights and one match up in the game of tennis. They had not even spoken to each other about themselves and the day was going.

"Do you have a boyfriend?" he blurted.

"No." The eyes stayed shut and the body did not move.

"I don't have a girlfriend."

"Good."

"Are you looking forward to America?"

"I've never been there before."

"And the show?"

"I hope it succeeds."

"Where will you go from there?"

"Probably Hong Kong." She smiled and opened her eyes to look at him.

"You want to come back?"

"Oh yes. Maybe we all belong here. It isn't a crime to have mixed blood in Hong Kong. I don't know about New York. They chased Adam out of England. It's easier for the family having us both out here... Will the breeze come up?"

"Probably not. I'll use the motor. Do you want to be an actress?"

"I think so. There doesn't seem much else really, and it's better than shorthand and typing."

"You must be very good to have landed the part?"

"Time will tell. I'm not naïve. The package may make money. The ancient family saga that comes to life. They're always looking for shows to make money... The music is good..." She thought of Blake and was unable to control the hurt at the image of him thrashing around in a bed with Roz... or did it no longer matter?... but she knew it did. The warmth of their love had gone for her, but now they would be working together. And how was she going to keep Richard D'Altena under control?

And there would be others. She had read about New York. Would it really matter if she gave in to Richard? He wanted her so much and he was a kind man. Or would that be worse, giving him a little, or would once or twice slake his thirst and send him off again chasing something new? She did not know enough about men to answer that question. It was so much easier when she'd first met Blake. Then, they'd both been innocent of the world. She was still a virgin, but that didn't prove anything. They'd raped her mind instead.

And now Dan had fallen under the same spell and was unable to see the wood for the trees. Or rather, he wanted her body, and that was for certain... Would she change when she gave it to someone? Who should it be? Would it have been better to have given in to Blake? She had asked herself that question plenty of times... If she had, would he be with her now? Would they have the same happiness they had shared in Ashtead Woods? Should she be looking at Dan with a proper eye? 'Have you a boyfriend?' No, she had answered. Was that the beginning and end of their relationship? 'Keep it light, Tammany,' she told herself.

"Let's go down into the cabin and fix some supper. Can we motor back in the dark?"

"No problem," said Dan, delighted with the idea.

"Then we have hours together... This little bay makes all those people seem so far away."

.   .   .

"HOLD IT, HOLD IT," said Reggie. "Never lay down the law when you are negotiating, which I presume you are."

"Of course," said Ted Cornwell.

Reggie looked at him steadily. "Your company, and you in particular, were employed by *Jive* as their promotions consultant, so that you would have your freedom. You still have it, so don't involve *Jive* shareholders in your ambitions. Certainly if you wish to go into competition with one of your clients you are welcome to do so, but if you fail in the rag trade you'll find it difficult to go back to consultancy. Prospective clients would feel nervous...

" I agree," Reggie went on, putting up his hand to stop Ted interrupting, "that you created for yourself a good client who pays well and should always be grateful to you. Let me explain one fact of business. The only indispensable man is the one who puts up the risk capital. There are plenty of bankers who will lend you the money if you have the collateral in the ratio of two to one. All the best ideas and people require money to develop them and with your ideas and energy you're going to need a lot of new capital. Luckily, we have it and are constantly looking for vehicles in which to invest our burgeoning profits, but there aren't many companies like ours that feed straight out of gold and diamond mines."

He got up and walked across his office. "Thelma," he called into the outside office, "Can you rustle up some tea?... Now. Where were we? Were you offering to buy out *Jive* shareholders or were you going into opposition? On both counts, where are you getting the money from?"

"The banks."

"Some, but not enough. You have to have your own money as well. You're still in your twenties. There's plenty of time. I know your feeling of looking at *Jive's* balance sheet and looking at all those profits that you think you created on your own. You're suggesting I don't put anything into the business apart from money, but you're wrong. You forget the hairier schemes you've come up with that didn't check out with our financial team. You forget our systems of cost control and financing of the retailers. You forget who put a factory into Hong Kong. You forget what the clout of Beaumont Limited means to the big chain stores. With my money behind you, they feel comfortable. It's easier for them to rationalise and say a *Jive* product is going to sell to the public. You're the one who talks of all those beautiful links in the business chain. Take us out and you'd flounder. The big stores will stay with me. Not all, but most. And who's going to design your stuff?"

"I have a girl who's brilliant. She'll knock 'em."

"Brilliance and products that sell don't often go together. Sure, she may become another Isabel Beaumont, but if that is the case why aren't there hundreds of them now? Isabel is a fluke. She never got involved in anything before, so when she came up with an idea it was pure original."

"What happens if Isabel leaves the company?"

"Fortunately she's family. She is probably designing clothes in Africa right now. A safari look. Artists can work anywhere. It is their one advantage. And Ted, the one thing I've learnt in business is not to be greedy. You are doing all right. Now, how do we stand?"

Ted thought very carefully before giving an answer. "You're probably right."

"Coming from you, I will take that admission as very important. You and I are the same kind. Stick around. We're only just getting to know each other."

"Do you know, Mr Beaumont, I have never been able to win an argument with you?"

"I never argue, Ted. Now, if that's what you had to tell me, may I have the floor?"

"You want to talk about Hong Kong?"

"Not particularly. It's about a musical. Against my better judgement, the family have been drawn into producing a musical. You do know about *1066*?"

"Of course. It's damn good. I know a bit about music."

"Thank you for your confidence, though it is not your musical opinion that I am after. How the hell are we going to sell it to the Americans? Like *Jive*, I'm assured the product is good, but now it has to be promoted. The best product can stay on the shelf for years because nobody knows about it. First they're producing off Broadway, but I think the main promoting should start now. We must titillate the press and the television networks. We have to launch the complete campaign. If the family are in then they're jolly well going to win. What I thought you might like to do is go to America and work this damn musical up to the biggest thing the Yanks have seen since the revolution. The Americans are very fond of the British and anything that smacks of a joint heritage. We have a couple of Beaumonts who went to America. I think they were killed in the First World War. Find some relations. I want the American public to become personally involved in tracing the descendants of Sir Henri de Beaumont. There's more to this musical than song and dance."

"You want me to go to America? What about *Jive*?"

There was a slight smile on Reggie's face. "No one is indispensable... Thank you, Thelma... Milk and sugar?" he said to Ted.

"One sugar and just a little milk."

"How does it sound?"

"A promoter's dream."

"You'll be reporting to my American partner, Chuck Everly. He's married to Isabel's sister. You'll like him. Good sense of humour. He'll give you all the help you need and Thelma will give you your ticket when you leave."

Ted began to laugh. Reggie watched him carefully.

"Not only have you got what you want, but you've stopped me rocking the *Jive* boat."

"I will only get what I want when you deliver a smash hit on Broadway."

THE PARTY TO celebrate the return of Peter Escort from the war in Malaya started at ten o'clock in the morning. There was a plateau of land in front of the house. At its edge, with a view of bush and farmlands for twenty miles, stood a row of spits with four black men tending them. Oil drums had been cut in half and the wood fires inside projected a good heat over the turning meat.

Under each carcase was a basting tray to catch the juices. The first was a sheep's carcase, its zipped-up belly crammed with cut oranges, limes and fresh herbs. There was a young calf, two bush pigs Clay had shot a couple of days earlier, a haunch of kudu, a line of trussed guinea-fowl from the Zambezi Valley, a row of ducks that had been double-barrelled by Clay down on B-section dam, and, as the *pièce de résistance*, an ox over a specially dug pit, turned on a monster spit high enough to keep the legs out of the basting tray. The mingling smell that wafted across the lawns was delicious. Wine and honey were being added regularly to the drip-trays, used for basting, to give the meat its tangy crispness and the rich toffee colour.

A marquee had been set up on the lawn. On top, one at either end, flew the Union Jack and the flag of Southern Rhodesia – green and white, with the Zimbabwe bird emblazoned in the centre.

THE NIGHT BEFORE THE PARTY, Clay and Isabel became lovers in the truest sense of the word. They had made love with their minds as well as their bodies and woken up together at peace with the world and themselves. If Isabel had been missed in the big house, she was not going to worry about it. At noon, they left Clay's house to join the guests on the lawn. They looked out over the expanse of Africa, ploughed for crops here and there but otherwise untouched; the blue mountain range in the distance shimmered in the heat haze.

"It's so peaceful," she said to Clay.

"That's Africa. The sun makes people content."

"Quite a party. That food. I would never have thought to cook an ox for a day."

"I'm going to have a farm like Greswold. Two more seasons and I'll have enough to buy nine thousand acres and put up some barns. There's a new block opening to commemorate the birth of Cecil

Rhodes. They're calling it Centenary. Plenty of water, and the soil's a light sandveld. Perfect for tobacco... Could you live in Africa?"

"There isn't that much for me in England. My daughter's independent. Merry Hall accepts me under sufferance and Reggie stopped looking at me twenty years ago."

"Why don't we get married?"

"Don't be ridiculous, we barely know each other, and I'm a bitch."

"And I'm a bastard. I want five children."

"You've picked the wrong one for that at my age."

"We could always try."

"Are you mad? Life's meant to begin at forty and that..."

"I'm serious, Isabel. All these women can talk about is servants and babies. None of them are women to my mind. Nice people and I'm fond of them, but they don't think. Look at their husbands." He pointed at the bar. "Bored with their wives, so they sit up there to get drunk and talk tobacco. I want a woman as my wife."

"Ted wants to buy my shares."

"Who's he?"

"Helped me start *Jive*... I could design freelance."

"Are you saying yes?" said Clay, turning her to him.

"I'm thinking."

"Have you anything better to do with your life?"

"We wouldn't have to wait two years for a farm."

"Why not?"

"Do you know how big *Jive* has become?"

"You said you had a shop in Carnaby Street."

"It's that and a whole lot more. We're budgeting for a taxed profit of four hundred thousand pounds."

"You won't want to come to Africa with that to look after."

"We've got a lot to think about, or maybe nothing. I don't know. Do you know something, Clay, I don't think I have ever been happy before... Come, Jake Escort's going to give his speech."

. . .

BEAU FINALLY SLEPT with Lindley Starr their last night before arriving in Cape Town. She was the only girl on the boat worth looking at and he was not sure from Raoul's reports whether he would find many girls where he was going. After the sea voyage, there was work ahead of him, years of it, before he would return to England and the kind of life he intended to live. Having chased and conquered Lindley, he was quite happy to write her into his diary and leave it at that. From his experience with well-worn debutantes, she was not very good, and his excitement had been her pushing him away with her hands and pulling him back with her dark, almost black eyes that drank in his sex. She was on her way home several months after her last term at boarding school, she and her friend with the large, almost audible pimples.

The top deck of the *Braemar Castle* gave Beau his first sight of Africa. The captain had deliberately waited until a glimmer of dawn had begun to outline Table Mountain before bringing the ship into harbour, with even Beau, who had not gone to bed other than briefly with Lindley, excited by the beauty. Impulsively – a rare mistake for Beau – he took little Lindley's hand in his and the two of them gazed together at the flat-topped mountain.

"Beautiful," said Lindley, and the tears came into her eyes for the parting. "There's a train leaving from Cape Town for Johannesburg at ten o'clock."

"I'm not going by train," said Beau.

"Then you can fly." She was gazing at the beauty of the bay and the blood-red sun of morning. "I'd never done it before," she said.

"You should have told me."

"I didn't think it was going to happen."

"Every girl says no when she means yes. It's a stage of life, Lindley... I'm going by car."

"Can I come too?"

"Your friend?"

"Lives in Cape Town. They have a wine farm."

'All right,' thought Beau, thinking of the long, unknown drive on his own.

"We'll have to stop on the way."

"Oh."

"I'll be careful now that I know."

"I won't fall pregnant?"

"I've had plenty of experience."

"Of getting girls pregnant?"

"No." She reminded him of his cousin Roz when she giggled. He'd always wanted to bed his sexy little cousin.

"Are you hiring a car?"

"Brought it with me, along with a lot of other things."

"I'll show you Cape Town before we drive north."

"Lovely. The car comes off the boat first."

"Super-duper! What do you think of Africa?"

"I haven't set foot on it yet." The boat's fog-horn let off a sonorous note that folded away from the ship, across the bay, telling Cape Town the mail boat had arrived. Two tugs put out from the docks.

"Let's get some breakfast," said Beau. "I'm starving."

"So am I... You can stay with us in Jo'burg."

"Don't you think...?"

"You can tell my father you put the car on the train. He won't have to know about the stopover."

"I see."

"He'll like you."

"Why?"

"Everyone in Johannesburg has heard of Sir Reginald Beaumont, Bart," she said, using the term for baronet that those in the know loved to wield to show off their knowledge.

"I see."

"I just think Mummy will... Why didn't you mention your uncle, by the way? The cabin steward told me."

"Bully for the cabin steward," said Beau, and stopped himself smiling. The five pound note had hit home after all.

"He said you are Sir Reginald's heir."

"Did he?"

"Is the title really a thousand years old?"

"Not quite. Eight hundred and eighty-two, to be exact."

"Golly. That's older than the Queen's."

"There were kings of England before Beaumonts."

"It's terribly exciting."

"Breakfast, Lindley," said Beau, who had got enough from his five pound bribe.

"Oh yes," she said, smiling up at him faithfully.

THE BRISTOL CAME out of the forward hatch in a sling and was pulled up free of the ship's superstructure and swung away to the dockside where the crane driver, high up in his cabin, wound it gently to the ground. To Beau's relief, it did not bump the dock, and he gave the 'thumbs up' to the driver.

"What is it?" shouted the man.

"A Bristol."

"Never heard of it."

Beau drove through customs, the car having been pre-cleared by Reggie's shipping agents. In the boot were Lindley's and Beau's overnight bags; the rest was going up-country by train.

"Where to?" said Beau.

"Keep driving. I'll give directions."

"How come you know Cape Town?"

"We have a bungalow at Clifton beach. Every summer holidays. You have to get out of Johannesburg... This is the most beautiful car I have ever seen. Did your uncle give...?"

"No."

"Of course. Old money. Your family..."

"This is my money. My company."

"Don't be silly."

"I told you, Lindley. I have come out here to make my fortune."

"Left into Strand Street," she directed. "With a car like this who needs more... Do you have a lovely big mansion?"

"The family do."

"And one day it will be yours?"

"That's the idea."

"You must have lots of girls running after you," said Lindley, realising her problem.

"THERE IT IS," said Lindley when they got out of the car at the Rhodes Memorial. "Cecil John Rhodes wanted to build a railroad from Cape to Cairo for Queen Victoria. He was younger than you when he arrived in Africa and he didn't even have a motor car. When he died in Muizenberg, that's fifteen miles from here, he was one of the richest men in the world, with a country named after him."

"How did he do it?" said Beau, gazing up at the monument, which was looking sternly into the hinterland of Africa.

"Father says everyone did what he wanted them to do..."

"That's a good ingredient. Why, though?"

"No one knows. He was a fat little queer with a squeaky voice."

"Maybe he had a big enough vision for others to see."

IN TEN YEARS, Carl Priesler, Managing Director of Beaumont Limited, South Africa, and one of the founding partners with Reggie in the holding company, had overcome his weight problem and felt a lot better in the process; carrying eighty pounds excess fat was not a good look for a wealthy bachelor. Puzzled, he put down the white phone and smiled across his desk at the middle-aged man sitting opposite him.

"I must go," said Jonathan Starr, holding up his hand. "We are going round in circles. See you tonight. Lindley's due back from school. I'm picking her up at the station. Don't like her flying. You haven't seen her for a while, have you?"

"Not for a year... Maybe we'll develop our record companies individually. Joint ventures look good on paper, but we forget the personalities. We have the RCA label and you have HMV. Someone has to press records locally and someone has to make the sleeves and labels. Why don't you put up a pressing plant and we'll put up a specialised printing shop for the sleeves and labels? You press for us, we print for you."

"Pressing takes more capital."

"Then do it the other way round."

"Seven-thirty tonight?"

"I'll be there." He picked up his phone. "Send in Mrs Beaumont."

Jonathan raised an eyebrow.

"Reggie married?"

"No," laughed Carl. "Must be Isabel, Henry's widow."

"It is," said Isabel as the two men rose from their chairs. "How are you, Carl? You've lost weight."

"Thank you," he said. "Isabel Beaumont. Jonathan Starr. Opposition trying to find some common ground," he said to Isabel in explanation.

"Nice meeting you, Mrs Beaumont."

"Yes it is."

"Well, I'm away. Seven-thirty."

"Fine... Tea or coffee?" Carl said when the door closed. "What a surprise. When did we...?"

"The Victory Ball at Merry Hall. Almost ten years ago. Are you married?"

"No. Reggie would have told you."

"Reggie doesn't always want to talk to me. I've come for some help," she said, and immediately launched into telling him about Roz and her promiscuity and her turning to lesbianism.

Carl was acutely embarrassed and kept looking at the closed door, hoping his secretary would come in and save him.

"I'm sorry, Isabel, but..."

"You remember the evening after Brett's?"

"Yes," said Carl, looking at her carefully.

"Henry wasn't able to have children. We tried for years to produce an heir. Roz is your daughter, Carl."

"Don't be silly, Isabel. That was years ago."

"Kids don't stop growing just because it was years ago. You can check dates. You can even ask Reggie if you want. I told Reggie. We thought it better for the family and Roz to..."

"Isabel... It was a long time ago."

"I can't knock any sense into her. Maybe you can."

"Me!"

"You are her father."

Carl got up and looked out of his window at the traffic in Fox Street. "Johannesburg is becoming quite a city. The mining camp is changing its coat... Still a mining camp, though. Where are you staying?"

"Dawson's. Reggie..."

"He would... There's one big problem staying a bachelor. No children. You have to have children to be sure you leave something behind... Are you absolutely sure?" There was a faint smile on his face.

"Absolutely, Carl."

4

———

*C*lay Hunter and Peter Escort had every intention of getting drunk. Apart from the old couple, they were the only whites left on Greswold Estate. Raoul had gone into Salisbury to meet his brother's train, which was due from Cape Town in the morning, not knowing Beau had changed his plans. Lorna had gone to Johannesburg with her aunt and then flown to America for the off Broadway opening of *1066*. Peter hoped the musical would be a huge flop and she would stop changing her mind about settling down with him in Rhodesia. And in spite of thinking he'd never have Isabel, Clay had lost all interest in other women. He was also not looking forward to the arrival of Beau Beaumont, who was going to disrupt his life even more. Cindy was away at university in Cape Town: one less problem to think about, at least.

In front of the veranda of Clay's manager's cottage were a herd of eleven kudu, the third largest antelope in Africa, their short, stubby tails flicking at flies as they grazed across the old maize land.

"That herd's been around for years," said Peter.

"Everyone wants stability. Even the buck."

"Beautiful animals."

"Beautiful."

"Is this brother for real?"

"I've checked. Fifty thousand acres leased to him for ten years at no rental, one hundred thousand pounds capital and a bank facility of twenty thousand pounds."

"Barely out of his teens."

"Yes, barely out of them."

"Why doesn't he stay in England and leave us poor colonials in peace?"

"Funny how the game came back," said Clay. He was watching the kudu. "They said that once the Umvukwes was opened up the game would disappear forever."

"Everyone has to adapt if they wish to survive. They look happy enough."

"Happier. More food. Plenty of maize kernels in all that stubble."

"Maybe we should get some sleep," said Peter, changing the subject.

They sat and looked at the bush, sipping at their beers. The sun was going down behind the distant range of hills.

"Better light a lamp." The light went quickly when the sun went down.

"Leave it," said Peter. "Too many moths after the rains."

"And didn't we have some rain."

"Are you going to join Beau?"

"I think so. The risk is not mine. If ranching tobacco doesn't work, as it probably won't, he goes broke, not me. If it comes off, my bonus will buy me a farm."

"But you like working here."

"Pete, you can't have both worlds. Either your family run their farms or they go to pot. You can't expect a faithful manager who's any good to work for you all his life. You will have to resign your commission."

"I was hoping..."

"You've had a good run at playing soldiers. Now the game's over."

"I hope you're right, Clay."

"What do you mean?"

"We were sent to Malaya to learn how to fight a guerrilla war. The commies are backing the nationalists here. Only a matter of time."

"What is?"

"War in the bush."

"Don't be ridiculous."

"That's what the planters in Malaya said."

"Pete, I've got enough problems right now without becoming paranoid. Have another beer."

"Okay."

"That's better."

"Nothing ever stays the same."

"Maybe that's the real excitement in life."

"WHY DIDN'T you tell me Carl Preisler is your godfather?" asked Beau. The party was in full swing at the Starr residence.

"Why didn't you tell me you were Sir Reginald Beaumont's heir?" replied Lindley. "You should live in Johannesburg instead of going off into the Rhodesian bush. Do you have a house up there?"

"Not yet."

"Where on earth are you going to live?"

"In a tent. We have to get the barns up first and builders are scarce. Won't you visit me in my tent?"

"I don't like bugs."

"I will also have a suite in Meikles Hotel. That's Salisbury."

"I do live in Africa, you know."

"Weekends," he said. "Raoul says I won't have time."

"Daddy thinks you should join Uncle Carl. You can play cricket. We have a very good ground here at the Wanderers. You might get into the Transvaal side... When are you leaving?"

"Dawn tomorrow. Straight through to Salisbury."

. . .

"WHAT A COINCIDENCE," said Carl. He and Isabel were on the other side of the room.

"Nothing is a coincidence with Beau," said Isabel.

"Lindley's told her father that Beau is Reggie's heir. I thought the next baronet was..."

"Adam. So did we. Beau found out that his Uncle Tug doesn't have a marriage certificate. Or a birth certificate for Adam. The Japs. But he won't get Reggie's money."

"Hence the launch into tobacco farming?"

"Merry Hall needs a lot of money," said Isabel.

"When are you flying to London? I'll come with you. We can both talk to Rosalyn. I went through the family album. My grandmother on father's side. Very similar."

"Really? That's a relief to hear. Good... You'd better warn Lindley about Beau."

"He can't be that bad," said Carl, laughing.

"Worse."

"The boy showed me figures. How he's going to do it. It might just work. The price of tobacco is good this year. I checked."

"Oh, it will work. Beau would never put up with failure. I just feel sorry for Adam."

"We all have to fend for ourselves."

"I should be in New York, you know. That musical of Tammany's is finally happening. They're opening very soon. Lorna's gone. Reggie said he'd try to be there."

"Musical?"

"*1066*. Based on the original Beaumonts. Haven't you heard?"

"Not everything filters out to Africa... I wish you had told me about Rosalyn."

"It seemed right at the time not to tell you."

"Did Henry know?"

"I don't know. Probably. Men like that aren't as stupid as they look. Poor Henry."

"Poor Isabel. You had to live with it."

"Yes. I've done enough damage for one person. It's why I'm going home."

"Who's the new one?"

"A lot younger than me."

"You always were unconventional."

"We can't just suddenly have what we want. Life doesn't work that way. There's always a price. It is one of the few advantages of getting older. You know you're not going to get away without paying. Why haven't you married?"

"Too comfortable as a bachelor. You don't have to get married these days, and after forty the urge to reproduce slackens off. I'll die a lonely old man. Very rich, maybe, but very lonely."

"Maybe Roz can help."

AT SEVENTY MILES an hour the Bristol left a dust trail a mile long. Beau sang at the top of his voice and whooped every time the wheels hit soft sand and started to slide, making him correct deftly until the 3-litre engine powered the sports car back onto firmer road. The air-conditioning was on full blast to combat the 117-degrees Fahrenheit heat outside the car.

"Look at all the empty space," he shouted to himself. He had not seen a soul for fifty miles, just dirt road and long brown grass and the trees solid on either side of the car. "And the world is starving for food. Add capital to this and everyone gets rich. No wonder the Americans got excited about the West." And softer, more intensely, he went on: "This must be the last spot on earth that hasn't been developed. Fallow for eternity and waiting for me." He looked again at the milometer. "Nearly there."

"You'll need a compass," they'd told him in London. "The beacons were put down fifty years ago. You'll find the cairns if you scratch enough. You may need a surveyor." Beau had gone out and done a short course in surveying and here he was, ready to rip out the trees, plough the land, build the barns, drill for water, pump up from the rivers, build dams to hold back the rains, then roads, and last, a house to live in. "Five years and this land will give me what I want."

Looking for a shade tree, he stopped the car by the side of the road. Grass was growing in the middle and trying to swallow up the tracks encroaching from both sides. He got out into the heat and shot the sun for his position, consulting the map and the sections of aerial photographs that he had pinned in the overlap to a board so that when he looked through the stereoscope the bush leapt up at him in three dimensions. He got back into the car and drove on for ten more minutes before stopping. The easy ride was over.

"Like being in the army," he told himself, whistling away happily now he was standing on land that belonged to him by lease for the next ten years.

He adjusted his backpacker and the wide-brimmed hat they had told him went with the job and with a .375 slung comfortably over his right shoulder he struck off the road through the long grass, heading for the river his aerial photographs told him was six miles away. Unseen doves called to him from hidden trees and the sun pressed down and the heat sucked the sweat from his body, soaking the back and armpits of his khaki shirt. In his light-weight running shoes, strong and ventilated, he went off between the trees, checking his army compass regularly. He had marked the position of the car clearly on the photographs. With a stick he prodded the long grass for snakes and then forgot about them and relied on his trousers for protection. After three hours of heavy going, he was happy to sink down on a flat rock beside the Mutwa River.

"Bilharzia," they had warned him. "Don't swim in the rivers, and boil your drinking water. Gets in through the skin and attacks your liver. The brain sometimes, if you're unlucky... Stay out of the water."

Before the sun went down, Beau had his firewood gathered and had cleared a small patch of ground for his tent. He put on a pot of water over the open fire and listened to the crickets singing from the long grass. For the first time in his life he was at peace with the world and his surroundings. He ate a supper of canned sausage and beans and washed it down with three mugs of coffee before crawling into his tent. 'I wonder if Sir Henri de Beaumont felt like this when they gave him six thousand acres?' he thought to himself. Within a minute he was sound asleep and the night sounds of Africa built up around him.

He added wood to the fire several times during the night, waking at dawn with the sound of the birds. Every bone in his body ached from sleeping on the ground. The air was tangible and he felt he could reach out and take a piece, the silence of Africa was so strong. He added more wood to the fire and cooked breakfast before making his libation to Africa by trickling rich black coffee onto the dusty earth, which pleased the ants and the beetles that staggered over the wet blades of brown grass to drink it.

"A little for you and a lot for me," he intoned, and shirtless, shoeless, bollock naked to the sun, arms stretched up to get the feel of the place, he began to laugh. A bush buck, a small pixie-faced duiker with two of the tiniest devil horns, broke cover from across the Mutwa River and leapt away to find a safer place.

Packing the tent and carefully putting out the fire as he had been warned to, he felt the solid, satisfying feeling in his gut that came from the knowledge of hard work ahead and a job worth doing.

CLAY HUNTER HEARD the Bristol from the grading shed, where he was supervising the baling. Africans in tattered, cast-off clothes were standing at tables grading the tobacco leaves ranging from pale lemon with just a little spot to the darker, mahogany red that went into the richer, continental cigarettes and pipe tobacco. As the grades separated, they went into wooden boxes that were emptied by the women and the tobacco tied into hands, with the seventeenth leaf tied round the stems. The hands were then packed into a large box and compressed into two-hundred-pound bales of tobacco.

The chatter of the gang ceased abruptly and Clay looked up

from the bale ticket he was marking to see a young man looking around the shed as if he was about to make an offer to buy the place. The man stood his ground at the end of the grading tables.

"I'm looking for Raoul Beaumont."

"He's in Salisbury."

"You must be Clay Hunter or Peter Escort?"

"Peter's just gone back to his army unit."

"Beau Beaumont... I like the smell of tobacco."

"Some people find it nauseating."

"Not me."

"Raoul went to meet your train."

"Oh dear. Can I phone the station?"

"Not worth it. Takes three hours to get through if the line isn't down. One thin telephone line and a lot of bush."

"Plenty of bush."

"Yes," said Clay, accepting the outstretched hand. The handshake was strong.

"I hope you are going to work for me," said Beau. "Have you made up your mind?"

"Not yet." Clay turned to the bossboy and spoke to him in fanagalo, the lingua franca of southern Africa. "Come on," he said to Beau. "He knows how to grade."

"Why stand in the shed?"

"They expect it. We call the others 'stoep farmers', the ones who drink beer on their verandas and expect the gang to do the work. The bloke next door gave his gang five hundred bags of fertiliser and told them to spread it over eighty acres. They dug one big hole and buried the lot and spent a week sitting in the shade. He'll go bust if the Land Bank doesn't bail him out again. Is that your car?"

"Yes."

"Not suitable. You need a Merc or a Land Rover."

"Clearance is good," said Beau, taking his briefcase out of the boot of the car.

Clay got down to have a look underneath. "Surprising."

"Not really. Had them move the exhaust. Raoul warned me."

"Can anyone tune that thing?"

"Me."

"You a mechanic?"

"Spent three days at the factory."

"Three days isn't much." Clay got up into the cab of a one and a half ton truck. "Get in the other side. Your car will be safe."

"How many acres do you grow?"

"Eighty on the home farm."

"Is that enough?" asked Beau in surprise. He climbed up next to Clay and slammed the passenger door.

"Don't want to kill the soil. The Escorts have been here for fifty years. The old boy came in with Rhodes and then went farming. You can't take more out of the soil than it wants to give. The blacks do it. Did you see the Tribal Trust Lands on the road up? Not a blade of grass."

"Too many goats."

"You know about Isabel?"

"Saw her in Johannesburg. Remarkable woman. Never looks her age."

"I want to marry her."

"Don't ask me, old boy. Ask Aunt Isabel... What's that over there? Looks like a waterless swimming pool six times too big."

"Where we dry the maize cobs."

"You grow maize?"

"Two hundred acres."

"Why? Tobacco's the cash crop."

"Adds a bit to the gross."

"Why not put in tobacco?"

"Not enough tobacco barns."

"Sounds like a lot of effort. I'm putting up two hundred barns."

"Take you plenty years."

"This year."

"Impossible."

"Why?"

"Bricks. Money. You can't get skilled labour."

"You can buy labour."

"Not skilled labour."

"You have to do sums. I'm planting a thousand acres in January next year and another in October. That way we'll get two crops through the same barns."

"If it rains early enough, which it never does in these parts. The rainy season's too short... Here we are. How does bacon and eggs, sausage, kudu steak and sheep's kidney sound?"

"Perfect... We'll just have to extend the rainy season."

"How long have you been in Rhodesia?" asked Clay, and bellowed his breakfast order to the invisible cookboy. "Kitchen's at the back. Taguma's been with me ten years."

"Two days," said Beau, smiling.

"You can't build two hundred barns just like that."

"You can if you bring a contractor from Jo'burg."

"Cost a fortune."

"Well, not really, if it's done in bulk."

"And water?"

"Boreholes. The rivers. Another bunch from Jo'burg start drilling tomorrow."

"Do you want a beer?"

"Before breakfast. Oh, why not?"

"Have you brought a flock of witch-doctors from Jo'burg to make the rains come early?"

"What's to stop us watering the seedlings in the lands?"

"A thousand acres! Do you know how many plants there are to an acre?"

"Four thousand."

"So every five days you are going to individually water four million plants?"

"Yes. Plenty of unskilled labour. Anyone can be taught to slop water out of a bucket."

"The beer's cold."

"Can I use that table?" said Beau, pointing. "I gave each job a separate sheet. This is the building programme."

"How many sheets are there?"

"One hundred and eighty-seven. When you separate the problems, they shrink in size. I'm in a hurry. As General Manager you will receive five per cent of the gross. Two, thousand-acre crops of Virginia at twelve hundred pounds to the acre, averaging three and four pence a pound grosses four hundred thousand."

"Twenty thousand pounds for one season?"

"You'll have worked for it. Problem is, I know nothing about growing tobacco... Three year contract. After that you can go off and buy Salisbury. I'll know how to do it after three seasons."

"And you trust me?"

"I don't trust anybody."

"What do I say to the Escorts?"

"You've had a better offer."

"Who'll run Greswold?"

"Peter. My sister wrote about him. Very capable. Better to give time to the family estate than the army. You should just see how far it's got my father."

"But he's a general."

"Pity for him. They pay him five thousand pounds a year plus perks. What do you think I'm doing in Africa? If father had gone into the city like Uncle Reggie I wouldn't be here."

"Some people like playing soldiers."

"Each to his own," agreed Beau as Taguma brought in the breakfast.

THE CHRISTMAS VAC at the University of Cape Town had begun with Cindy Escort putting her Mini on the road and heading north. A fellow student drove alternate hours and the seventeen hundred mile journey was tolerable. They did not stop in Johannesburg. At nineteen, Cindy had turned into a woman and being away from her family and sharing a student flat in Mowbray had given her independence and a new aspect of life. Her studies were mostly interesting, but so was the social life, and her relationship with Raoul had begun to fade.

She had dropped her travelling companion in Salisbury and driven straight to the farm, where she was told by the servants that her parents were at the club watching tennis. She looked for Raoul, but he and his car were gone. The truck was parked outside Clay's cottage, which surprised her, as he normally ate his breakfast in the grading shed.

"Clay," she called, and pushed through the screened door to be stopped dead by the chemistry created with the man eating breakfast with Clay. Her stomach lurched and the moment stood still for both of them.

"Cindy," said Clay, getting up. "Come and meet my new boss."

"We've met," said Beau, standing up at the table. "Hello, Cindy. You've changed since Merry Hall."

"So have you." The words were tight in her throat.

"Hopefully for the better," said Beau cheerily.

Clay pulled out a seat. "Breakfast?"

"Please."

"Taguma!" bellowed Clay.

"Yebo, baas. Food coming." He had seen Cindy drive up to the cottage.

"Leaving Greswold after all," she said to Clay, composing herself. "Isn't that selfish? You have a good job and..."

"He's not his own man," said Beau tactfully.

"He'll be less of his own man working for you. Raoul says..."

Beau interrupted. "What does Raoul say?" He was smiling, which increased her irritation and buried the turmoil in her stomach.

"You like other people to do your work."

"Certainly. That is the first principle of good management."

"You can't walk into Africa and take people out of their jobs. Daddy worked hard to build..."

"Then why doesn't Peter run the farm?"

"He prefers the army."

"Isn't that selfish?"

"Not if Clay…"

"So Clay must shoulder Peter's responsibilities? I only want Clay for three years. After that he will have more than enough cash to buy his own farm."

"But you want to pick his brains."

"Certainly, but I'm going to pay for them. Are you not being selfish denying him the opportunity to have what your father has? Better tell your brother he has a job of work to do. It's not as though I'm leaving Greswold without an alternative. I appreciate you taking in Raoul. He tells me he's had a good training. In the end we can all meet as equals. As owners. Nothing selfish about that, Cindy."

She looked at Clay and then back at Beau. "You could be right. Where is Raoul?"

"In Salisbury looking for me. Seeing as you're his girlfriend, why don't we drive in together?"

"The Mini's pretty…"

"We can go in my car."

"Where are you staying?"

"In a tent on my farm."

"Where's Clay going to stay?"

"In another tent."

"You didn't tell me that," said Clay.

"I haven't told Raoul either. Barns first. They tell me you get used to sleeping on the ground."

"Are you taking any of the gang?" asked Cindy.

"No. On that I give you my word."

"Taguma will come," said Clay. "He was mine anyway."

"When do you start?" Cindy asked Clay.

"As soon as he's worked his notice," replied Beau.

"Who will look after everything?"

"Your father. He will have to until Peter decides what to do."

"He hates it."

"It's his tobacco," said Beau and looked up at Taguma, who was standing with a new plate of breakfast. "Do you have some more steak?"

"Yebo, baas."

"What does yebo mean?" said Beau to Clay.

"Yes, in Zulu," answered Cindy, looking at Beau again and realising that life was full of complications.

PART IV

JANUARY TO SEPTEMBER
1955

1

$\mathscr{A}$dam flicked the mooring rope from the *Seacatcher*, letting the twenty-two-foot ketch drift away from its floating buoy in the hurricane-proof yacht basin at the Royal Hong Kong Yacht Club.

"I've got it all worked out." His eyes were soft and sentimental as he looked at Ruby seated next to the mast. She was wearing a bright red jumper that highlighted the perfection of her porcelain skin. "I'm going to go on living just like this. No more. No less. A job in trading. Salary every month. No worries. I don't need big deals in China or America, and Merry Hall has lived without me for hundreds of years. Hong Kong is made for Eurasians." He looked around the teeming harbour, enjoying the contrasting sounds and smells. "We're not going to get far today. No wind."

Ruby smiled. She would not think of her past.

"Live for today," said Adam. "To hell with yesterday or tomorrow. We have a flat, a car, a share in a yacht, a job I enjoy, and each other. What else can we want? All this striving for more leaves me cold. Just let people leave me alone."

BLAKE EMSWORTH SAT in the bar four hundred yards from the

theatre. There were two drunks further down and the barman was reading the sports page of the afternoon paper, not a worry in his world. Blake's nerves were raw. He had given birth and in one hour's time the baby would belong to the public. *1066* was over for him and if it went off right he would write another musical, and if it sank he would go back to the Stock Exchange, which would please his father but not Charles Ainsworth. He was always upsetting someone.

He thought of Tammany, and it no longer mattered whether he wrote musicals, sold stocks and shares or played the guitar in the gutter. They were strangers; friendly, joking, going out together, discussing the musical, many things, but never more. Their bond had broken. They had grown up. There were no more oak trees, bicycles, small fires and talk through the night when the world had belonged to them. Laughter. So much joy. So much joy... A man sat down on the barstool next to him without being noticed... What the hell was success, money, even fame, without Tammany? It was a rotten little theatre but he had his name in lights. Tammany's name was in lights. He smiled ruefully at that one.

The man turned to him. "At least you haven't lost your sense of humour."

"Ted! Ted Cornwell. What the hell are you doing here?"

"Looking for you. They said you might be here. It'll be all right."

"What?"

"*1066.*"

"Oh, that. That's the least of my problems."

"What are you worried about?"

"Tammany. Me and Tammany."

"Now that is a problem... Mr Barman, could I interrupt the football news and order a drink?"

"What you say?"

"A drink, Mr Barman. One of those," he said, pointing to Blake's drink, "and a plain whisky, Scotch. Black and White. No ice. No water."

"You learn quickly," said Blake, trying a bad laugh. "How long have you been in New York?"

"Two hours."

"Why?"

"Reggie Beaumont sent me. He tried to send me a while back but friend Heron didn't want us interfering."

"He's only interested in Tammany."

"As we thought. Where is the great actor/director, Mr Richard D'Altena? His name's not on the programme."

"He only wanted Tammany. Cheers. Good to see you. The play's a mess, by the way. Heron's been toying with her. Last thing he wants is a success. Richard saw that and walked out. So did the leading actor. Zach took over. Nobody knows Zach. Or Tammany. It'll flop, Ted."

"Maybe this time."

"Heron's papered it. Sent out free invitations. Three hundred dollars at the box office."

"Where's it advertised?"

"It isn't. Heron's office handle the business side of everything. They said the newspapers got the dates wrong."

"What's the real reason?"

"Tammany turned him down. Said she wouldn't marry him even if he was studded in diamonds. That was last week. Haven't seen him since."

"She should have waited a week."

"He wouldn't let her. That man's gone right through the bag of tricks to get her in the sack. Never thought he'd offer marriage. Worth half a billion. Not bad looking. Old enough to be her father, but who the hell cares these days?'

"She must have someone else."

"She met someone in Hong Kong. He's serious, she's not."

"And you?"

"Nothing. She doesn't feel a thing for me anymore."

"What's it all about?"

"A career. She's changed. That beautiful, soft Tammany's gone as hard as nails."

"Can't be too hard if she turned down Heron. And D'Altena?"

"Same thing, except with all his ex-wives he can't afford her. Good to see you, Ted. What really brings you to America?"

"*1066*. I'm going to promote it properly."

"Whose money?"

"Sir Reginald Beaumont's. We're going to buy Heron's rights. If it flops tonight, Heron'll want nothing more to do with it."

There were thirty-seven people in the five-hundred-seat theatre when the curtain went up. The seven-minute overture still echoed round the empty space. Heron had told his staff not to bother with the invitations and had gone off to the East. Or rather, an ex-Indian Army type had gone off using a British passport that had cost sixty-five pounds sterling. From the start, the players tried their best and sang lustily, which only resulted in making the music sound peculiar once the first wave of notes had gone off and come back again instead of being absorbed by the audience.

At the interval, Ted went out round the bars offering complimentary tickets, but drink proved more interesting than theatre. The second and third acts were plain embarrassing, and no one bothered with a curtain call. The only satisfied person was Ted Cornwell. His ear for music was very much in the popular vein and he had enjoyed the melodies that Richard D'Altena had crafted into place during his period of chronic infatuation with Tammany. Heron could take his contribution with him, but the music was there for keeps. Ted had anticipated the debacle and had ordered quantities of food and wine sent over, and though none of them had enjoyed the show, everyone enjoyed the party. They laughed heartily when Ted joked that at least the venue was paid for by Montague Heron. When they were all a little drunk, Ted addressed the cast, explaining that he spoke for Reggie Beaumont with his full backing.

"The music is lovely and that's what counts. Let's look at tonight as the first dress rehearsal. Mr Heron has nothing more to do with the show. What you need is a promoter and that's where I come in. Heron got you English cast 'green cards' to work in America. Lovely. The revival of *Carousel* fell flat on its face at the Adelphi. Lovely. And I'm in America. And that's really lovely. What's good for *Jive* is good for *1066*. We go on in Broadway when the show they brought forward at the Adelphi comes off. We'll be using real horses and real knights and oak trees the size of skyscrapers.

"And three days from now, we're launching an American-wide campaign in conjunction with *Jive* jeans to find every descendent of Sir Henri de Beaumont in the world. There's going to be a Beaumont banquet in New York the night we open on Broadway proper and every member of the family, however distant the cousin, will receive a certificate to say where he stands in line to the baronetcy. We all know who's eighth cousin to the Queen. Now we're going to find out who's twenty-third cousin to Sir Reginald Beaumont. There will be the number one in line right down as far as we can go. And when the certificates have been given out, the curtain will go up on *1066*. Mr Caterer, please open the champagne. Thank you. Good luck."

They cheered him off the table.

"What about the argument between Adam and Beau?" Tammany asked, passing him a glass of champagne.

"That's the whole point. It's a promoter's dream. We'll have every American wanting to be a cousin and the build-up to proving who's the heir will cap the excitement."

"Who's paying for it?"

"Reggie, of course. Or rather, *Jive*. You can buy a whole lot of promotions on five million jeans at three dollars wholesale."

"You are too much."

"Thank you, darling. What's with you and Blake?"

"That's over."

"Is it?"

"We blew it, Ted. Good and proper."

. . .

ADAM HAD NOTICED the trading pattern changing for months. It took Craig Craig a little longer to talk about it and call a meeting. "Like eating soup with a fork," Dan had commented. "Everything slips away." The two of them, Adam and Dan, had written down case descriptions and the failures were all the same: the buyer or seller lost interest; on two occasions Adam proved the buyers paid more for the same commodity through another broker. It was as though there was a squeeze out on Beaumont, Hong Kong, and if it had not been for their long established customers and in-house business they would have been in trouble by the time the letter from Sir Reginald had arrived.

Dear Craig, what's the matter? Reggie.

They had all known what the letter was talking about, but the customers refused to talk. Everyone said they were busy and could Beaumont's get off the line as they had business to do.

"It's only Beaumont, Hong Kong," said Craig at the meeting. "Reggie says business elsewhere is fine. I asked Swires and Jardines: Hong Kong has never been better. What the hell is going on around here?"

"Make offers in another name," said Adam. "Form a separate company through nominees. Everything's done on the phone. No one knows I'm Adam Beaumont unless I tell them so. I'll move into another building. The Beaumont connections can be fed to me and offered to the market by a brand new company. In fact, we'll form three companies simultaneously to confuse the issue further. We can do back-to-back letters of credit. It just means an extra set of papers."

"Do you know what is happening?" asked Craig.

"Possibly. Probably. But it doesn't help."

"Who is it?"

"Someone who wants me to join his company."

"Why?"

"The man has some perverted idea he was in love with my mother."

"Perry Marshbank?"

"He has a world-wide legitimate empire trading in billions. Needs an heir. Funny, isn't it, with all this 'find the heir' in America."

"He can't have so much influence?"

"It takes years to build a reputation and one good rumour to destroy it. He's told the market we are not to be trusted in Hong Kong. He's told the banks. Every one of our deals goes through a bank. The bank just says do or don't. No reason. If they gave reasons for declining finance they'd be in the permanent litigation business. And banks report problems to each other very quickly. Our nominee should not be a bank."

"Bring someone from Australia," said Dan.

"Leave it to me," said Craig. "You'd better go over to the factory," he said to Adam. "The *Jive* sponsorship for the 'Search for the Heirs' has made them put on three shifts. Bloody clever. Like an ongoing cricket match. Everyone wants the score. Each new cousin is a big event."

THE NOMINEE COMPANY did not make any difference. It traded for two months, ran up a healthy telex and telephone account, but was unable to complete a transaction. The manager went back to Australia with a year's salary, totally confused. Kim-Wok Ho put the word back to his cousin that Adam Beaumont wished to talk to Marshbank. Craig Craig had been specific.

"I'm running a business, dear boy. So is Reggie. If you are an impediment then in all fairness you will have to resign. This other stuff is none of my doing. I can't fight your battles for you."

The meeting was arranged in London and Adam found himself on an aeroplane going back to the other half of his roots. The following day, business at Beaumont, Hong Kong, returned to normal and by the end of the week the enquiries were distinctly bullish.

"Someone is rubbing his nose in it," Craig Craig confided to Dan with a genuine smile on his face. "He must have a lot of money."

"Who?"

"Marshbank, or whoever he calls himself."

A week after Adam's arrival in London, he received a handwritten note telling him to take a train to Guildford where he would be met at the station; he had not left his London hotel or told anyone of his arrival but had sat in his room watching television and missing Ruby.

At Guildford Station he was left for three hours and only after he came back from the men's room did he find a ticket for the following day that would take him further into the country. He booked into the Mitre for another frustrating day. By the time he arrived on the platform at Cranleigh Station he was totally frustrated.

"My car's outside." He recognised the voice but not the face or build of the man who was talking to him.

"Why the hell couldn't we...?"

"I wanted to show you something. Tell you a story. Is that all you have?" said Perry Marshbank, pointing to Adam's grip. "Do you know these parts?"

"Ashtead's only twenty miles..."

"Here, I meant. Beautiful village. Village green. Church. Pond. That type of thing."

"Why did you lean on my job?"

"To demonstrate power. To show what can be done when you have a lot of money. Put the grip behind the seat. Do you like Jaguar XKs? Wasted on English country lanes. Have you decided?"

"About what?"

"My job offer."

"I wouldn't work for you in a fit."

"Well, you certainly won't work for anyone else. I thought I had demonstrated that quite clearly. Where I went to school," he said and pointed at the well-kept lawns sweeping up to the school buildings on the ridge of the hill. "Father was the local bank manager. You remember? They put him in jail and when he came out society prevented him from getting a job. Nobody said anything. Just the jobs fell through. He couldn't confront anything because there was nothing to confront. You have been experiencing that feeling. Finally, he burnt himself to death with my mother. I was paying the rent on the flat. Your father gave me a lot of sympathy, but then the establishment in the form of Gray's wife found out my background. Same process, only less subtle. I was left with very few nice feelings.

"There are many ways of destroying a person without giving him drugs. And in the drug process at least the taker has some fun. Shall we go and visit the new headmaster? Have a chat in the common room? They didn't think much of me when I was at school. Thought I worked too hard and gave up on the sporting side. Their most famous pupil, I suppose. There was one before me. Champagne Charlie. Don't know his proper name. Educated at Cranleigh and Borstal.

"There's a new science laboratory behind the chapel. We can't see it from the road. I never have seen it. Cost me one hundred thousand pounds. Despite themselves, Cranleigh gave a damn good education. It was the smug complacency I liked. Instead of creating a day boys' house they put six of us into each of the existing houses and hoped we wouldn't be noticed. Not the thing to be poor at an English public school. But they use my science lab all right. The school magazine crows about it every year. They came back through my front man and asked for a swimming pool. We had an indoor one in my day they didn't heat. Called it the colds. What the hell. Let the rich little buggers have a nice big pool. This Ted Cornwell wants me to testify your parents were married. Clever promotion. Your sister will like the applause."

"You know nothing about Tammany."

"I do. I've taken an interest in your family."

"Of course," said Adam, turning in the car. "You're Montague Heron."

"Don't be silly."

"There is always a soft spot in any man's armour and my mother was yours. You even proposed to my sister. You're sick."

"No more than anyone else. Sigram's is a massive corporation. The origin of all big money is shady."

"You want to buy me and screw my sister."

"She told me to get lost."

"And the money stopped."

"Reggie's backed the musical instead."

"I'm surprised you haven't stopped that one."

"Reggie has power... I want to talk to you about drugs. About our society. How its rules are made. The skilful indoctrination. The manipulation."

"I don't want to..."

"Hear me out. I'm no more sick in the head than the rest of you and I am certainly a lot more honest."

Leaving the car under a tree, Adam followed in single file down the path that took them over a stile and into a meadow, rich in yellow buttercups and humming with the soft sounds of summer. A tree, Adam could never remember what kind of tree it was, dominated one corner of the field and gave them shade to sit under. Nothing of man's making was visible, only the sound of man, a motorbike, a long way off and nothing to do with them or their business.

"If it wasn't for drugs, would you join me?" Perry Marshbank had sat himself on the grass.

"I have travelled twelve thousand miles to stand under this bloody tree."

"Don't be rude. The young are full of righteous indignation... Morals change. What is punishable now is old hat in twenty years. Steal a rabbit from this meadow two hundred years ago and you were deported for life."

"Drugs kill people. Ruin them for life. Destroy families. We have been through this before."

"Don't we have the right to decide for ourselves? Freedom of thought, religion, movement? We demand freedom and the new society applauds. Every man has the right to determine his own future. Equal rights. We shout it out. Abolish public schools. Equal education. Remove the elite. Socialism. Communism. Take from the rich. Man's vested right. Self-determination. So why should he not have the right to self-destruct? There are so many ways. Drugs. Booze. War. Suicide. Those that cannot cope will find their way. There are millions of Americans taking drugs at this moment and those with self-control will decide on their own future.

"Do you know why governments hate drugs? They can't think of a moral way to make it legal and slap on the tax. Shame on them. But they will. In fifty years' time, my criminality will be the same as the rabbit stealer. You can't stop anyone getting what he wants. I created the product, Adam. I did not create the market. It is not just the odd person. Millions, Adam. Intelligent people. All walks of life. There will always be a percentage. The abuse percentage. Go and have a chat with Alcoholics Anonymous. This little exercise is just another prohibition, because if man wants it enough he'll change the laws, and he will. Oh, he certainly will. And then I'll be just another distillery owner and you will have thrown away your chances."

2

*T*ammany and Lorna left the Australian television studio complaining of splitting headaches. The traffic in George Street was terrible but they managed to find a cab; they were on their own for the first time in two weeks.

"Where you going, ladies?"

"Elizabeth Bay," said Lorna and gave him the address of the Beaumont company flat that they had to themselves now Ted had flown back to England. The first thing they did in the flat was take the phone off the hook, giggling like schoolgirls.

"I really thought you did have a headache," said Tammany. "Let's change into jeans and a blouse and no bras."

"Where are we going?"

"The Grape Escape. I've never been to a wine-bar. Nor any other bar on my own. Quite all right in Australia. I like Aus."

"What was it like after the war?"

"Too much emotion with Dad in the jungle and no one knowing about Mum. It was tough going through those years. Adam still likes the place. Do you think anybody will try and pick us up?"

"When they've finished drinking."

"Come on, the cab's waiting."

"How far is it?"

"How the hell must I know? Freedom. Absolute freedom... Lorna! You can't wear that blouse. It's too see-through."

"You do want to be picked up?"

"What do we tell them?"

"Anything but the truth. You're the actress."

"And if they recognise us?"

"English aristocrats don't expose their breasts."

Downstairs, the taxi was waiting patiently but the cabbie did not even think of getting out to open the door; then he looked at Lorna, shook his head and let out the clutch. Lorna gave him the address.

"If they rape you, lady, it won't be no crime... Lucky bastards," he finished softly.

The Grape Escape was so full they could have been wearing nothing and it would not have made any difference. The short-skirted waitresses were even more provocatively dressed than Lorna. The men were up one end of the bar drinking and Lorna and Tammany joined the girls.

"Go for your life," said a girl as she elbowed her way back from the bar-counter with four glasses and a carafe of wine.

"Two sherries, please," said Lorna politely.

"Anything particular?"

"Nothing particular." The service was swift. "Are you going to get back with Blake?" asked Lorna with their drinks. "That table's free. Grab it."

"I don't know. We don't talk anymore."

"Have you told him that brother Beau was setting you up?"

"Does it matter? He certainly slept with Roz. He wants a good time. They all do."

"All?"

"Men... Look at this lot."

"So what's wrong?"

"Everything, with me."

"Don't you like it?"

"What, Lorna?"

"Sex, of course."

"Never tried."

"Don't be silly. In America you were wined and dined in forty states. You liked that guy in LA. What was his name? I can help you sort out a contraceptive if that's what...?"

"I don't want to be like the others... No offense."

"You must want it. You do like men? Roz is..."

"No. She had an influence. Look at her. Look at her mother."

"Aunt Isabel has enjoyed her life. There's this bloke in Rhodesia."

"Ten years younger. I want a permanent marriage. Kids. A family. I don't want to be worrying about getting old and not being sexually attractive. I've seen them. They chase you hell for leather and six weeks later they're after someone else."

"Can you ever be sure of anyone?"

"I want to be. I know I can be sure of myself. Blake was like that. Before Roz he was a virgin. We could have done it together. Now I wish I had. Poor Blake. He was so frustrated."

"Then why?"

"Everyone has been insinuating all my life that my mother was a whore. She wasn't, Lorna. Daddy loved her. Do you know, I can still remember that feeling of peace in Sarawak when I was little. I was at peace with Blake until..."

"Growing up's a hell of a game."

"I want more than sex. I want to belong to someone. I look around at the others and tell myself I don't want to live their lives. Uncle Reggie rushed from pillar to post. He's not happy. He can't be. He's got no one to be happy with. That dancer wants Beaumont Limited, not Reggie Beaumont. Lovely lady. Hard as nails. I'll be glad when opening night comes round and stops me thinking of myself."

"And if it flops again?"

"With Ted's promotion?"

"Ted's selling lots of jeans. *1066* will have to stand on its own."

"Blake's music is so beautiful. It will work. I have gone through so many emotions with *1066*. Now I can look objectively. Zach wrote a good script. It may not run forever but it's good enough. Did you like that interview today? 'Do you think your brother will inherit the title, Miss Tammany?' 'Are you asking me if I am a bastard?' Poor man couldn't look at the camera, and it was live."

"Do you mind?"

"Very much so. You know that. If we didn't have a dark skin the subject would never come up."

"Does it worry you?"

"Being Eurasian?"

"I suppose that's what I mean."

"Try it yourself for a week and you'll know how to answer. That's part of the problem. Men don't want me as a wife and mother of their children. They look at you with that knowing look that expects sex. Your mother did it, so why not you? Half the men I meet treat me like a whore. Very polite but very determined."

"They try all the tricks on me as well," said Lorna, "and there's one coming over right now. Let's enjoy ourselves, Tammany. We've got two weeks holiday in glorious Australia and we may just find us some long lost cousins."

"Do you really think Roz is not my cousin?" asked Tammany.

"She's mine, whoever the father. She took off for Africa quick enough. Always had her eye on the main drag. Her girlfriend was not amused. I'd like to know who got the bigger shock, Roz or Uncle Carl. He's damn nearly as rich as Uncle Reggie. Bully for Roz. I'll bet my brother Beau has another look at her, first cousins or no first cousins."

"Do you think his farming gamble will pay off?"

"Everything Beau does pays off one way or the other. His barns are up and the crops in the ground. Peter's quite impressed."

"Are you going to marry him?"

"I just don't think I could live on a farm all my life. You marry a lifestyle as well as a man, however much you think you love him. There's no rush. I'm becoming more realistic and less romantic as the months go by. He's a very lovely man. Who knows."

"Excuse me," said a man standing next to their table. "My name's Kerry Beaumont and the fellows over there bet me a quid I was wrong. You are the English girls on the television programme?"

"What show, mate?" asked Tammany in a passable Western Australian accent.

"In Town Tonight."

"A good line, though. Pull up a chair."

"Where you from?"

"Perth. Friend here's from England. Cousin of mine, you know."

"On holiday?"

"Yah."

"So are me and the fellows. Going up to Cairns. Barrier Reef. Been up there? Want to go?"

"They told me Australians were fast," said Lorna with a straight face, picking up Tammany's story. Kerry signalled his friends and four chairs were plonked at the table and sat upon in thirty seconds.

"Lost my quid, fellows. Girl's Aussie. Other side, though. Perth."

"Western Australia play good cricket," said one of them.

"Not bad," conceded Kerry. "We're all from New South Wales. I've asked the girls to come on the hike. You two got any money? Petrol, that kind of thing. By the way it's your shout, Merv. Least Merv can do is buy you a grog."

"He's bloody marvellous," said Merv.

"You should have seen these girls on the telly," said Kerry, ignoring him. "Same surname as me. Trying to trace their cousins. Some baronetcy back home. You must have heard?"

"Oh, that," said Lorna. "Promoter's gimmick."

"Funny if we were related," said Kerry whimsically.

"Who?" said Lorna quickly.

"Those girls on the TV."

"Were you born in England?"

"Not likely. First Fleeters, us. Never been out of Aussie. Good on you, Merv." Merv put down the drinks. "Next shout's mine. Funny thing is, they called my granddad the aristocrat."

"The only aristocrat in Australia," said Merv, "is a man who can trace his ancestry back to his father."

"Very funny."

"Not far off, mate."

"What's a First Fleeter?" asked Lorna.

"People who emigrated with the first two fleets that arrived in Botany Bay down the coast a bit. Politer way of saying deported."

"Was your grandfather the First Fleeter?" asked Lorna.

"Not likely. Five generations Aussie, me. The convict must have been my great-great-grandfather."

"Do you know where he came from in England?"

"Surrey. A place called Ashtead, wherever the hell that was. None of the family ever been home. Couldn't bloody well afford it. Dad got up to New Guinea during the war. You know a place called Ashtead in Surrey?"

"I was born there," said Lorna, and received a kick under the table from Tammany.

"Do you know where this Henri de Beaumont fellah came from, seeing you're English?"

"Ashtead, in Surrey."

"You're kidding."

"You'd better get one of those forms from the TV Network and fill it in. Are there any more male Beaumonts in the family?"

"Fact is, no. Dad never came back from New Guinea... What a bloody laugh. If they can trace back from the First Fleeter I'll get a free bash in New York."

"What's your name?" said Merv.

"Lorna. Lorna de La Rivière."

"And you're English?" asked Kerry.

"Norman stock."

"How long are you going up the coast?" said Tammany, changing the subject.

"A week. Maybe ten days. Provided the bloody car gets there. You also a de La whatever?"

"Rivière. That's right. First cousins."

"Mind if we go to the jazz?" said Tammany.

"Pulling out?"

"Not likely. Your round's next. Then it's our shout." Kerry got up awkwardly as Tammany stood up with her bag. "Don't run away," Tammany said to the men.

"Not likely," said Merv, watching the perfect form of Lorna's breasts as she got up wishing she had put on something more decent. "Over there to the right of the bar." And as the girls walked away they heard him say: "Good line, Kerry. Best looking Sheilas I've seen in a while."

When they reached the toilet, Tammany and Lorna broke into a fit of giggles.

"You can't be serious?" said Lorna.

"Why not?" said Tammany, keeping with her Australian accent.

"You'll never keep up the accent."

"I'm an actress, darling," she said in her English accent. "I'm sick of being treated like a celebrity and they look like good, normal guys."

"What about Ted?"

"We need a break."

"We have interviews in Melbourne."

"So we go AWOL. Poor Ted. He'll think of something."

"What if they try and rape us?"

"They won't. They're honest. Didn't try and buy us. Refreshing. It will be a giggle." Lorna followed Tammany back into the bar.

"What's the verdict?" asked Kerry when they returned to the table to the obvious relief of Merv. "Girls' talk in the toilet," he said in explanation.

"Got yourselves a couple of hikers."

"I've got a guitar. Can you sing?"

"I hope so," said Tammany, almost losing her accent.

THE KOMBI WAS CRAMPED with six of them – the surfboards were tied on the roof – but the journey north to Surfers Paradise in

Queensland was idyllic. They had one change of clothing and a bathing costume each; for Lorna and Tammany, the pressures of international travel and television studios disappeared in the sun and the surf, the boys spending hours in the water catching waves while they watched from the sand. At night they searched out a suitable clump of trees near the water, tied up a sheet of canvas to keep off the dew and slept on beds of leaves in the balmy warmth. No one had a problem in the world.

Kerry bought the Sunday newspaper to read the comic strips, and there they were on the back page.

"You sure look like those girls," said Kerry. "They've disappeared," he said, reading.

"Another promotion," said Lorna.

"Not this one. Police are looking. This musical it's all about is opening in six weeks, and the dark one sings the lead. Right bloody pickle. Who wants to read a newspaper, anyway? Come on, Merv. I've counted the waves. There's a big one on the way." The men picked up their boards and ran back into the water.

"Edward Cornwell," said Lorna, having read the article in full, "would turn anything into money. He's deliberately lost our note and told the police we're kidnapped."

"He'll have it in the American press," said Tammany. "I love him. He's just too beautiful. I'm surprised he never told us to get lost for a week. Leave it a couple of days and then we'll phone. I'll have a story for the press by then. Now that's what I call mileage, Ted Cornwell."

"Should we tell the boys?"

"What for?"

"And if Kerry is a relation?"

"We'll meet him in New York, darling. And that'll make a good story."

"You're as bad as Ted."

"No. I'm enjoying myself. Being natural is something people should work on more often."

. . .

BEAU, burnt mahogany by the sun, stood quite still: the dappled shade thrown by the msasa tree patterned his bare torso, touching the strength in the young muscles. Had the man a tail it would have twitched like a leopard watching its prey. Behind him, the newly built cottage was almost soundless in the clean sun of the African morning; it had rained heavily during the night and the air was so pure it was touchable. The only sound came from the diesel pump down the hill sucking water from the Mutwa River and rhythmically pushing it up the long pipe into the man-made reservoir behind the house. The sound of the water was cool in itself.

The small house on the highest hill of Beau's home farm looked out for miles over the dips and dales, the ridges and vlei, now green with tobacco as far as Beau could see. The wet part of the vlei and the soilless pockets of rocks were the only parts left untouched by the Caterpillar tractors. Beau's tobacco was perfectly even, patchworked into twenty-acre lands, and the tractors and trailers were out with the gangs of black labourers reaping the bottom leaves off the six-foot plants.

Beau wore a pair of brief shorts and carried a pair of binoculars round his neck; the binoculars were the most powerful he had been able to purchase from Germany. He brought them up to his eyes and immediately the tobacco-laden trailers leaped towards him and the black, human ants became people, bending and snapping off the wet, green leaves, tucking them under their sweaty arms, bunching five leaves and then passing them back to the boy behind, who hooked them onto the *mtepes*, the six-foot-long sticks of bush timber.

Beau picked out his brother and smiled indulgently; Raoul was a worker when told what to do. 'No imagination,' Beau said to himself, sweeping the binoculars round forty degrees to the row of new barns where the tractors and trailers were unloading tobacco. Once unloaded, the *mtepes*, with the tobacco leaves on either side, were being passed inside. The activity was properly concentrated and the work was running smoothly. Like a good conductor, Beau smiled again at the way of things: he could see Clay through the glasses for a moment, bossing up the barn operation; the man was earning his five per cent.

A dirt road had been made up to the house, winding around the rocks to the top of the kopje. Beau heard a bicycle being pushed up the hill and it reminded him of his breakfast. Resting the binoculars on his chest, he picked up the cup of coffee he had made himself and sipped the burning hot liquid, content for the moment with his world.

The cook boy came into sight, pushing his bicycle. "Boss Clay give me this," he said in fanagalo and handed Beau a large envelope. "Breakfast coming."

"For two," said Beau, absentmindedly turning over the foolscap-sized envelope with its American stamps before ripping it open, exposing the heavily embossed and expensive invitation. His name was written out in elaborate script.

"Boss Raoul get one too."

"Go and make breakfast, Sixpence."

"Okay, boss," he said in the only English he knew, and went off bare-footed with his bicycle, the old pair of torn, white-man's shorts barely hiding his genitals.

Beau opened the invitation and an airline ticket fell onto the grass and he had to bend down to pick it up. The ticket was made out in his name and scheduled Salisbury to London via Nairobi and Rome, with a separate ticket for the London/New York leg of the journey. Flight numbers and times were neatly docketed. It was a tourist class ticket for six weeks hence, the arrival date coinciding with the opening night of *1066*.

"What is it, Beau?" asked Sybil, coming out of the small house. "Any coffee?"

"Help yourself."

She stood looking out over the acres of tobacco for a moment, adjusting her eyes to the glare. "Do you always make them reap on Sundays?"

"Ask Clay. Nature doesn't stop the tobacco ripening on the Sabbath."

"From the Queen?" she said sarcastically, looking over his shoulder.

"Family gathering." He passed her the card.

"Wow! Some gathering. Who's paying?"

"Anyone who buys Aunt Isabel's clothing."

"Can you take a partner?"

"No."

"Maybe not," she said. "I prefer a small pond... Do you think Clay will marry your aunt?"

"No."

"You're sure?"

"He's looking forward and she's looking back. Never works. She's better off designing clothes. You can't have fun forever and suddenly change your spots."

"They said you'd never make it."

"Half the crops reaped, which covers expenses. What's coming in now is profit and the second planting area's as good as the first."

"Did you really feed an egg-cup full of fertiliser to each plant after eight inches of rain?"

"Did it twice. Eight and sixteen inches. Took the risk out of too much or too little nitrogen."

"They hate you at the club."

"They're fools. They think they're in Africa for good. Kenya's getting independence. Why not Rhodesia? I've just borrowed some land and grown something the people at home want to use. I'll go home when I'm finished."

"They'll never succeed without the white man."

"Fallacy, Sybil. They don't want to succeed."

"You haven't been here a year and now you're preaching politics. Do you think we could go back to bed while breakfast's cooking?"

"You have a one-track mind."

"There will be years in the future of my life when I won't feel like a good fuck."

"You don't want anything in return?"

"I've told you."

"Materially?"

"Dad's got plenty. Why must I worry? Life's too damn short for a woman. Had a long talk with your aunt. She told me."

"Clay?" said Beau, taking her hand.

"What about Clay?"

"When you've both finished screwing your brains out you should marry each other. You're both completely physical."

"Anything wrong?"

"Nothing. Thinking is a curse. People that don't think get through life much easier. If my brother had a thought in his mind it would be lonely."

"Did you screw Cindy?"

"Why do you ask?"

"She is such a little prude."

"A man should never talk about his conquests."

"She hates you for forcing her brother out of the army."

"He'll thank me. Ask my mother. A soldier's life in peace-time is very boring. Father was furious the Malayan war came to an end."

"And Lorna?"

"She's back in the arms of her actor."

"Poor Peter."

"Don't you marry him. He's far too nice. He's an honest man, Sybil. Always does the right thing. Thoroughly boring." He led her back into his bedroom.

3

*A*dam had also received an invitation; he used it as an excuse for a business holiday that would fly him round the world.

"I want to see those buyers," he told Craig Craig in his office. "Assure them that whatever information they have received from their bankers, they should talk to our bankers direct. Anyway, I have to go to England and see Dad and Gran."

"Won't they be in New York?"

"I don't know."

"What do you really want to do, Adam?"

"The man is dangerous, Mr Craig. Mr Kim-Wok Ho has been specific. So has my uncle. I require four weeks unpaid leave and will be back in Hong Kong two days after my sister's opening. Then you can decide my future with the company."

Adam's first job was to purchase a portable camera that would pick up sound as well as picture. Then he bought a hand-gun and went off with it to the pistol club; a portable screen completed his purchases. The papers had taken up the story of his argument with Beau and the press had interviewed him twice. Ted Cornwell was grabbing every possible avenue for publicity. Ladbrokes had opened a book on the inheritance and his cousin was the five to four favourite. There was doubt whether *1066* would have a long run, but there was no doubt about *Jive* having made a lot of money. Isabel, back in her London office, was churning out new designs by the dozen.

Despite what his Uncle Reggie had given them, Adam knew there was no way the College of Heralds would authenticate his birthright without the proper documentation. The final full stop had been the death of Lord Gray. Everybody knew he and Tammany were perfectly legitimate, but their father's word sworn under affidavit was just not enough should Beau challenge it in court.

'Of course your parents were married, Mr Beaumont,' he imagined being told. 'We do not question your father's affidavit, but what we need is the certification. Many people marry in the eyes of God, but they need a priest or a registry office to make it legal in the eyes of the law. Who do we have to corroborate the marriage in terms of British Law? You need someone in addition to your father to swear to this court that a valid British marriage licence was issued by the Colonial Authorities in Kuching. Good intentions are just not good enough, Mr Beaumont.'

Dan helped with the equipment at Kai-Tak airport. "What are you going to do with this lot?"

"Take photographs."

"Give my love to Tammany."

"Does she write?"

"Not anymore. What can you expect? A man's past catches up on him."

"What past?"

"Nothing serious. Too many girls. Couple of orgies. Drugs. Light entertainment. The good life of a Hong Kong bachelor."

"Who told my sister?"

"I've no idea."

"Someone with an axe to grind. What the hell has a past to do with a future?"

. . .

ADAM'S first stop was a clinic in the suburbs of Singapore run by the nuns of the Order of the Sacred Heart. It was not a pretty sight. Adam's camera and sound equipment recorded the birth of a baby girl to a fifteen-year-old heroin addict. The mother's thighs were the width of a tennis racket grip. The mother had been all belly before the child was born, and now she was nothing. Adam recorded it all automatically despite his horror as the nurse swabbed the five pounds of new life. The baby let out a perfunctory cry, then held its breath in a deadly fight for survival: the whole of its little body shook with delirium tremors; the baby was as addicted to drugs as the mother. Adam and the camera watched the child die seven minutes later.

"Probably best for the poor little sod," said the lay doctor. "No chance."

"She's dead," said the nurse.

"Not surprised. How can a human being be reduced to that?"

Adam had everything recorded, including the conversation between the doctor and the nurse. For the following three weeks, he toured the drug centres of the world recording the horror of human degradation. The personal problems that had come into his young life were as nothing. Each time he left a rehabilitation centre he breathed clean, pure air as if it were the first time.

"WE ALL HAVE TO BE PRAGMATIC," began Heron in his office. "Take a seat. Did you fly from Hong Kong? The musical, of course. Nothing to do with me anymore. The show will flop, but your uncle will have made his money. Money again, Adam... What is that?"

"A projector and a portable screen. I've come to show you something."

Heron picked up on the tone of his voice and his smile disappeared. "Are you coming to work for me?"

"No."

"You're a fool."

"Will you watch this movie?"

"Of course not. I have appointments."

"I want to show you why."

"Drug abuse films? I've seen dozens."

"I made this myself."

"Why don't you go to Alcoholics Anonymous and ask them to show you round their prize exhibits?"

"People are not born addicts."

"Here we go again. I know a man who hasn't had a drink for twenty-seven years. He knows one would kill him. He has the strength of mind and as a result he is one of my vice presidents. There are millions of drug takers who have not got down in the gutter. The weak become failures. The world doesn't need genetic failures. A weeding out process. Nature did it before and nature is doing it again. Your film. Can I show you mine? Down and out boozers who can't get gin so they filter methylated spirits through loaves of bread in order to escape from life. Sniffing glue if they can't get meths. Eating out of ash cans. Right here in New York. Want to see? Want to come now? A man who can get it all together kicks the habit. Never judge your fellow man by yourself, Adam. Others don't think like you. Don't get Swords of Honour. Don't fight racial prejudice effectively."

"You are a murderer," Adam spat at him.

"So is every politician who goes to war. Every man who makes cigarettes. Don't you bloody well moralise with me. Man is fundamentally dishonest. They all rationalise to their own advantage. Do you want to know the truth?"

"Of course."

"No you don't, young man, but you are going to get it. Before I offered you a job I did some research. As a result I know everything about you. You've been used by your so-called friends and relations with their calculated malice. I'm in business. You don't like one of my products. That is your prerogative. But I'll have you know I'm a damn sight more honest than them. You're only twenty-one. You'll grow up. It's about time your honeymoon with life came to an end... Don't interrupt. My turn to lecture. You can then work out for yourself who's sick. Let's start with the Royal Air Force. Why did they send you to OCTU? Why did they select you for the Sword of Honour? Because you were the best? I doubt it. There were hundreds of your age group just as good. You were a pawn. The British government has had enough of its colonies. It wants to give the problem away. India has gone and so will the rest.

"The ball game's changed. Some wise men in London have decided they can have their cake and eat it too if they are clever. Keep the trade and kick out the problems. Racialism: the problem of the second half of the century. They don't like wogs but they have to trade with them. They have to show the wogs they really are Worthy Oriental Gentlemen. The day you joined up at RAF Cardington, a directive was sent from the Colonial Secretary to the Air Member for Personnel to give you a commission, and when they saw you were competent another one told the same man to give you the Sword of Honour. Do I have to explain the reasons?

"So you see, you are not so bloody smart as you thought you were. You have a usable mix in your immediate ancestry. A tradable commodity. Ted Cornwell wouldn't have half as much fun if you were white. The public are scratching their prejudice with self-righteous ecstasy. If your mother had been English and married your father in Timbuktu the whole bloody thing would never have started. Even you can see that. And the Chinese cuddling up to you? Your boss in Hong Kong?"

"I'm going to blow your cover."

"No one will believe you."

"They will. They'll bay for the big capitalist's blood in the same way they scratch my colour problem."

"Go ahead. I don't give a damn."

"You do. You like power."

"Craig Craig isn't his name. What father would be dumb enough to christen his kid twice with the same name? He worked for me for ten years. How the hell does he afford to send his kids to public school? Reggie thinks the man has private means. Damn right he has. Your uncle and Kim-Wok Ho set you up. 'Get him out of England, old boy. Bloody embarrassment.' Ruby was planted on you."

"Not Ruby." Adam's fight had gone right out of him.

"She's a whore. Craig was told to pay her for a year. Daniel did the dirty work. The girl fucks for money. Ask her."

"She's in love with me."

"Whores fall in love. Now, my main point. Everyone gets a chance once in a life. Your sister blew it and you're blowing it too."

"I'm going to the police."

"Be my guest, and take your junky film with you."

"Was Ruby really a whore?" he asked when his leaden feet had got him to the door.

"Ask her. And don't slam the door."

Heron pressed his intercom. "Mrs Try, I'll be leaving now."

HERON WENT INTO HIS PRIVATE, permanently sealed bathroom. Half an hour later, a man took himself down in the lift, let himself out of the basement and took a cab to the airport. The man had never underestimated anyone and, though his customers might kill themselves by their own hands, he had never resorted to killing to solve a problem. The FBI would have a lovely time tracing back the ownership of Heron's companies to their final resting places in his numbered bank accounts in Switzerland. Big business had been getting boring anyway.

By the time the FBI came looking the next day, the man was enjoying himself on Ping-Lai Ho's veranda with an ice-cold Singapore gin sling and a view over the valley.

BLAKE EMSWORTH HAD REVERTED to his bohemian outfits, which pleased both the media and Ted Cornwell. The stockbroker had never existed. Sadly, Tammany watched him at the piano, remembering their rooms in Holland Park and their evenings busking at the Earl of Buckingham. Zachariah was pretending to sleep on the couch. She missed Mrs Stedham's threadbare carpet and the expectant ring of the phone in the basement that never made a sound. Well, they had arrived, all three of them, leaving behind Baxter, who was ensconced at Merry Hall. Even if the show flopped, there was no going back to their origins. They themselves had changed, the outside pressures had made them so different. She thought about this, concentrating on the problem of change. Blake was writing music for something to do.

"Scared?" said Zach, his eyes still closed.

"More frightened of where it will take me," she said.

"I have terrible stage fright."

"Who doesn't? My lines are so jumbled nothing will come out right."

"Don't think about the show."

"You brought it up."

"Sorry... It'll be all right, Tammany," he said softly.

"What?" She waited, but Zach said nothing. She glanced at Blake, but he was in a world of his own.

They had four hours before the curtain would rise on the opening night of *1066*. The three-bedroomed flat they now shared was quiet of extraneous noise.

"It won't flop," said Zach.

"No," she said. "No, it won't. You will be good tonight and everyone will get their money's worth." She jumped up as the doorbell rang and Blake stopped playing the piano. "Go on, Blake."

"I'd finished."

Zach opened his eyes as Ted Cornwell came into the flat, immediately disturbing the brooding peace of the place; the man was always so busy. Zach winced and closed his eyes.

"Why aren't you dressed, Tammany?"

She looked at him and shook her head, quizzically trying to understand a man who never took other people into consideration. "Zach and I are going straight to the theatre. No Beaumont banquet, thank you."

"But the public..."

"Can see me at eight-thirty on the dot. Have you no idea what it takes to psych up for a first night...? No you don't. Sit down and stop flapping that newspaper. Blake's going dressed as he is."

"There's a warrant out for Heron, that's what this is all about," said Ted, slapping the folded newspaper with the back of his hand.

"Whatever for?" said Zach and Tammany at the same time.

"He's Mr Big. Top of the drug pile."

"You're kidding! Have they caught him?" said Zach.

"No."

"Well there you are. How can you turn that into good publicity for *1066*?"

"I'm thinking of something."

Tammany suppressed a smile.

"Oh, there's a letter for you, Tams," he added. "From your father."

"He's not coming, is he?"

"No. He asked me to give you the letter now."

"Poor Adam."

"It's your big night."

"It's Adam's also. He'll know by eight o'clock if we are officially legitimate... Are we, Ted? You must know."

"I'm not saying."

"Then we aren't..."

"I'm not saying. Heron's on the run."

"Thanks," said Tammany, taking her father's letter.

"Hell, I'm bricking myself!" said Zach.

"I'd change places," said Blake, slamming the lid on the piano. "You lot can get another part."

"If this one flops, the next one won't. Genius will out. Have a drink. Your work's over."

"Number thirty-four and forty-two haven't arrived." Ted was back to business.

"Send them their certificates in the mail," said Zach.

"You don't approve of my methods?"

"Sure."

"The theatre's booked for three months. Full houses and no one's seen a review. If the reviews kill us we don't close."

"We do appreciate," said Tammany. "Our nerves are shredded."

"Good luck... You really won't come to the banquet?"

"No."

"See you all later then."

"Tell Gran I'm sorry," said Tammany.

"The American press just love her."

"They would. They think all her cutting remarks are upper class English wit."

"Sells theatre tickets."

"And jeans."

"And jeans. Have you seen Roz?"

"Yes." The door closed without further conversation.

Blake went back to the piano, Zach closed his eyes to stop the butterflies eating his stomach, and Tammany opened her father's letter.

"Ted had better be careful," said Zach. "Making you do a disappearing act in Australia was one thing, but Heron? That man's rich. You can't start rumours with the police."

"Do you think...?" began Tammany.

"Of course. Publicity stunt."

Tammany picked up the discarded paper. "No," she said, reading the report. "They say here Heron is Marshbank. Marshbank was best man at my mother and father's wedding. Go and ask Adam, not Ted. So now I know why Heron came into our lives."

"If Adam worked it out and told the FBI, he's dead. The drug business is not nice. I never did like the slimy bastard," said Blake, who was biased.

Tammany read the letter. "Poor Daddy. Says he's too much of a recluse to face so many people. His only life is that little house and his paintings."

"He must really have loved your mother."

"That point was never in question. He's sent over a painting for the banquet. He's built a guest room onto the cottage for his grandchildren."

"I'd better go," said Blake, standing up. "Good luck." And he was out of the door.

"What was that about?" said Tammany, looking at the closed door.

"Grandchildren," said Zach languidly.

REGGIE BEAUMONT HAD HIRED a horse and buggy in Central Park. The driver may have heard their conversation, hunched up on his board, but Reggie did not think so; the man was happily inebriated and the horse knew its work. Adam had talked for half an hour without interruption as the horse took a slow walk round the busy wide streets of central New York with the buildings towering up on either side of them. Reggie had a look up at Exxon Towers and cricked his neck.

"Merry Hall's very important," he said. "I can understand the big metropolis provided I have Merry Hall in the background of my life. I don't mind being closeted up for long periods, but I must have space at the end of it. I have to ask myself a lot of questions. Which is sicker, Perry Marshbank who takes pleasure out of other people's misery, or the society we've created that needs to take his drugs?"

"He said something similar."

"He was never a fool. It's his revenge on society, of course. Society made him a rebel and he over-reacted. There is a thin line between legitimate business and crookery. It's difficult, to be honest. The tax man is so efficient. I often wonder," he said, chuckling to himself, "if a king of old would have lasted five minutes if he had taxed so much and done so little in return. They've got us so well trained from birth that we hand over our wealth with little more than a whimper. Well, most of us do because we wish to be honest.

"The system, of course, has created its own cancer as people realise they're being cheated blind by their governments. Slowly, the insidious disease of corruption eats into us. Only the amateur gets caught. The authorities have as much chance of catching Perry Marshbank as they have of making him pay tax on his drug profits. If he was going to react violently to your disclosure he would have done so by now, so relax. He's sitting somewhere reading the newspaper and laughing up his sleeve."

"But it's not right."

"If the core of our society was not so rotten, I'd criticise Perry more adamantly, but people who live in glass houses should not throw stones."

"He kills people."

"He does, doesn't he. I was idealistic at your age and then I was made to fight in a war. I also killed people. The only difference between my killing in aerial combat was that I killed the best, good people, tomorrow's people. I don't think I have any more time for the weak than Perry. You can't mollycoddle people all the time. Or rather, you can if they vote for you."

"Is communism the answer?"

"Man has never found a way of governing himself that doesn't create strife. Society is imperfect and so are we."

"I don't believe it."

"Remember that when you're my age... I like New York. It's so damn commercial."

"What are you going to do about Mr Craig?"

"Nothing. His profits speak for themselves. He's a good manager. If I fired every dishonest employee I would be working on my own. The trick is to keep their thievery to manageable proportions. It gives Craig the feeling of free enterprise. Management is very difficult to find. I will drop a couple of guarded hints and he'll feel a twinge of remorse and make me some extra money to compensate. It will checkmate Perry very nicely. The RAF story is wrong. I spent six years in that service. Sure, they were hoping you would get a commission; I told your CO to kick your arse towards OCTU. Even told the training officer to give you every assistance. But you got the Sword of Honour, Adam. Didn't they tell you there were no bad airmen, only bad officers? They would never compromise that part of their system for a temporary, political expediency. If you were dumb, I'd have kicked you out of Beaumonts by now."

"And Ruby?" said Adam, turning to his uncle nastily.

"We thought you would be better off in the East. The family, that is. I know what it was that was eating you when you came to England after the war. Suddenly you found you were different. Our elders often make decisions for us, decisions made in good faith. The question was how to keep you happily in the East. Or, in the first place, to make you want to go back. You were sexually naïve. Ruby was not. I didn't expect you to fall in love. Very few men are monogamous."

"But to buy me a whore?"

"Have you confronted the lady with her occupation?"

"Not yet."

"I hope it doesn't hurt you any more than it already has."

"What do you mean by that?"

"Girls often say they love people when it suits them... Driver, back to the Waldorf... We have to change. We have a lot of new relations to get to know."

"Was the family parade your idea?"

"No."

"It's a circus."

"I don't think so. I asked my mother before I gave Cornwell his head. She thought it would be a lot of fun to find out if we had any more relations. Quite a crew, as it turns out. Ted Cornwell did an interesting exercise once he had all the cousins in place. He estimated the total wealth of living Beaumonts at over a billion dollars. Not bad for one Frenchman. It's proving quite a club, the Beaumonts, a very exclusive club."

"Do you know who Ted is going to announce as your heir?"

"Yes."

"You won't tell me?"

"No. Ted deserves his Oscar awards. It's the kick in business that keeps him going, and the money comes next. He's right, of course. If business isn't fun, forget it."

. . .

CRAIG CRAIG TOOK the call from Reggie Beaumont and was converted to a double agent, which kept his sons at Ampleforth. The call was transferred to Daniel, who made a call himself. Ruby began to pack, drained of emotion and hope. 'Damn,' she thought to herself. 'After three hundred years, I really thought they were letting us out.' Within an hour she was gone, with her clothes, her money and her memories. By the time Adam got through to their flat, the phone rang on indefinitely.

RAOUL HAD WANTED TO COME, of course, but his brother had explained how important the reaping season was to both of them and that he, Raoul, was the one who knew how to do it. Raoul had felt wanted. Cindy was already back at UCT without her virginity and her blind ideals. In her mind she actually thanked Beau for what he had done and threw herself into the university's social life with whole-hearted abandon. She told herself she had a lot of living to do.

ISABEL FOUND Reggie in his hotel suite.

"Isabel. What a surprise. Come in. Have a drink."

"I can't do any more at the theatre. Getting under their feet. Tammany had an acute attack of nerves."

"She's a professional."

"But still a young girl."

"Will it be all right?"

"Who knows? The public? Critics? People are fickle. It'll either turn them on or not. I've seen three dress rehearsals and don't know anymore. The whole damn thing's too personal. If nothing else, it's made me feel old."

"We are the older generation. From our side, we never see it. But we are. Are you going to marry this bloke in Rhodesia?"

"Does it hurt seeing Lee with Zach?"

"Yes. It made me realise a few truths I already knew."

"Why didn't you marry? God knows I would have married you at the drop of a hat."

"Timing. After Oxford I had to make money. We Beaumonts were broke. Enough to take us through a few more years, but Merry Hall was falling down. Then a war took up six years of my life and when I came out I knew too much about people. I could not find that young burst of love that would carry me through to a marriage and children. I didn't take people on face value. I kept looking for the warts and finding them. I've got used to being a bachelor... You haven't answered my question."

"I'll just have to get used to being a spinster."

"There's Roz."

"She prefers the idea of Carl to Henry. More money."

"Maybe she'll stop and have a look at herself in the mirror."

"It was all my fault."

"Probably. Do you know, in some ways I'm glad the sex drive is beginning to wane. Gives us more time. The amount of energy I have spent in my life in the pursuit of sexual gratification is scurrilous."

"But it was fun, wasn't it?"

"Oh yes," he said, brightening. "What'll you drink?"

BEAU WAS TOTALLY confident as he looked at himself in the mirror. The cable from the Standard Bank in Salisbury was in his pocket and he went to the writing desk in his hotel room and wrote out a cheque for five thousand pounds and put it in an envelope with the cable. Smiling, he crossed the room and took himself off to the banquet and his future.

"SHE CAN'T GO in that state," said Lady Beaumont, looking at her daughter-in-law. Lady Hensbrook was crying softly and Major-

General Geoffrey Beaumont was trying to remember the beautiful girl he had met at a tennis party back in 1933.

"I'll stay with her," he said.

"Did you know she was an alcoholic?"

"For some years. People change. She was left alone too much."

"I'm going to the party," said Georgina, bringing her eyes back into focus with an effort.

"No, darling. The party's over."

"I've ruined your life."

"It doesn't matter. We've been together a long time and this is just another crisis we will overcome together."

"The children?"

"Are old enough to look after themselves."

"Beau is going to inherit the title, isn't he?"

"It doesn't belong to him."

"But he will, I know he will."

"I'll stay with her," said Lady Hensbrook, pulling herself together. "She is my daughter."

"She is my wife," said Geoffrey, sitting down and taking her hand.

"Have you seen Beau?" asked Lady Hensbrook.

"Oh yes. I told him he was a ruthless little shit."

"Really, Geoffrey."

"I'm sorry, Mother."

"Come along, Mary. We'll be late. Thank goodness the children didn't see. When you've sobered up, Georgina, you and I are going to have a good talk. I'll talk to Reggie. There must be something we can do. I have never come across a problem in this life that cannot be resolved." The door opened and closed.

Outside the lift, Lady Beaumont said to herself as much as to anyone, "They all think I never have a problem. They never think who I can turn to."

"Don't be morbid, Alice."

"Well, you know what I mean. Do you think the Waldorf knows how to cook food?"

"I expect so." And the two old ladies, slightly bent, with old, crinkled faces and wise, surprisingly young eyes, made their way to the banquet.

BEAU HAD TRIED to see Tammany in her dressing room, without success. He had written a letter instead, addressing it to Blake Emsworth and giving it to the theatre manager for immediate delivery. He was going to be late, but called at the florist and sent off a bunch of flowers. He called his mother from the florist, but his father answered the phone, so he hung up without announcing himself. He was still trying to look at himself from the other direction and decide if he really was a ruthless little shit. "It's tough getting to the top," he said to himself, and walked out of the flower shop on his belated way to the banquet.

TED LAY in wait for Roz in the lobby. He had finished his promotion and it now only required him to introduce Sir Reginald at the banquet and he could go home; the show, the product, would have to generate its own momentum from now on. He was already thinking of what he could do next. A bevy of beautiful women passed through the lobby while he waited for the one that still sent his hormones dancing on the ceiling. He had just not had enough of her, he told himself. He had caught her in his office pumping away and jealousy had sharpened his appetite. He had avoided her for a year. The lesbian stories had even raised his interest. He knew she was not a lesbian. Kinky, but not a lesbian.

She came into the hotel with her mother, who gave an understanding smile while steering her daughter towards Ted. The girl looked even more luscious than a year ago. The press waiting to report the heir apparent brought their cameras up and captured her sexuality for millions of readers. Isabel stood slightly back from her daughter.

"What's your name, miss?"

"No surname." She loved the limelight. "Just Roz."

"The dress?"

"*Jive,* of course."

"Are you related to the Beaumonts?"

"By marriage, I suppose."

"How can you only suppose?"

"It's a long story... Hello Ted. Having fun? Shall we go straight in, Mother? I really do like America," she said, looking around the luxurious lobby of the Waldorf-Astoria. "It smells so rich."

"Are you a model?" said a reporter.

"Only for *Jive.*" She passed on into the banquet hall ahead of her mother.

Ted found a sofa and sat back, ready to shout with excitement. The power had gone. She was too damn obvious. The bit he had got of Roz was the only part worth having, and he thanked his lucky stars he had not married her because he was as sure as hell he'd have divorced the little bitch who'd just walked through the lobby.

"Wait 'til your looks go, darling," he said out loud, which caused the man next to him to turn round. The man was old and bent and favoured a walking stick; he got up and moved slowly to the double doors, showing the security guard his press card. Ted got up and followed him.

"Writers never stop writing," the man said in explanation.

BLAKE HAD GONE to the bar, the unread letter from Beau still in his pocket. "How can a man be so alone," he said to himself.

"You all right, mister?"

"I'm dead."

"Don't joke, mister. We're all dead soon enough. I'll buy you a drink, how's that?"

"I'd like that," said Blake.

"I know what it's like to be flat broke."

Blake sipped his free drink and tried not to think. "What time do you get off?"

"Eight o'clock. Been on since this morning."

"Do you go to theatre?"

"Sure do, when I can afford it."

"Married?"

"No. Barmen don't get married."

"Can you use this?" Blake passed his ticket over the bar. The barman looked at it.

"This a joke, mister? That show's booked up for months. Isn't tonight the first night?"

"Yes."

"Did you forge it?"

"No."

"They say the girl's quite something."

"She is."

"Have another drink on me. Wow: An opening night. Do I have to dress up?"

"I was going like this." He looked down at his bohemian outfit.

"You were? Don't you want to see the show?"

"Not anymore."

"Well, if it's going begging. Thanks, mister."

"You're welcome."

"You English?"

"Can you tell from my accent?"

They both laughed, which made Blake feel a little less like suicide.

Richard D'Altena, the old pro, had timed his entrance to perfection. As the last newsmen waited their turn to go in, a change in atmosphere told them to turn and have another look at the lobby. Lorna's dress was such that it was just as well her mother had passed out in the suite upstairs.

"May I present Lorna Beaumont, Major-General Beaumont's eldest daughter and niece to Sir Reginald. Is she not beautiful?" The famous smile took in the ravishing body that was tantalisingly covered in clothes Isabel would not have dared let her wear in London but were just suitable for the sophisticated glitter of New York. Her sex appeal screamed at the customers. "Lorna will be staying in America to further her career as a model. What do you think, gentlemen?"

"Are you taking her into films?"

"I'm taking her nowhere except this banquet."

"He is a friend of the family," said Lorna, enjoying the sensation they were causing.

"I've heard that before," said the journalist, smiling.

Lorna smiled and shook her head. "He is seated next to my Beaumont grandmother and no one sits there without an invitation."

"Are you going to *1066*, Mr D'Altena?"

"Of course. Isn't everybody?" he said, and proceeded to make his grand entrance into the banquet hall.

"Ladies and gentlemen, would you please be seated," said Ted Cornwell, the Master of Ceremonies. "I can't think that anyone would arrive after our guest of honour. Ladies and gentlemen, Mr Richard D'Altena, who all of you know by sight. May the banquet begin."

The press tables were on either side of the long, family table. The authenticity of forty-five cousins had been proved by Ted Cornwell and there were one hundred and forty-seven people seated at the table whose surname was Beaumont, either by birth or marriage. The one hundred and forty-eighth guest was Richard D'Altena, as Lady Beaumont had insisted that without him there would never have been a musical and a reason for the search. The table was a miniature United Nations and the mingled ancestry of many of them was not all Anglo-Saxon; the Beaumont from Birmingham, Alabama, was a whole lot darker.

The seated guests immediately fumbled to undo the beautifully tied scrolls. To make it more interesting, the scrolls not only stated they were a fourth cousin three times removed from Sir Reginald Beaumont, Bart, but they were forty-second in line to the title.

Beau looked across the wide table at Adam, as if the outcome was of little concern: neither of them had been given a scroll.

Reggie got to his feet to welcome his guests. "The thing that strikes me," said Reggie, "is that if Sir Henri had been killed at the Battle of Hastings, not one of us men would be here tonight. Makes you think, doesn't it? We all have a lifetime to get to know each other personally, and I offer all of you the hospitality of my home, Sir Henri de Beaumont's home. You will all be welcome at Merry Hall. I give you Sir Henri de Beaumont." They all stood up and drank in silence. Then Reggie sat down to thunderous applause.

Kerry Beaumont was puzzled and kept looking at the beautiful woman who had arrived on the arm of a film star. The girl reminded him of someone very much, but every time he tried to catch her eye she looked away. Throughout the meal, he kept up the eye battle without success.

During the fish course, a message was given to Ted Cornwell which made him glance at Beau and Adam alternately. Reggie also caught the exchange. He knew the name of his legal heir and could only put the fuss down to Ted's style of publicity until he received the note in Ted's handwriting.

A document has been handed to reception which changes the position of Beau and Adam. I had been warned by telephone that it was on its way and withdrew the College of Heralds' adjudication on Adam's legitimacy. I was told a legal document, purporting to have originated from Perry Marshbank, was on its way, swearing presence at the marriage of Adam's parents and giving detailed information regarding Marshbank's early relationship with you and Tug, information that would only be known to the three of you. The bulky envelope has arrived and is the proof Adam searched for in the East. Do you wish to make the announcement?

Reggie turned the note over and wrote:

No, not until I have read the document. This business has been going on for long enough.

Lady Beaumont raised her eyebrow at her eldest son and received a queer smile in return.

When the poultry course had been cleared away, the barons of beef were brought in shoulder high by the kitchen staff. Ted gave a signal and the painting which had stood in darkness on its tall easel at the end of the function room was lit up. Conversation subsided, and heads turned towards where the spotlight was showing them a curtain covering a picture ten feet by seven feet that had taken Tug the best part of six months to complete. It was his special contribution to the evening. Ted was pleased with the gasp of surprise as the cover was removed to reveal a painting of Merry Hall, set up on its hill where Sir Henri de Beaumont had first put it in all its splendour. No one, including the press, had to be told what it was; the Hall spoke eloquently for itself.

The wine flowed and by the time the toasts to the Queen of England and the President of the United States had been drunk, the guests and press were nicely merry and in good spirits for the musical. A long line of limousines waited outside to ferry them to the theatre and the bonhomie was thick as glue. They were correctly seated in the theatre five minutes before the curtain was due to rise. Expectations began to surge, especially for those closest to the production. Adam sat with both fingers crossed for his sister. When the lights dimmed and the orchestra began the overture, the butterflies in his stomach all ran wild at the same moment and he clutched his grandmother's hand for comfort. Lady Beaumont was totally relaxed, having no doubt that a granddaughter of hers would carry off the show very nicely. In the row behind them, the old, bent reporter had hung his walking-stick on the seat in front. Next to him sat the barman.

Within five minutes of Zachariah Booth riding a seventeen-hand stallion onto the stage, both of them in full war armour, Richard D'Altena recognised a sensation. When, half-way through the first act Tammany made her first entrance, he was certain, and so was the audience. Even those cynical of the run-up publicity changed their minds, and by the second act, everyone was settled back enjoying themselves, transported into another world that should have been a fairy story but everyone knew to be true. The final chorus, with the majestic Zach splendidly dressed next to Tammany, had the audience on their feet. Nobody noticed the old reporter excuse himself, favouring the stick he had taken from the seat in front of him.

Back in the bar, while Tammany, Zach, Lee and the rest of the cast were taking their eleventh curtain call, Blake finally gave his drunken attention to the letter in his pocket.

THE IMPROMPTU AFTER-SHOW party was thrown in the spacious apartment of Phillip Beaumont, an industrial chemist who had made some money out of detergents.

"Well," said Beau, holding out his hand to Adam, "it seems I can't call you a bastard anymore without being sued for libel. What are you going to do with the old place?"

"Uncle Reggie is very much alive."

"You see yourself as squire of the Hall?"

"I never wanted Merry Hall."

"Then what was the argument about?"

"There was no argument I started."

"Merry Hall belongs to an Englishman."

"You really are obnoxious."

"The one spot that hurts."

"Not anymore. I am what I am and must live out my life accordingly. The slant of my eyes is of little importance."

"You don't mind people's opinions?"

"Not yours, Beau. You've created enough bad blood."

For a moment Beau was left in the centre of the room on his

own. "You win some, you lose some," he said to himself, remembering the envelope for his uncle that had yet to be delivered.

"Something for you, Uncle Reggie," he said, barging into the conversation Reggie was having with Isabel. Reggie took out the cable and the cheque made out to himself for five thousand pounds. "I used a commercial grader," said Beau, smugly. "The tobacco auctions opened on Wednesday and the buyers were hungry. We sold seven hundred bales the first morning. My bank has credited your account with one hundred thousand pounds plus interest. That cable is your confirmation."

"And the five thousand pounds?"

"Your usual raising fee. I hate being obliged to anyone."

"If you go about life with a less aggressive attitude, you will find it more pleasant. Frankly, I am delighted you are not my heir."

Beau turned on his heel and left the room. No one even noticed he had gone.

THE DAY WAS BREAKING when Zach and Tammany left the party.

"Are you and Lorna finally over?" she asked in the cab.

"She doesn't want me any more than Peter Escort. She wants Lord Barnstable's son."

"He doesn't exist."

"Oh but he does. Somewhere. She'll find him... Cabbie, can you stop at that newsstand?"

"I'm sorry, Zach."

"So am I. Hell, I deserved it." He got out of the taxi and came back with all the morning papers. They went on to the flat in silence.

Blake opened the front door before Zach could turn the lock and handed Tammany Beau's letter. Zach pushed through with the newspapers.

"He sent me flowers to my dressing-room," she said, finally handing back the letter of apology.

"Can we start all over, Tams? I know I can't undo what I did. I was jealous. Just so damn jealous."

"Wow! Look at these reviews," called Zach from the lounge.

Tammany was crying, looking at Blake, who was silently crying as well.

"You two going to close the front door? Here's another. They're raving about us. Hey! Did you hear me...? Well about time," said Zach, coming back. "I want to be best man... Please laugh, one of you. Can I open the champagne now or later?"

"Now," said Tammany, pushing Blake away from her as she tried to laugh.

"That sounds better... Look at this." He pointed to a report on the front page.

FIND THE HEIRS REPORTER MURDERED

An old man was found dead in the men's toilet at Dulles airport. In his pocket was an invitation to the Beaumont Banquet together with a programme for '1066', the new smash hit at the Adelphi. The man had been shot through the back of the head in a typical mob killing. His trousers had been removed and a walking-stick pushed up his rectum.

Five months later, Adam received a letter from the Union Bank of Switzerland.

As sole heir to the estate of Mr Peregrine Marshbank, we have to inform you of an inheritance exceeding one billion Swiss francs. Following Mr Marshbank's last instructions, his shareholdings have all been realised and the money is held in this bank pending your further instructions.

"How much is a billion francs?" asked Dan when he had read the letter.

"The money is dirty."

"Clean it up. Make it good. If you hand it over to the government they'll squander the lot."

"At least we can afford to go over for Tammany's wedding."

"Not me. I'm staying in Hong Kong."

"You really did fancy my sister."

EPILOGUE

*a*t the time Tammany and Blake were kneeling at the altar of the Norman Church half a mile from Merry Hall, Perry Marshbank was enjoying a sundowner with Ping-Lai Ho on the other side of the world. The young cook had just taken back the evening menu with their order.

"She may be communist, but she's a damn good cook," said Perry.

"Perfect. There is something rather erotic about perfection that can't be touched. How's your drink?"

"I'll have another one. The valley's so peaceful."

"For two million a year we should have some peace."

"Why do the Chinese call you Ho Ping-Lai?'

"Family name should come first. When will your bungalow be finished?"

"Can you put up with me for another week?" Perry accepted his refill.

"Will the boy accept the money?"

"Money has a life of its own. Gets hold of people. It's what everybody wants. Being rich is a very nice feeling."

"Who was the old man in the toilet?"

"He wasn't so old. Good make-up. That was luck. The bloody

fools tried my trick. When Adam went to the police, the mob decided to take out Perry Marshbank. They thought I might go to the opening. The disguised reporter went there to kill me. For that evening, I was the seventeenth Beaumont in line for the title. People are ridiculous."

"Shall we go in to dinner?"

"Whoever said crime does not pay was a damn fool. Even the FBI think I'm dead this time."

Arm in arm, chuckling happily at the way of things, they went in to supper.

PRINCIPAL CHARACTERS

~

The Beaumonts

Lady Alice Beaumont —Matriarch of the Beaumont family and Reggie's mother

Reggie — Sir Reginald Beaumont and owner of Merry Hall

Tug — Reggie's younger brother and heir

Tammany — Daughter of Tug and Tammany Beaumont

Adam — Son of Tug and Tammany Beaumont (blue eyed)

Geoffrey —Reggie's youngest brother

Georgina— Geoffrey's wife and Lady Hensbrook's youngest daughter

Lady Mary Hensbrook— Georgina's mother who was married to Baron Hensbrook

Beau— Geoffrey and Georgina's eldest son

Lorna — Geoffrey and Georgina's eldest daughter

Raoul — Geoffrey and Georgina's youngest son

Karen — The youngest child of Geoffrey and Georgina

Isabel — Lady Hensbrook's daughter

Rosalyn (Roz) — Isabel's daughter

Other Principal Characters

Benedict Bellamy — Friend of Roz's at the Debutante's Ball

Blake Emsworth— Zach's friend and Tammany's love interest

Charles Ainsworth — Beau's friend

Chuck Everly — Married to Isabel's sister and Reggie's American business partner

Cindy Escort — Raoul's girlfriend who is the cousin of Megan Strong and great niece of Major Gerald Escort

Clay Hunter — Rhodesian farm manager of Greswold Estates

Craig Craig — Managing Director of Union Mining House, Beaumont Limited, Hong Kong

Daniel Chang — Works in the Honk Kong office of Union Mining House, Beaumont Limited

Edward Hemming —Lorna's eligible escort after the Ball

Hal Radley — President of Sigram Inc., America

Jake Escort — Father of Cindy and Peter and first cousin of Megan Strong

Kim-Wok Ho — Very rich Chinese business man; Reggie's friend and business partner

Lee Tuchino — A twenty-two year old American dancer

Lindley Starr — A girl who Beau has a shipboard romance with

Mandy — Isabel's business partner

Miss Ellenbogen — Craig Craig's secretary

Montague Heron/Guy Faulkner/Tobias Stratton —The many disguises of Perry Marshbank

Perry Marshbank — Fabulously wealthy and powerful man who has many disguises, and a wanted man

Peter Escort — Cindy's brother and lieutenant in the British army

Ping-Lai Ho — Kim-Wok Ho's cousin and wealthy drug dealer amongst other business pursuits

Richard D'Altena — A doyen of British film and theatre, actor and director.

Sybil Crane — Clay Hunter's lover and girlfriend of Peter Escort

Taguma — Clay's bossboy

Ted Cornwell — Jive's promotions consultant, and Roz's boyfriend
Zachariah Booth — An actor and friend of Tammany

DEAR READER

~

Reviews are the most powerful tools in our kitty when it comes to getting attention for Peter's books. This is where you can come in, as by providing an honest review you will help bring them to the attention of other readers.

If you enjoyed reading *Each to His Own,* and have five minutes to spare, we would really appreciate a review (it can be as short as you like). Your help in spreading the word and keeping Peter's work alive is gratefully received.

Please post your review on the retailer site where you purchased this book.

Thank you so much.
Heather Stretch (Peter's daughter)

PS. We look forward to you joining Peter's growing band of avid readers.

ACKNOWLEDGEMENTS

∿

With grateful thanks to our *VIP First Readers* for reading *Each to His Own* prior to its official launch date. They have been fabulous in picking up errors and typos helping us to ensure that your own reading experience of *Each to His Own* has been the best possible. Their time and commitment is particularly appreciated.

Hilary Jenkins (South Africa)
Agnes Mihalyfy (United Kingdom)
Derek Tippell (Portugal)
Daphne Rieck (Australia)
Andy Gentle (United Kingdom)

Thank you.
Kamba Publishing

9 781916 353466